# Orabelle

## The Keepers of Imbria Book 1

## J. Barrett

For my mother, thank you for your unwavering belief in me.

# THE KEEPERS OF IMBRIA

The sky had darkened with bloated clouds of ash that cloaked the last hours of sunlight from the horizon. Darkness crept at the edges of the battle like a looming monster waiting to pounce over the red swathes of raging flame that lit the destruction. She pushed herself up to one knee, wiping blood and dirt from her eyes. She was breathing heavily and could feel the pulsing wound in her back with each beat of her heart. But at least her heart was still beating. She tried to stand and cried out with the effort, falling back to her knee.

"Get up!"

She could not tell where the voice had come from amidst the chaos. The war churned around her, a violent mess of blood and bodies. Everywhere she looked there was death. The ground was soaked with it, the air fouled with the cries of it, her senses assaulted by it. These were her friends, her companions, everyone she had ever cared about and they were strewn about her, torn apart callously like discarded, broken toys.

She tried again to stand, struggling unsteadily to her feet even as the pain threatened to engulf her. She reached to unclasp the breastplate that protected her heart and let it fall to the ground with a heavy thud. A steady drip of blood ran down her face and fell from her chin and she watched its rhythmic cadence as it fell upon her discarded armor. It was too much. It was all too much. She turned her head away from the sight of her own blood and squinted through the thick blankets of smoke and fire. She thought she saw the figure of a wolf leaping, its strong jaws snapping at its enemies' neck. She took a step towards it and it was gone, either swallowed by the fight or perhaps it had never existed, a trick of the flickering flames and her battered mind.

"You have to stop them."

Was the voice in her mind? She could no longer tell. She looked about frantically and there was only the battle, the awful clamor of weapons against armor, the cries of the dying.

"Stop them!" it shouted again.

"I can't!" she screamed back, shrieking into the premature night. "I can't, I tried and I couldn't stop any of it!"

"You are the only one who can."

She hung her head, her matted hair falling over her face. She could smell the burnt flesh that clung to her as she tried to breathe, to find the strength to go on.

"I can't," she whispered. A tear slid from the corner of her eye, painting a golden streak down her stained cheek. She wanted to stop, to fall back to the ground and close her eyes and let the darkness overtake her. She didn't want to face the pain, the awfulness of the afterward, of knowing they were all gone. She didn't want to feel the loneliness again and she longed for the numbing nothing that would come with death. All she had to do was stop, to fall back down, to let them have their broken world and let them burn it to the ground.

Something cold touched her face. Then again. She tilted her head to look up. There was a break in the heavy curtains of smoke and far above them she saw grey storm clouds rolling across the sky. Another raindrop fell and it ran over her cracked lips, tasting bitter in her mouth. Silvery light bathed the landscape and for a moment the horrible redness of the flames was dimmed. Her throat knotted with emotion and she felt her lips tilt up into a smile as more tears fell from her eyes and mingled with the falling rain. Something inside her stirred and she bent forward, screaming out with every muscle in her body, her lungs burning with the sound of it, her fists clenching. She felt the strength gather within her and she screamed again, the sound echoing over the ravaged field. She would not let them have this world without a fight. In the distance she heard a name called out in fury and terror and her smile widened. The name of the one who had changed everything all those years ago, the one who had started it all.

*"Orabelle"*

# 1

Moonlight fell in slanted shards across the white sand beaches that formed the eastern shore of Lehar, the largest of the islands that were scattered like stars throughout the Southern Sea of Imbria. A warm breeze lifted off the sea and draped a gentle veil of mist over me as I stood on the upper deck of the ancient, beached ship that was my home, idly caressing the grey pearl that hung from a silver chain around my neck and wondering what I could do to forestall the future that seemed to be inevitably bearing down on me. I was Orabelle, Queen of Lehar and the Keeper of Water, and one of the four rulers of Imbria who had been passed the responsibility of controlling an element. The Pearl I wore was the amulet of my element, the connection between myself and the water around me. It was not the source of my power, but the conduit through which the power flowed so that I was able to harness it and bend it to my will. Yet despite all of this immense power, I still felt tossed about by the whims of others, like a tiny boat trying to navigate the raging tides of ambition and deceit that swirled around me.

I sighed as the breeze wove its subtle touch through the long, pale braids of hair that cascaded down my back, staring out over the ocean with eyes that were a deep, bottomless blue.

My eyes were ever-changing, their color reflecting my moods and the infinite colors of the sea. They were ringed with a heavy fringe of pale lashes and tilted up at the corners giving me the exotic look that was customary of the Leharan people. My high forehead and strong cheekbones would have made my face look haughty were it not for the full lips that softened my appearance. I would tell you that I was not traditionally beautiful. My mother had been beautiful and so was my sister, Maialen, but I was something different. There was something darkly arresting in my countenance that people seemed drawn to.

A sound like a quiet moan moved through the misty air and I could sense my Sirens nearby. The Sirens were my servants, creatures that had been born of the ocean at my command. They were the personification of my emotions, small pieces of my soul given life. They served me willingly and faithfully, taking on the shape of women when they needed, but always part of the sea. Even in their human forms the Sirens' movements flowed like water. Their pale blue skin shone with moisture and the tangled green tresses of their hair were eternally damp from the sea. They never spoke words, only sang out notes, even and steady, the tone and pitch of their song befitting their moods and mine.

"The Sirens seem mournful tonight," a voice spoke from behind me. I closed my eyes and let the sound flow past me caressing my skin. The voice was rich and deep like heavy velvet.

"They have much to mourn," I replied, keeping my back to the man.

"I suppose they do," he agreed quietly. He moved to stand beside me and I still did not look at him though I was aware of every inch of his body. Together we watched the ocean as it lapped calmly at the shore. The peacefulness of the tides was the only thing that seemed to subdue the emotions raging inside of me.

"Perhaps I should leave you to your thoughts," the man said after a long while, turning to leave.

"Tal, no," I protested. "Don't leave me. I do not want to be alone right now."

Tal nodded and returned to stand obediently beside me, tall and proud and silent. I wore a simple white gown that shone like the moonlit sand, my arms bare so that his long, pale hair brushed my skin and I once again closed my eyes, feeling his proximity like the rush of energy before a storm. Tal was my Guardian, my chosen protector and the commander of my army. He was Leharan and like me he was golden skinned with slanted eyes. His hair was a silvery white that fell like silk past his shoulders and matched the color of his irises. He was lean and muscular, standing more than a foot taller than me. That night he was barefoot and wore a loose linen shirt, the laces open at the neck. His black pants fit snugly, showing the long muscles of his legs and the only adornment he had was the silver belt slung around his waist that carried his sword.

I let my mind float back into the hazy past and I remembered the first time I had seen Tal. It had been nearly ten years ago, on my sixteenth birthday when I was to choose my Guardian. The day had been hot, the southern sun beating down on a cove teeming with ships from the four kingdoms of Imbria. Brightly colored flags flapped in the breeze and anticipation sparked through the air as people streamed through the coralstone walls beneath the citadel into the vast open courtyard. The ancient citadel was the heart of my kingdom, a towering structure that ascended into the sky and presided over the southern islands like a silent sentinel. It had been carved centuries before from gigantic pieces of coralstone that jutted up from the ocean floor and it dominated the otherwise serene landscape with its magnificent presence.

From its height one could look out over all the islands, even seeing the distant edges of mainland Imbria across the sea.

The crowd that gathered that day had spread itself around the edges of the square beneath the shadow of the citadel, and people were chatting excitedly and making loud, friendly wagers on who the chosen man would be. Groups of hopeful candidates clustered on opposite sides of the yard, stretching and punching the air, wielding weapons and practicing maneuvers.

I sat on a raised dais that had been erected at one end of the field, my eyes traversing the men who had gathered below. Many of the candidates were unremarkable in appearance and I glanced over them without interest until my eyes came to rest on one enormous man from Veruca, the region ruled over by the Fire Keeper. The man's ruddy skin and heavy beard, along with his massive size, made him stand out among the smoother-skinned races of the other realms. The man caught me watching him and leered at me, flexing his enormous muscles as I quickly turned my head away in embarrassment.

My father, Chronus, sat beside me in an ornate and overstuffed chair that I suspected he had brought with him all the way from his own kingdom of Kymir. He wore his usual attire, rich robes of green laced with gold, a viridian shirt with jewels adorning the collar and brown pants stitched with gold thread. His hair was a thick, chestnut brown that was starting to grey at the temples and his harsh features supported a trim, pointed beard. On his wrists were the heavy golden cuffs he always wore, the emeralds that encrusted them dazzling in the sunlight. I had always hated the wrist cuffs for they had made his hands heavier when he had struck me as a child.

"Why are there no women competing?" I asked him, inwardly bracing myself for I knew the question would stir his ire.

"What a ridiculous thing to ask," he scoffed in response.

I glanced again at the Verucan man who still continued to leer grotesquely in my direction. I made a noise of disgust.

"What is the matter with you now, Orabelle?" Chronus asked, bending towards me so that his breath had hissed in my ear. I made a vague gesture at the vulgar man. Chronus followed the line of my hand. "Oh, that is Raynor, a fine warrior. I believe he may be our winner today! I know he is Verucan and it is customary to choose from your own kingdom, but there is no rule saying that you must. He is my personal choice for your Guardian."

"That is not surprising," I had muttered under my breath, refusing to look at the beastly man again and instead letting my eyes roam through the crowd of spectators.

"What was that?" Chronus demanded sharply.

"What? Oh, nothing, father," I tossed back over my shoulder, ignoring him. I could practically feel him reddening with anger but I kept my back stubbornly turned, not caring. I knew that Chronus was a politician above all else and he would not want to cause a scene with me here where so many people were gathered.

My eyes came to rest on a silver haired man who stood far back from the others, leaning against the coralstone wall of the citadel with his arms crossed over his chest. He wore loose white clothing and a silver belt hung on his hips. I could barely see the hilt of a sword where the shadow of the fortress tower slanted across him. He didn't appear to be much older than I was but he watched the warriors in the yard with a calm detachment that made him seem experienced beyond his years. His eyes moved from man to man, studying them, his expression never changing.

"Father." I flapped a hand at Chronus while keeping my eyes on the man. "Who is that?"

"Orabelle, stop swatting at me like a fly. I swear you have the manners of a Tahitian," Chronus said disgustedly.

"But father, I want to know-"

"Quiet!" he snapped, his irritation beginning to border on anger. "I have heard enough from you for the day. Sit and try to be more like your sister if you can."

My eyes flashed pale blue at him and I glanced to where Maialen sat demurely, hands folded in her lap, looking straight ahead and smiling pleasantly. I rolled my eyes then settled them back on the man with the silver hair. He was handsome but there was something else about him that drew my attention, a hum of energy that circled him, like something savage and fierce was lurking just beneath his calm exterior.

The trumpeting of a conch shell interrupted my thoughts and I pulled my gaze reluctantly away from the man. The beating of drums echoed over the courtyard and a cheer rose up from the throng of spectators. The demonstrations were about to begin. The warriors would pair up to spar, showing off their skills and after each round I would select the winners, narrowing them down till settling on one who would become my Guardian. The first groups came forward and began to fight their mock battles. I watched for a few minutes but I quickly grew bored. I had yawned loudly, much to Chronus's dismay and he had glared at me balefully. I smiled sweetly at him and once again sought out the silver haired man. I found him staring back at me, his face still immobile, not having moved but for a slight tilt of his head. I straightened my back and lifted my chin so that I could look down my nose at him to show him my superiority. To my astonishment a smile flashed across his face and his shoulders shook gently with laughter. My mouth fell open in surprise and I furrowed my brow in indignation, wondering how he could possibly have the gall to laugh at me. He continued to smile and shrugged his shoulders helplessly. My own laughter escaped my lips before I could swallow it and I clapped a hand over my mouth.

"For the gods' sakes, Orabelle!" Chronus cried out, throwing his hands in the air and bringing them down hard on his knees, the gold cuffs flashing garishly.

"Sorry, father," I murmured, still struggling to suppress my laughter.

Chronus grabbed my arm and I flinched involuntarily as he jerked me closer to him so that he could snarl under his breath, "Do not embarrass me further, daughter, or I shall become very angry with you."

His grip tightened painfully and I pulled my arm sharply from his grasp and rubbed at the red marks he had left on my skin, saying stubbornly, "I am Queen here, father. You forget we are on Lehar. This is not Kymir and I shall laugh if I want to."

"You are Queen with the Council's permission and with our supervision. It is several years till you are twenty and can rule on your own, Orabelle, an edict that I and the Council can overturn. If you do not curb your temper I shall see that you are forced to wait until you are fully mature," he threatened, adding with disdain, "if such a thing is even possible."

I remained silent knowing that he was right but still feeling the anger boiling inside of me. I despised the fact that I still had to defer to him. The edicts of the Council of Elements had been written long ago by the ancient ones and had never been challenged. I was the first exception that had ever been made and I often wondered what that meant for me. Keepers were only allowed to rule after they had lived one era and were the age of twenty and then they could only hold power for two eras. After that the amulets and the rule had to be relinquished to the next, who was chosen by the current Keeper.

My eyes glanced over the crowd to see if anyone had noticed the uncomfortable exchange with my father and hoping they had all been too busy watching the competitors. The man with the silver hair was staring at me intently, his eyes narrowed. I realized I was still rubbing my arm where Chronus had grasped it and I dropped my hands to my lap, focusing back on the hopeful warriors in the courtyard just as the conch sounded again. The round was over and I was to select the men I wanted to continue on. Since I had not paid any attention to their demonstrations I waved randomly at a few of them. Cheers went through the crowd and people began making bets for the next round. Again two groups came forward from either side. The great beast Raynor was there, facing off against a tall, solid looking man from the Air Kingdom of Samirra who carried a long broadsword. Raynor circled the man menacingly, tossing his battle axe from hand to hand. The other man was following the axe with his eyes and Raynor struck out with his left foot, kicking the Samirran squarely in the chest and sending him flying across the yard. Raynor immediately grabbed the closest man and struck him on the temple with the flat of his axe. The man crumpled to the ground and the Verucan roared loudly, moving to the next opponent.

"Enough!" I yelled, standing up on the dais. Chronus cursed heartily but I pretended not to hear. The men stopped fighting and the spectators grew silent as everyone turned their attention to their little Queen. "I have had enough of watching you bash at each other to impress me."

I gathered my skirts in one hand and swung myself over the rail of the platform landing lightly on my feet and striding into the courtyard. The men gaped at me in shock then hurried to move out of my way. I imagined the apoplectic fit Chronus must be swallowing and I suppressed a smile.

"Queen Orabelle," one of the men asked, "What on Imbria are you doing?"

I looked around at each of them, feeling my eyes begin to cool and darken as I called to my power. My voice echoed across the coralstone. "Attack me."

An astonished murmur rose from the crowd and the men looked at each other, perplexed.

"Attack me, you cowards!" I ordered again, laughing at them. "I have seen you beat on each other and I am unimpressed. You who wish to protect me should be man enough to challenge me! Or are you afraid on one little woman?"

I lifted my arms to either side and drew my element to me. The morning dew, the dampness in the air and the cool drops of sea spray all moved to do my bidding. I flicked my wrist and a plume of water slammed into the closest warrior, knocking him off his feet. I then settled my gaze on Raynor and crooked a finger at him.

Raynor gave a loud roar and charged at me, axe held high. I braced my feet, hands in front of me ready to repel the attack. I was unafraid, the naiveté of youth making me think that I was invincible. Raynor swung his axe and just as I lifted the water to shove his weapon aside a flash of white blurred across my vision and there was a loud clang of metal. The man with the silver hair was standing in front of me, his body blocking me from the massive Verucan. He held a long, wickedly curved sword whose blade was etched with whorling designs. As I watched he moved around me with fluid grace to counter each of Raynor's moves. He had a confidence that only comes from the complete awareness of one's self. His sword danced in front of him in long arcs, his body curving to follow it. Raynor had deliberately charged me with a blow I could easily have deflected, after all he would not risk injuring a Queen, but now he grew furious at the other man and growled and charged, swinging the axe with all his might. The silver haired man spun me out of the way then dropped to the ground, kicking out at Raynor's legs and rolling underneath him as the huge man tumbled to the ground. The Verucan ended up in a heap near my feet, the silver haired man's sword at his throat.

Raynor howled with rage. "Get him!" he yelled to the other men who were watching uncertainly. They charged forward, surrounding us.

I was mesmerized as the silver haired man fought the men back one by one all the while keeping me safely behind him. Finally they relented and he stood, one arm around my waist, the other holding his sword, panting from exhaustion and soaked in sweat. His lip was bleeding and one slanted grey eye was swollen and darkening to a bruise.

I grabbed his hand that held the sword and raised it into the air. "This man shall be my Guardian!" I announced defiantly, my face shining with pride while his remained expressionless. The crowd surged in around us, the men congratulating him and clapping him on the back heartily.

Chronus came storming through the crowd, elbowing people aside rudely. He strode directly up to the silver haired man and shoved a finger in his face. "Just who do you think you are?" he demanded to know.

The man drew his hand from mine and sheathed his sword. He bowed low, his long hair nearly sweeping the ground. "I am Tal, Guardian of Orabelle, Water Queen of Lehar." As he rose from his bow he locked eyes with Chronus and said in a voice barely audible above the noise surrounding him, "And if you ever bruise her skin again you will answer to me."

The sound of his words wrapped around me like a comforting embrace and I knew in that moment that this man, whoever he was, would protect me with his life. I had repeated his name silently to myself letting it roll off my tongue. It was from the ancient language, Tal, a language that few still spoke or understood. He was named for the rain.

The memory of that day faded from my mind leaving a bittersweet taste lingering in my mouth as I let my eyes follow the coastline past the assemblage of silent, furled ships that were rocking peacefully in the harbor, up the sloped beaches to where the great citadel rose in the distance. I wondered what memories were weaving their way through Tal's mind or if he thought only of the future, his past left behind in discarded remnants of what could have been.

"Tomorrow it begins," I murmured aloud.

"I know well what tomorrow brings, my Queen," he replied stiffly.

I turned to him finally and studied his profile in the moonlight. His face gave away no hint of emotion, save a shadow that darkened his grey eyes. I looked back to the sea and did not try to keep the contempt from my voice as I continued, "The old bastard will be there, of course, presiding over everything and strutting around in his ridiculous robes like a tyrannical peacock."

The corners of Tal's mouth twitched and he leaned forward, bracing his hands on the smooth wooden rail of the deck. The muscles of his shoulders strained against the fabric of his shirt and I watched the long lines of his body from the corner of my eye as he spoke. "You do have a way with words, little Queen. Though I can't imagine your father would be pleased by you comparing him to a peacock."

My eyes flashed pale as my temper flared. "There are worse things I could compare him to! I am nothing to him but a pawn. Something to be auctioned off and sold to a man I despise so he can further his own agenda while hiding behind some ignorant, outdated tradition."

Chronus had arranged my marriage and that of my sister, as was the tradition for women in royal families. A tradition, in my opinion, that served to keep the powerful women of Imbria in their place and to remind us that we were still subject to the rule of men. Chronus had betrothed me without my knowledge or consent, caring nothing about who or what I wanted. Tomorrow we would be traveling to his kingdom of Kymir for the festival that was to celebrate my imminent union to Blaise, Fire Keeper and King of Veruca, a man I had always loathed.

"Your father wants what is best for you, Orabelle."

"Ha!" I scoffed. "After all this time you cannot possibly believe that! Chronus does what is best for himself, not for me. He must be hoping that idiot, Blaise, will tame me and make me meek and obedient so that he will have full sway over the Council."

Tal raised an eyebrow. "I don't believe anyone would use the words meek or obedient when referring to you, my Queen."

"Do not tease me now, I am angry!" I snapped. "Blaise has been after me for years and if my father has finally decided to hand me over then I can promise you that he has attained something valuable in return. Once I know what that is, I will do everything in my power to make sure that he never gets it." I began to pace the deck back and forth in agitation trying to determine what it was that my father could have asked for in exchange for agreeing to the marriage.

"You're torturing yourself. Stop this. If your father did request something in return for your betrothal there is no way to find out what it is tonight."

"How easy for you to say, Tal. I am the one who has to marry that impudent little upstart. He is arrogant, cruel and conniving and has no right to his throne or to me! He coddled a dying, heirless old man to get his hands on the Fire Opal and elevate himself from a grunt in the Verucan army to a king!"

"Blaise was very close with the former king, one of his closest advisors," Tal pointed out.

I stopped pacing and stood directly in front of Tal, shoving my braided hair back from my face. "I don't care! I don't want him! Where is my choice, Tal? I am Queen, why must I do as they say? I am the one giving up my freedom and my life! Why? And what if I don't, what if I refuse?"

He sighed. "We've been over this, Orabelle. Your father has maneuvered you carefully into this position. You are already promised to the Fire King. The peace between Lehar and Veruca has always been an unsteady one, especially since the incident with the Tahitians. Your marriage will bring security, whereas throwing him aside could bring us to war. He would see it as a very serious insult and Blaise is a proud and vain man."

"I don't care what he sees it as!" I said vehemently. "What can he do, Tal, attack us? We have the best army on Imbria. Besides that, Lehar is an island. They can't reach us if I don't want them to. You know what my power is. I would destroy them all at sea."

Tal was perhaps the only person who knew the full extent of my powers as the Water Keeper. I had taken over my element much younger than the Keepers before me. I was thirteen when the former Queen, my mother Ursula, had fallen ill and was no longer able to rule. I had been forced to take the element seven years before I should have. As a result I had grown powerful, able to use and control the water in ways the former Water Keepers could never come close to. My father and the rest of the Council knew that I was powerful but I had kept many of my abilities secret.

"You would go to war so easily?" Tal asked, frowning.

I refused to meet his gaze knowing that I would see consternation in the grey eyes. It was ironic that the man who commanded my army, one of the greatest warriors Imbria had ever seen, was one who would do anything to avoid war. Over the years he had drawn me away from conflict, soothed my temper and convinced me to grant mercy when I would have shown none. There had been one incident in particular where Tal had been the sole reason that I had not plunged us into a mire of conflict with the other realms. We had been sailing along the western coast of Imbria, part of a convoy that had journeyed to the other kingdoms as a token of goodwill, when another ship had appeared on the misty horizon. It had been just after dawn and the fog hung low over the water, obscuring the dark shape of the vessel that glided towards us. I had been woken from my sleep by Tal who had wrapped a warm cloak over my shoulders and led me onto the deck. The ship was eerily silent as it approached, the rigging creaking and one sail luffing in the breeze.

"Where is the crew?" I had asked Tal.

"We signaled them but received no response though their bearing is bringing them straight for us."

"Which means someone is steering that ship. Signal again and have the crew ready at their stations," I ordered. Tal bowed his head slightly and saw that my commands were followed as I stayed on the windward rail, watching the ghostly ship. It began to come around so that it would pull up beside us and suddenly there was a shout and a spark of fire flashed in the cool dawn. A loud thud caused me to glance over my shoulder at an arrow that was embedded in the main mast just above my head, a thin wisp of smoke trailing up into the air. I felt my eyes pale with anger and Tal shoved me aside just as another fiery arrow pierced the morning.

"That is a Verucan ship!" I shouted to him as I pushed myself up from the deck.

He yelled something back in response but the cacophony of the water I called up from the sea drowned out his voice. I reached out for the black-armored ship, the water clawing up the side and tearing at the vessel like a great monster from the deep so that it began to roll under the waves. There were screams from the crew as they fought to hold on desperately and I felt laughter bubbling in my throat.

"Orabelle, stop!" Tal's voice was close to me and he gripped my arm, trying to pull me around to face him. I shook him off and stood defiantly on the deck, savoring the feel of my power as the Verucan ship began to shudder and the masts dipped underneath the water. I would rip it in two and toss all of those who dared attack me to the mercy of the sea.

"Orabelle, no, remember Tahitia!" Tal insisted, grabbing me again. This time I looked up into his grey eyes and I felt reason returning, washing away the anger. I stopped abruptly, the water receding from the ship in a rush and the vessel swinging upright so that the masts were once again pointing to the sky.

"They attacked us."

"I know but you have the heard the stories," Tal had warned. "If you kill them you will put yourself in danger with the Council. Take these men in and demand answers from the Verucan King."

I had done as Tal had asked me to and spared the lives of the men who had tried to kill me, bringing them on board as prisoners and calling for a meeting of Council to confront Veruca. Blaise had smirked and as I expected he claimed no knowledge of the attack, saying the men were mercenaries and hadn't known I was on board but promising that they would be punished for their actions. The memory of it still infuriated me and I felt my temper rise once again at the image I conjured of Blaise's smug face across the Council table.

I shook my head in agitation. "I have maintained peace, I have bitten my tongue and bowed to their demands in the Council and still they ask for more!"

"Calm down, Orabelle, you must think of what is best for Lehar." Tal laid his hands on my shoulders and the feel of his warm skin on mine tied my stomach in knots. He quickly backed away, letting go as if I burned him.

"They will destroy Lehar if I give them the chance," I said with a shake of my head. "Chronus and Blaise are threatened by this realm. The Tahitians have already been banished. I am afraid that if I go through with this marriage then I could stand to lose everything."

"By not going through with it you could lose more than that."

"So that is the end? That is how it will be?" I demanded. "I have no choice and you will just let him have me? You would give me away like I am nothing?"

"You are everything to me, Orabelle. You know that." His voice had deepened and his hands were fisted at his sides.

"Then prove it!" I shouted at him.

"You are not mine to take or give! You are the Queen, the Keeper of Water, ruler of Lehar. You cannot start a war among the Council of Elements because of me!" he shouted back.

I grabbed his hand and slammed it to my chest, holding it just above my breast so his palm covered my heart. "I am yours, Tal! How can you let me marry another?"

He stared into my furious eyes and felt the quick beating of my heart under his hand. He spoke softly and firmly. "I wish that things were not so but I cannot change who we are, Orabelle, and you must."

I flung his hand away from me. Tears fell in sparkling rivulets down my cheeks as I tried to swallow the knot in my throat. I felt my eyes darken to the hard, flat blue that conveyed more than any words how hurt I was. He reached for me but I stepped away from him, shaking my head.

"No," I began defiantly, wiping the tears from my face. "Do not touch me. Never again will you touch me, Tal."

"Orabelle-"

"No!" I interrupted, feeling as if my heart was being torn from my chest. I took deep breaths, making my voice calm and steady. Then I said cruelly, wanting to hurt him, "You will not touch me again because I will belong to another man. You will not feel my lips or the touch of my skin. Instead you can take your morals and your reasons and they can comfort you at night while HE touches me! While he kisses me, while he holds me, while he-"

"Enough!" Tal cried. His eyes were bright and wide, his golden skin flushed. I stopped and lifted my chin stubbornly, holding his gaze. He stared at me for a long time, his breathing matching mine. When he finally spoke his velvet voice was rough with emotion. "Orabelle, I would willingly give everything I have for things to be different. Your wedding will destroy me. The thought of your wedding night is unbearable. But I cannot let you jeopardize everything that you have, all that you love, your kingdom, for me. What kind of man would I be then?"

The raw sound of his torment broke against me, washing away my hurt and anger. It was all too much, too unfair and I didn't want to think about it anymore. I stepped closer to him, wrapping my arms around his waist and laying my head on his chest. He crushed me against him, holding me tightly.

"Stay with me tonight, Tal. One more night," I whispered.

He nodded and lifted me effortlessly, taking me down the steps to the lower deck where my quarters were. He carried me through the curtained doorway that led to my bedroom where the moon shimmered through the gossamer fabric coating everything in a pearlized haze. A single candle burned on the bedside table and I damped it out with a wave of my hand, loathing the sight of its warm glow in the cool night.

Tal lowered me to the ground and we stood facing each other. I gazed upon the strong, determined lines of his face and felt desire wash over me like the caress of the ocean breeze. A longing rose in me that I had never felt with anyone but Tal. I ached for him so that my skin hurt with the need for his touch. My lungs drew air only to breathe him in. My eyes were blind but for the sight of him and my throat thirsted for his taste. I wanted to watch his cool reserve desert him. I needed to feel him tremble beneath me. My eyes turned a deep blue-green and my lips parted, my breath quickening.

He watched me, standing perfectly still like a beautiful statue, a quiet tension in the air the only hint of my effect on him. Tal's self-control was impeccable, save when he was alone with me. Like an intoxicating wine I would drink in the sight of him losing himself to me. I pulled my dress over my head, the adornments in my hair chiming against one another. I stood before him, drowning in my own need. His eyes moved over me, my skin flushing beneath his gaze.

He reached for the clasp of his belt and set his sword on my dressing table. He tugged at the laces of his shirt, loosening them further so that he was able to take it off in one quick motion, his eyes never leaving me. A heavy sigh escaped my lips at the sight of his silver hair raining down over the golden skin of his shoulders and chest. My fingers twitched against my sides with the yearning to touch him and I curled them into my fists. A smile played at the edges of his mouth as he slid out of the tight black pants, kicking them away. We continued to face each other, waiting for the desire to build until it was nearly unbearable, each waiting for the other to give in. My breathing grew deeper and he watched the rise and fall of my breasts. My need was filling me till I thought I would go mad if he didn't touch me, that my heart would stop beating if he didn't come to me.

"Tal," I whispered.

"Ask me," he said. His jaw was clenched and I could see how he struggled to restrain himself from me. The sight of him standing there silent and proud, barely holding himself together, brought another rush of desire crashing through me.

"Please, Tal. Please come to me," I begged. He made a noise deep in his throat and was in my arms. We fell on each other in desperation, neither of us able to get enough to quench the bottomless thirst that rose between us. My senses whirled as I felt the smooth hardness of his body against mine. I tasted him like succulent poison, pulling myself closer, wrapping my body around his and making him groan. He gripped my thighs and lifted me, draping me back across the cool silk of the bed. He climbed over me as I lay trembling beneath him, his warm body sliding across mine. He propped himself up on his elbows so that he could look down on me. His hair brushed my skin and I shivered, pressing my hips against his.

"You captivate me, Orabelle," he murmured and I looked into his eyes, seeing a tenderness there that I recognized as his giving in to me. I opened my mouth to speak and he stopped me with a long, deep kiss. "No," he said. "No more words tonight."

I nodded and arched my back as he began to move. I wrapped my arms around his neck and pulled his face down to mine so I could see the look in his eyes. I could feel the breath in him as the sweet sensation of his body poured over me. I moved with him, wanting to be closer, close enough to touch his soul with mine. I wanted to lose myself completely to him, to let him possess me. I cried out as he brought me further and further to the edge of myself. Then finally he pushed me, crying his name, over the edge and into the abyss that was him.

# 2

The great trees of Kymir towered above us as we made our way from the docks to the Royal City. Tal walked beside me, flanked on either side by the Leharan Guard. The Guard were Tal's personal soldiers and my bodyguards, a group comprised of ten of the strongest and bravest in our army, including Colwyn, his second in command. The Guard, like Tal, were dressed in their military finest, their crisp white shirts threaded with pale silver, tall polished boots covering dark blue breeches and silver swords gleaming at their sides. My own gown matched their uniforms, shimmering deep-sea blue at the neck and fading to the silvery white of the Leharan sands at the hem.

Behind us stretched a line of Leharans composed of regents and noble families all clad in their finest attire to represent our island. Following them were the villagers carrying baskets of fruits and fish, gifts to the festival from my people. They formed a shimmering ribbon of blue and white that flowed behind me and I was proud to be their Queen.

I kept my eyes forward as we walked and did not glance at Tal. I had woken that morning to find him gone, already at the fort preparing the ships to sail. There had been no goodbyes, no promises nor any regrets, only the emptiness of the bed beside me. I had dressed slowly, letting the Sirens weave their colorful baubles through my hair, trying not to feel his absence like a slap in my face.

A heavy wave of nostalgia flowed over me as the lofty wooden houses of the Kymir Royal City became visible in the treetops, pushing thoughts of Tal from my mind. The smell of evergreens and the musky scent of earth filled the air. I had spent my childhood divided between Lehar and this place, the happy, carefree years before my mother had fallen ill. I looked up, straining to see the room where for years Ursula had wasted away in solitude as the sickness slowly ate at her. It was still there, a tiny roost just above my father's own lavish dwelling. The abandoned structure sagged with decay and vines had begun to tangle around the walls.

I could not help but remember the first time I had made my way to that room. I was thirteen and my mother had been sick for several months. Maialen and I were forbidden from seeing her as her illness was a mystery and contagion a fear. My father had come to me one morning while I sat on the forest floor, braiding flowers through my sister's thick, wavy hair.

"Orabelle, come with me now," Chronus had ordered, holding out his hand as his long shadow slanted across us. There was something in his face and the tone of his voice that had frightened me. I had cowered behind Maialen, staring up at him in trepidation.

"Come with me, now!" he had repeated sternly and I had stood, biting my trembling lip and ignoring the offered hand.

"Can I come too?" little Maialen had asked, blinking her huge green eyes solemnly. I watched our father's hard face soften into a smile as he knelt and patted her head.

"No, darling Princess. You stay here." He then rose and led me up into the trees, climbing the roped staircase that bypassed his own house and heading for the room where my mother was kept.

"Am I going to see mother?" I had asked excitedly, joy suffusing my face at the thought.

"You are," Chronus replied, opening the door. I had rushed past him nearly knocking him off balance and eliciting a string of irritable curses.

"Mama! Mama!" I cried in elation then stopped abruptly, clapping my hands over my mouth in horror. My mother lay in a large bed, eyes closed, her golden skin pale and waxy. Her beautiful white hair that had once billowed around her like a snowy cloud now lay in sweaty clumps on the pillow. She was thin and frail and the room reeked with the overwhelming sour stench of decay and sickness. I approached the bed slowly, afraid that even a loud noise would damage her further for she looked so fragile.

Chronus stepped into the room as her red-rimmed eyes fluttered open. She looked at me and the ghost of a smile passed over her dry, cracked lips.

"Mama?" I whispered hesitantly.

"Orabelle," she sighed in a hoarse and raspy voice I didn't recognize.

"It is time, Ursula," Chronus said, coming to stand beside me at the edge of the bed. "Give her the Pearl."

"The Pearl?" I had asked, looking up at him in confusion. I knew that one day the Pearl of Water would be mine, that I would be Queen, but that day wasn't for years to come.

"Yes," Chronus answered me, "your mother is too ill. The Council needs someone to control the element and she has grown weak. She has insisted that it be you so you shall take the Pearl and begin your rule under the Council's supervision."

My head spun at his words. The only thing I could grasp was that my mother wasn't going to get better and that was why they wanted me to take the amulet. I shook my head stubbornly. "No! I don't want it."

"Orabelle, now is not the time to be childish! Those days have passed," Chronus snapped irritably. He seemed in a hurry to be out of the room and had barely glanced at my mother, showing her no signs of sympathy.

"But she will get better!" I had insisted. "You will get better, won't you, Mama?"

She smiled again and the feebleness of her tore at my heart.

"Ursula, I haven't got all day. Give her the damn Pearl," Chronus ordered callously. I saw my mother's eyes brighten with what might have been anger had she been stronger.

"Orabelle," she said to me in her strange, dry voice, "you will be Queen now. Lehar belongs to you, my daughter. Do not let anyone take it from you. And do not let them control you. You need to be your own woman."

I nodded my head, my face wet with tears. She coughed and the sound scraped through her throat painfully. She lifted her hand and pressed the Pearl into my palm. I stared down at the dark silver orb in wonder, feeling the first stirrings of power. My mother coughed again, spittle dribbling down her chin. I tucked the Pearl into my dress and reached over to wipe her mouth with my sleeve. She caught my arm in a surprisingly strong grip and brought me closer to her face, her feverish eyes burning into mine.

"There is something else you must know," she rasped. "Your father-"

"What are you doing, Ursula?" Chronus interrupted, jerking me back by my shoulder. The force of it spun me around and I slammed into the wall.

"Chronus, don't," she pleaded. "I need to tell her!"

He turned on me, his face red with anger. "Get out!" he yelled.

I pushed myself away from the wall and tried to shove past him to reach my mother but he had used his body to block her from me. "But father," I had started to protest and he had grabbed a handful of my hair and flung me towards the door. I cried out, stumbling to my knees on the hard wooden floor.

"OUT!" he roared, coming at me. I scrambled awkwardly to my feet and fled through the doorway. I had not been allowed to see my mother again until she had fallen into a wasting sleep that had lasted till her death. For years I had pleaded with Chronus, begging him to let me take her home to Lehar where perhaps the sea air would help her. He had stubbornly refused, even going so far as to post his soldiers outside her door when I had threatened to take her without his permission.

I felt a fresh wave of hatred flow through me at the memories. One day soon I would make my father answer for the things he had done. Maialen was taking over as Keeper of Earth and Chronus would no longer have any power in the Council. I only hoped that I would be able to curb his influence over my impressionable younger sister.

"Queen Orabelle. I am so pleased to see you well," an oily voice interrupted my thoughts. A man was hurrying down the path to meet us.

"Damek," I greeted him with a nod. Damek was one of my father's closest advisors and in my opinion a sniveling sycophant not to be trusted. He was small and spindly with lank, dark hair that hung over darting eyes. He had always reminded me of a spider or some other crawling, lurking insect.

"Your father regrets that he could not be here to welcome you to Kymir himself," Damek said, taking my hand in his bony fingers and pressing my knuckles against his thin lips.

"I'm sure he does," I replied, surreptitiously wiping my hand on my skirts. Tal noticed my movements and the corner of his mouth twitched as he hid a smile.

"Oh, he does," Damek insisted. "Now, would you like me to show you to the rooms we have prepared for your visit?"

"No. Have our things taken there from our ship. I am anxious to see my sister," I said dismissively, moving to step around him.

"Yes, of course you are. I will take you there now," Damek offered, reaching to halt me. Tal's hand caught his thin wrist before he could stop me and I sailed past him.

"Do not touch the Queen," Tal advised coldly.

Damek looked up at him and nodded furiously. "Of course, yes, I meant no, nothing by it, of course. I was only going to escort the Queen and, well-"

"Escort me or chaperone me to make sure I don't cause any trouble?" I called over my shoulder as I kept walking, the sounds of the festival growing loud. I reached the edge of a huge clearing that teemed with people from all over Imbria. Brightly colored ribbons decorated the trees and garlands of berries hung everywhere. I scanned the crowd for Maialen but I wasn't tall enough to see past the first group of revelers who blocked my path.

"She is over there," Tal pointed out, joining me.

"Where?" I leaned on him to see from his perspective and peered through the throngs of people.

"Over there, with your father."

"Wonderful," I muttered and started to move off.

"Orabelle." Tal caught my hand to stop me. "About this morning... Please don't be angry."

I pulled my hand from his. "There is nothing to discuss," I said coldly and turned away into the crowd. I had nearly reached Maialen when Blaise stepped in front of me, resting his hands on my hips with too much familiarity.

"There you are, my dearest fiancé," he said with an easy smile. He was dressed in black, as he usually was, his bright red curls shining above his handsome, chiseled face. He was tall and broad through the shoulders, though still shorter than

Tal by several inches. His amber colored eyes were smoldering with an intensity that belied his casual smirk.

"Let go of me, Blaise. I am not your dearest anything," I said disdainfully, trying to peel his hands off of me.

"Now, now," he chastised with a shake of his head. "You don't want to cause a scene and embarrass Daddy."

"Let go of me," I repeated more insistently. "And if you think that I care in the least about embarrassing my father, you are quite mistaken."

He laughed and as always there was an edge to his laugh as if it could turn into a shout of rage at any second. "But you do care about your lovely little sister."

He inclined his head to where Maialen stood nearby at the edge of the wooden stage that had been set up for the festival. She looked beautiful, her bright green dress adorned with a pattern of vines that fitted her perfectly and her thick brown hair falling in loose waves around her shoulders. Her green eyes sparkled with happiness and the warmth of her smile could be felt all around the clearing. Beside her was her Guardian, Gideon, a giant of a woodsman whose gentleness was at odds with his intimidating appearance. The Guardian hovered near her protectively as she spoke to my father and another woman that I did not recognize.

"Who is that woman?" I asked Blaise. She had a thick mane of coppery hair and light golden eyes and the curves of her body exuded sensuality. Her full red lips were smiling at Chronus while she trailed long fingernails up and down his arm.

"That is my cousin, Loagaire. Seems she and your father are getting along very well," Blaise informed me with a suggestive leer.

I frowned at them. "How utterly revolting."

He laughed again and stepped closer to me. "Ah, how I have missed you, Orabelle. You always make me laugh."

"And you, Blaise, always make me nauseous. Now, I would like to see my sister, will you be so good as to get out of my way?" I asked with deceptive sweetness.

"I will accompany you," he said, sliding his arm through mine. I felt a flush of annoyance wash over me but I let it go, allowing him to lead me to where my family stood.

"Orabelle!" Maialen exclaimed happily, throwing her arms around me and effectively pushing Blaise aside. She let go of me and stepped back, clasping my hands, pushing Blaise even further away. "I am so happy to see you."

"You look wonderful, little sister. The Earth Emerald suits you." I gestured to the large stone that now hung from her neck.

She touched it gingerly with her fingertips. "Thank you. I....I am not quite used to it yet. Though father has been helping me prepare and he is so patient with me!"

"You will make a wonderful Queen," I assured her. I turned to Chronus, looking at the woman, Loagaire, who had draped herself against him. "I see you are doing well, father."

"And you, daughter, are a lovely bride to be," he replied, his words dripping with sarcasm. "Now that you have arrived I think we shall make the marriage announcements. Gideon, would you find the Samirrans for me?"

I narrowed my eyes at him. "Isn't it a bit early for the announcements?"

"I am eager to share the joyous news of both my daughters' engagements," Chronus offered expansively. I felt my face redden and I swallowed back the scathing remark I was about to throw at him. Instead I turned my back and waited as Gideon went to fetch Astraeus. Blaise moved to stand behind me, leaning over so that he could whisper to me.

"You will be mine soon," he said, his lips brushing my ear. I remained stubbornly silent, refusing to acknowledge him. I stared out at the gathered people and my eyes found Tal's. He was watching us, his face emotionless and showing no sign that anything happening that day concerned him in the least. Blaise followed my gaze, running his hands over my bare shoulders. "Who are you looking at?"

"No one," I said flatly. I turned my head and focused my attention on Maialen, who was rushing forward to greet Astraeus as he approached with Gideon and the Samirran Guardian, Favian. The Air King had never been of much interest to me but my sister was hopelessly infatuated with him. He had clear blue eyes and dark hair that contrasted dramatically with his pale skin. Lean and muscular, I could see why she found him attractive, though he had always been a bit lacking in intelligence and imagination for me. He seemed to rule his kingdom effectively enough and I suspected this was largely due to the influence of his mother, Irielle. Her quiet, regal demeanor hid a sharp intellect and it was well known that for years before her son had taken over she had managed the affairs of the former king, her husband, Astus.

"Hello, Astraeus," Maialen said breathlessly, staring up at her future husband, her face glowing. He took her hand and kissed it gallantly, flashing her a winning smile.

"You are radiant as always," he flattered her and her cheeks pinkened prettily.

Chronus moved up the steps to the platform and stood in the center of it, clapping to get everyone's attention. "People of Imbria!" he boomed, raising his hands in the air and smiling benevolently. "As you know, we are gathered here for a celebration! It is with great joy that I have invited all of you today, from all of the four realms!"

"The old man puts on an excellent performance, doesn't he?" Blaise chuckled in my ear.

"Let him enjoy it while he can," I said bitterly. "Maialen has taken over the element. He has no more power."

"I would not expect him to just fade into the background. You should know your father better than that," Blaise cautioned. "By the way, Daddy is calling you."

Blaise motioned towards the stage where Maialen was making her way up the steps to Chronus who was holding out his hands to her. He kissed her on the cheek and she beamed at him and they both looked to where I stood. I sighed and joined them reluctantly on the platform. Thankfully, Chronus did not attempt to embrace me with a show of paternal love but instead continued to orate to the crowd. I watched the gathered faces of the Imbrians as he droned on about his pride and his legacy and uniting the kingdoms, my eyes involuntarily seeking out Tal once again. He was standing with Colwyn and the youngest member of the Guard, Kaden, who made a rude face as Blaise was called to the stage. I lowered my head to hide a smile and the crowd cheered as the Fire King took my hand, mistaking my expression for one of happiness with my intended husband.

"And now," Chronus was saying, "Let them lead us in a dance!"

"Will these torments never end?" I muttered under my breath, throwing Chronus an icy glare. I allowed Blaise to lead me off the stage as the trill of flutes filled the air and the people moved back, clearing an open space for us to dance. Blaise swept me into his arms and as we moved his smoldering gaze became fixed on some point over my shoulder. He spun me around and I was startled to see Tal as the object Blaise was staring at so intently.

"You belong to me," Blaise swore in a low voice, his eyes still locked on Tal.

"I belong to no one," I responded haughtily.

He laughed. "Tell yourself what you will, Orabelle, but no matter how powerful of a Queen you are, you are still a woman."

I glared at him. "It bothers you not in the least that I don't want to marry you?"

"Not at all," he answered with the easy grin that was at odds with the fire in his eyes. "It matters little to me what you want. I am getting what I want and that is what concerns me."

"You want someone who loathes you?"

"As I said, I care not how you feel about things. Now, be silent. I have had enough of your venom for one night," Blaise ordered, tightening his hold on me.

"You are not my husband yet and even when you are I will not be so easily silenced!" I snapped at him, pulling away as the song thankfully ended.

Maialen hurried over to us, Astraeus in tow. She was flushed and smiling beatifically but the corners of her mouth tilted down when she saw my face for I was having a difficult time keeping my temper in check. She glanced at Blaise and then back to me. "Sister, would you care for some refreshment?"

"Yes, thank you, Maialen," I answered gratefully. She paused to squeeze Astraeus's hand then followed me through the crowd to where long tables had been set with casks of wine and carved wooden goblets. She passed me one and I sipped it as we stood back from the press of people.

"You really hate him, don't you?" she asked, her big green eyes full of worry.

I sighed. "I do not want to marry him."

"Have you talked with father? Surely he would not force you if he knew how you felt!"

I stared into the dark liquid of the wine as it swirled in the goblet and marveled at her innocence. "He knows how I feel about it and he does not care. It is done. He has made the announcement."

"Oh, Orabelle, surely he does not know!" she insisted. I gave her a disparaging look and she bit her lip, her eyebrows drawn together. "If only the two of you would try to get along!"

I gave a short burst of laughter. "That would be a sight. So you are happy with father's choice for you, the Samirran King?"

She blushed and looked down. "I am very taken with him."

"I had noticed."

"You did?" she cried, her head snapping up. "Oh, I am so embarrassed! Did everyone notice?"

"I don't see how they could miss it. Don't be embarrassed, Maialen. It has made everyone very happy to see the two of you and it distracts people from noticing my animosity towards Blaise."

"Orabelle.... can I ask you something? But you must not be angry!"

I raised an eyebrow. "Now this sounds interesting. What is it?"

She hesitated. "Well, it's just that... well, some people say... and then I saw you watching him... and, well... Gideon, he doesn't look at me that way, or rather, I do not look at him. We do not look at each other."

"Gideon?" I asked in surprise.  "What in the world are you talking about, little sister?"

"Oh, I don't mean Gideon. I just mean that when Gideon looks at me or I look at him, it is different from the way you are...with Tal...." she said, her voice trailing off. I did not answer but continued to sip my wine. She waited, growing more agitated with my silence. Finally she burst out, "I did not mean that there was something wrong! I was just asking if maybe the way you look at him has something to do with why you don't want to marry Blaise."

I shook my head. "You are mistaken, Maialen. Tal wants to be nothing more than my Guardian."

"And what do you want?" she asked softly.

"I thought I knew. Now I am not sure of anything."

# 3

Blaise watched as my sister and I moved away. Chronus approached him, clapping him on the back and ignoring the grimace on the Fire King's face as his heavy gold cuff bit into the younger man's shoulder blade.

"Congratulations, boy. The announcement was made and you have what you want."

Blaise continued to scowl. "There seems to be a problem, Chronus."

"What is it now?" Chronus asked wearily, tired of his eldest daughter and the constant headache she was to him. The sooner she was married off to the Fire King, the better. Then she would be the Verucan's chore to deal with and as far as Chronus could tell he was probably the only man in the four kingdoms who would be able to manage her.

"Your darling daughter is not agreeable to the marriage."

"You knew that already and you still wanted her. You have changed your mind now? Surely, Blaise, you are not so sentimental," Chronus chided.

"No. I do not care how she feels about it. I only care that her reasons may include more than just her antipathy for me," Blaise explained, his eyes fixed on some point in the crowd.

"What are you getting at, boy? Speak plainly for I do not have all day to worry that Orabelle has wounded your pride yet again."

"Do not make jokes, old man!" Blaise responded vehemently. "I am not concerned about her scathing tongue or what her feelings for me are! What is of concern to me is that man!"

The Fire King stabbed the air angrily with his finger, the line of his arm pointing at the stoic figure of Orabelle's Guardian, Tal. Chronus seethed inwardly though his face remained carefully bland. That damned girl would be the death of him. He had heard the rumors surrounding the Water Queen and her champion but he had hoped that the whispers of their affair had not reached Veruca. Chronus feigned confusion, asking, "Who, her Guardian? What has he to do with anything?"

"Do not play dumb with me, Chronus! I will not tolerate this! She belongs to me and I will not have anyone else touch her!" Blaise ground out through clenched teeth, his fury apparent in his bright amber eyes.

"Calm down, my boy. There is no need for concern. I am sure that you are merely imagining things," Chronus said soothingly. "I will handle this."

"See that you do!" Blaise turned on his heel and stalked away. Chronus took a deep breath and pressed his fingertips to his temples.

"Something wrong with my cousin?" Loagaire purred, her hips swaying enticingly as she circled around Chronus.

"He is merely acting like a foolish boy."

"You seem a bit upset for it to be just boyish antics," she observed, running her fingers over his arm.

He caught her hand and brought it to his lips. "Nothing for you to be concerned about."

"Is it your eldest daughter again?" Loagaire asked, looking up at him from under her long lashes.

"Most of my troubles these days center around Orabelle."

"Would you like me to speak to her? I know that she has no mother, perhaps I could-" she began and was interrupted by his derisive laughter. She closed her mouth, swallowing the rest of her words.

"You?" Chronus chuckled derisively. "Talk to Orabelle as a mother? I do not believe that she will be inclined to take maternal advice from anyone, least of all from you. No, I will deal with her."

"I was merely thinking that if you tried reasoning with her instead of ordering her around, you might have better results. She does not seem to respond well to authority," Loagaire pointed out, lifting her chin and hoping he would not laugh at her again for it was not easy to keep the anger from twisting her mouth out of the benevolent smile she had plastered on. She had learned early in life that it was better to be underestimated by your opponents. Blaise himself had made that mistake many a time when they were still children and commoners. She would deliberately let him win at their childhood games. Over and over on their little hand-carved game boards with sticks and leaves for playing pieces she would sacrifice her warriors while she waited and watched. She learned everything about him, every move he would make, every twitch of his face before he made a decision. And then one day she decided she was ready and would win. Blaise had been furious at his inability to beat his ignorant cousin, the girl who could not even read or write. He had swept the board clean, scattering her warrior twigs to the ground and grinding them under his heel. She had cried out and shoved at him and he had laughed, tossing the carved gameboard into the hearth fire before striding away. Loagaire had watched it burn, tears streaming down her dirty cheeks. Hers was a life of few pleasures and fewer gifts and the game was one of the meager things her parents had given her over the years and now it was gone. But she had won.

Chronus was shaking his head, "You do not know her as well as I do. There is no reasoning with Orabelle, she wants to do exactly as she wishes with no heed to consequence. You would be wise to not concern yourself too much on the Water Queen's behalf. It does not fit into your plans for you to strike up a friendship with her."

"You are right, darling," Loagaire nodded, continuing to smile obligingly and allowing him to believe that she would do just as he wished. "I do not need to befriend her. Your younger daughter, on the other hand, I believe would make a very useful friend indeed."

Chronus smiled back at her as she molded her curves against him. "I agree."

# 4

There was a stirring in the air behind me as Maialen was pulled into another dance by her fiancé and I turned to find Raynor looming in the shadows of the trees. The great, grizzled beast of a man was Blaise's Guardian now and every bit as repulsive to me as the day I had first met him.

"Well, well, well," he grumbled, absently rubbing a glossy red apple between his huge, calloused hands. "It seems as if there is some truth to the gossip of old women."

I straightened my back, setting my half empty goblet on the edge of the table. "You should not listen to idle gossip."

Raynor raised his heavy eyebrows. "Idle? Perhaps for once the rumors bear some credence. There has been talk that your dear Guardian is besotted with you. Now I see that it appears to be true."

"You see nothing, Raynor," I said contemptuously, moving away from him. He grabbed my wrist, his fingers hot on my skin.

"Let go of me," I commanded, beginning to draw my power subtly around us. The air grew heavy and dense with moisture.

Raynor released my arm. "I am only trying to warn you, Water Queen," he claimed as he began tossing the apple back and forth in his hands.

"I heed no warnings from you. Perhaps you are still angry at being second best," I suggested, deliberately reminding him of his failure to become my Guardian and his defeat at Tal's hand.

Raynor flushed with anger and he threw the apple to the ground, crushing it under his boot. "You will belong to my master soon. Just how long do you think he will allow the two of you to be near each other? Tal will be cast out and sent back to his pathetic little village where he belongs."

I smiled. "And if we are sending people back where they belong, exactly what slimy pile of refuse will you be returning to?"

"You forget yourself, woman!" Raynor snarled.

"No," I said softly, my eyes flashing, "it is you who have forgotten who I am. You would be wise to remember your place, servant."

"As Tal would be wise to remember his!" Raynor retorted.

"My place is by my Queen's side," Tal's velvet voice spoke as he stepped between me and the furious Verucan.

Raynor grinned malevolently at him. "By her side, not in her bed."

Tal's hand moved to his sword so that it was partially unsheathed, the etched silver blade glowing in the light from the setting sun. "One more insult to her and we will finish what we started years ago. Only this time it will not be a game."

Raynor's eyes moved between Tal and the half-drawn sword as pride battled with reason. He wanted to fight but he knew he would most likely lose. Tal was the most skilled swordsman on Imbria and Raynor's brute strength was no match for him. His reason seemed to win out and he brushed past us, whispering in my ear as he moved by, "I'll be keeping an eye on you."

I shuddered as I watched him walk away and Tal slid a comforting arm around my shoulders. I leaned into him without thinking and I caught my father's newest lover, Loagaire, watching us with undisguised interest. Several other people were staring, their attention drawn by the surge of power when I had begun calling my element.

"I need to get away from here, Tal," I said, stepping out of the circle of his arm and feeling as if I had been dropped in to a nest of vipers.

"Of course, my Queen," Tal obeyed and followed me as I skirted the edge of the clearing. I felt Blaise's gaze burn into me and I avoided him, ducking down a narrow path that I knew would take me around to Maialen's personal gardens where no one was allowed to enter. I needed a moment of quiet, the silence of the falling night. There was a little creek that ran through the garden and I was aching to feel the serene comfort of the water.

I followed the dirt path past magnificent tangles of flowers and majestic, ancient trees to the edge of the creek where I slipped off my shoes and waded into the cool water. I relaxed, letting the peace flow through me as the liquid swirled around my ankles. The last remnants of the setting sun reflected brokenly off the surface of the water, throwing gashes of molten light across us.

"Is that better?" Tal asked, waiting at the edge of the creek.

"Ah, yes. Much better," I sighed. The feeling of claustrophobia that had begun to bear down on me at the crowded festival was dissipating. I could still hear the noise, the echoes of laughter and the melody of flutes, but I was able to breathe again.

"What happened back there with Raynor? What was he saying to you?"

I ignored him, looking down at the tiny ripples that flowed outward from me. I lifted a finger, moving it in a slow circle through the air. The water whirled at my command and rose up in a column to touch the tip of my finger.

"Orabelle," Tal prompted. The water fell in a cascade of sun-reddened droplets as I lifted my eyes to look at him. He shone like burnished gold silhouetted against the deepening purple of the approaching night.

"He knows, Tal," I answered quietly. "They all know."

I waited for him to react, to say something that would ease the weight I felt bearing down on me again. After a long moment he merely said, "I am sorry."

All the frustration I felt welled up inside of me. "You're sorry?!" I exploded, splashing through the shallow water to stand inches from him. "That is what you say to me? I tell you that everyone knows, that my future husband knows about us, and all you can say to me is you're sorry?"

"Yes, Orabelle, I am sorry!" he said, keeping his voice steady though his grey eyes glittered with emotion. "I should have left a long time ago, as soon as I learned that you were to be married."

"Left?" I repeated incredulously.

"Yes. I should have left Lehar, left the army and left you."

His words cut through me like a thousand knives. "I had no idea you were so eager to get away from me. If you wanted to leave so badly, why didn't you?" I demanded.

He bowed his head so that his hair hung in a silvery curtain over his face. He breathed deeply then lifted his gaze to me, his eyes haunted. "Because I couldn't bear it. Because I love you."

I opened my mouth then closed it abruptly, caught off guard. Tal had never spoken to me that way before. There had never been those sort of words between us.

"I love you, Orabelle."

"And you are sorry for that?"

"No!" he denied fervently. "For that I would never be sorry. I am only sorry that I wasn't strong enough to leave you. I knew that it couldn't last, that you could never truly be mine, but I couldn't let you go."

He took my face in his hands and his eyes searched mine. I could feel his breath like the cool sea on my lips. I remained silent and still, fighting the urge to throw myself against him, afraid to move and shatter this rare glimpse behind in his stoic facade.

"Orabelle," he continued, the velvet sound of his voice barely a whisper. "I have loved you since the moment that I saw you. You own my body and my soul. I thought that I could do the right thing, that I was a good enough man to do what was best for you and ignore my own selfish needs but I am not."

"I don't understand," I told him, my head reeling. Tal pulled me closer so there was only a breath of space between us.

"I am not the man I thought I was. I cannot give you up. I cannot watch him take you from me and do nothing. I should have left a long time ago but I didn't and now.... now I am being torn apart from the inside out. Every time that man is near you, every time he speaks to you or puts a hand on you it drives me insane. I cannot take it anymore."

I shook my head. "But you wanted me to come here. You said that I had to and now you tell me this? What do you expect me to do? What do you want from me, Tal?"

His face was anguished as he let go of me and dropped to his knees. "I was wrong before. I should have listened to you. I know it is not right, it is not fair of me to ask you this now but please, please say you won't marry him, Orabelle. We can go back to Lehar, we can stand against them, whatever happens."

I was scarcely breathing, trying to hold at bay the wave of hope that was rising in me. "What if the Verucans go to war against us?"

"I am your Guardian, your soldier. I will go to war for you. I will fight every man in the four realms if that is what it takes," Tal vowed.

"And what if you change your mind?"

His hands tightened around me. "I was a fool before, Orabelle. You are my life. I breathe only so that you may breathe. I stand only to stand by you. If you go back with me now, little Queen, I will never again risk losing you."

I blinked back the tears that gathered in my eyes and leaned over to stroke his silken hair.

"Tal," I said, placing my hands over his and drawing him up to stand before me. "Take me home."

Relief flooded his face and he grabbed me, lifting me up and spinning me in a circle. We laughed together as he lowered me back to the ground, his body brushing against mine. I felt the stirring inside me that only his touch could bring and I closed my eyes, parting my lips for his kiss. His arms encircled me and held me close and his hands moved up my back, caressing my skin while his kiss filled me with promise. Suddenly he jerked violently, biting my lips so the coppery tang of blood filled my mouth. I gasped and stumbled backwards splashing clumsily through the water.

At first, I did not understand what was happening. My eyes were seeing what my mind could not grasp. There was blood and it mingled with the dying rays of the sun so that the world seemed bathed in it. Tal was staggering back from me then he spun around and I could see the massive wound across his back. It looked as if huge strips of muscle and skin had been flayed off where his white shirt gaped open, soaking with blood. He reached for his sword as a dark shape blurred toward him. He dove sideways but whatever it was that came at him caught his shoulder with a sickening crunch of bone. I began to scream and Tal fell to one knee, clutching at his useless arm. It was then that I saw Raynor. His face was splattered with blood and bits of flesh dripped from his beard. He was grinning evilly, a cruel black battle mace swinging to and fro before Tal. The large spiked ball was mottled with gore.

Raynor's eyes flicked to me and his grin widened. "Say goodbye to your lover," he laughed, raising the mace into the air and swinging it violently. I lunged forward and shoved Tal onto his side, the mace missing his head by inches. He cried out as his wounded shoulder collided with the hard ground. Raynor grunted and laughed again.

"So you want to play too?" he leered, hefting the mace and stalking towards me as I backed away, slipping on the muddy edge of the creek.

"Orabelle, run!" Tal ordered me, blood dripping from the corner of his mouth and pouring down his arm as he fought to stand, using his body to shield me.

"No!" I shrieked as the mace fell in a wide arc, catching Tal in the chest and tossing him backwards. Raynor paused to glance at the torn body then focused again on me. I wanted my power, I needed to call it but I couldn't concentrate. My vision was flooded with blood. I could feel it all over my skin. Tal's blood. It was everywhere, drowning my senses.

"Can't say I didn't warn you," Raynor chuckled malevolently letting the mace swing like a pendulum in front of my face as I stared at it in horror, pieces of Tal clinging to it.

Maialen's voice reached my ears and I could hear the sound of running feet. She was shouting my name as Raynor raised the weapon above me. I watched him numbly for all I could think about was Tal's crumpled body lying a few feet away.

All at once the earth around us began to tremble and Maialen burst through the trees, my Sirens close behind her. Gnarled roots shot up from the ground like skeletal hands and wrapped around Raynor. The vines snaked up his legs and across his torso to his arm and the mace fell from his grasp. I shook myself and let my power flow into me finally, prompted by the energy of Maialen's element. The water of the creek rose into the air, leaving the bed dry and littered with pebbles and twigs. It roared like a great waterfall surrounding me and Tal.

I could barely hear Maialen calling my name over the cacophony of the water. The wails of the Sirens rose in protest, piercing the night as I crawled over the muddy ground on my knees to where Tal lay on his side, the gaping wound on his back facing me.

"No, no, no, no," I mumbled to myself as my hands hovered over him, unsure what to do or where I could touch him without hurting him further. I crawled around so that I could see the other jagged tear on his chest. His arm was crushed and bent at an impossible angle underneath him and warm blood spread out around us, soaking my dress. I leaned down so that I could see his face, pushing his hair aside as I begged, "Tal? Tal, please! Please answer me, Tal!"

Something irreparable broke inside of me as I looked into his lifeless eyes that stared back, unseeing. He was gone. I shrieked wildly, the screams tearing through me as I gathered his bloody, broken body against me, resting his head on my breast. Tears streamed down my face as I smoothed his hair back from his brow and pressed his eyelids closed with my fingertips. I rocked slowly back and forth as the pain in my chest grew till I thought it would suffocate me. The pain crushed me, my whole body ached with it and I cried piteously. I couldn't hear anything but my own sobbing and the word no spilling over and over again from my lips. The immense grief engulfed me, it poured down my burning throat, drowning me.

I don't know how long I held him while the water raged protectively around us. The sky had darkened to a deep black when I finally laid him down gently. I bent over, kissing him softly, tasting blood and tears. I sat back on my heels as the water began to dissipate and flow back into the creek, leaving

Tal and I exposed to the crowd that had gathered. I tried to stand, nearly blind with tears, and fell back to my knees.

"Orabelle," Maialen spoke cautiously, coming to kneel in the mud beside me.

"He's dead," I choked out. "I couldn't save him."

Maialen's eyes glittered with sympathy as she held out her hands. She said, "I am so sorry, Orabelle. Come, let me help you."

I ran my own hands over Tal's face one last time, closing my eyes and tracing with my fingertips the strong lines that I knew so well. I turned to Maialen and she helped me stand, supporting my weight as I tried to regain my balance. I leaned on her, waiting for the dizziness to subside and for the blood to stop roaring inside of me. I waited for the knot in my throat to ease and for the anger to fill me. I wanted to feel the cold, hard rage that would overwhelm everything else.

I stepped away from Maialen and looked at Raynor where he stood rooted to the ground by the vines that snarled around him. "Take him," I commanded, my eyes flashing to the Sirens. They quieted their mournful howling and moved with liquid grace to stand on either side of Raynor. The crowd gasped and fell back as the Sirens changed shape before them. Their hair whipped wildly around their heads and their fingers stretched long and thin till they became like tentacles. They wrapped around Raynor making him cry out in agony as thousands of tiny barbs pricked his skin.

"You coward!" I spat at him. Maialen reached for me but I shrugged her off and went straight to Raynor, raising my hand and striking his face. My nails dug long, bloody streaks across his cheek. I struck him over and over till his face was covered in jagged red lines.

I heard my father's voice yelling "Stop her!"

"Orabelle, please," Maialen pleaded, pulling on my arm. I turned and shoved her away, sending her sprawling against

Gideon who had just forced his way through the crowd. The brawny woodsman caught her easily and set her on her feet, then stepped around her coming towards me. I ignored him and raised my hand again but his iron grip caught my wrist and he pulled me against him, pinning my arms to my chest. I struggled, the rage still boiling inside of me, not yet ready to recede. I wanted to hurt Raynor, to destroy him, to carve up his face with my bare hands.

I clawed viciously at Gideon's arms, shouting at him furiously. "Let me go! I will kill him! He will pay for what he has done!"

"Stop this! You must stop, you must calm down, everyone is watching," Gideon whispered in my ear as he held me fast. I stopped struggling and slumped forward as if I had fainted, forcing him to bend over me to hold me up. When he did I shoved upward, the back of my head slamming into his face. I felt warm blood in my hair and he released me abruptly, covering his nose and cursing. I threw myself at Raynor, jerking his hair back with one hand to expose his throat. I dug my nails into the flesh on either side of his jugular.

"Look at me, Raynor," I hissed, my face inches from his. "Look at me while I kill you. I do not attack from behind like you, coward. I want you to see my face as I tear your throat out!"

I squeezed harder and blood ran down my arm from his neck where my nails pierced the skin. The Sirens cooed appreciatively, urging me on while Raynor writhed frantically. With each twist of his body the Sirens' tentacles embedded their barbs further into his skin and he began to make pitiful mewling sounds for help.

"Damn it!" Gideon cursed again, grabbing me as blood continued to run from his broken nose. This time he pinned my arms behind me with one large hand and wrapped the other arm around my neck so that it was pressed against my windpipe.

"I am not trying to hurt you, Queen, but you must stop," he insisted.

Maialen stood in front of me, her gentle face strained with shock.  She pleaded with me, "Orabelle, that's enough. It is enough. Please, you must stop this. Everyone is watching. He is a Guardian, this matter must be decided in the Council. Please."

I stared at her, heard her words, but my mind was filled with a lust for revenge so great that nothing else made sense to me. I tried to calm down, to quiet the rage inside me. Gideon loosened his arm and I took a deep breath.

"You are right," I said, my voice raw. Raynor raised his head at my words and relief filled his face. The sight of his hope was more than I could stand. He had shown Tal no mercy but had bludgeoned him from behind when he was unarmed.  "Yes, Maialen, you are right. That is enough."

I looked at the Sirens, letting them feel the full extent of my hatred, my suffering, my anger. They keened in response and I shouted to them, "Tear him apart!"

A great cry arose. Raynor's pathetic, pain filled screams mingled with the Sirens' high-pitched wail. Maialen was yelling and from the crowd came shrieks of terror as the Sirens flung their arms wide, their barbed tentacles ripping through Raynor's flesh, sending pieces of him scattering through the forest. I watched, never blinking when others turned away in disgust, till there was nothing left of him save those parts that were still rooted to the ground by Maialen's gnarled vines. His screams burned through my veins, coursing through my body. I closed my eyes and darkness rained over me.

# 5

Gideon hesitated outside of Maialen's door, hearing the muffled sound of her tears from inside. He wished that he knew any words that would comfort her but he could think of none. She felt the blood from Raynor's death staining her hands for it was her element that had bound him even though it had been her sister who had actually delivered the man to his end. An end that Gideon could not help but feel had been well deserved. To attack the Leharans as Raynor had, in a gathering of peace, was cowardly. It was a betrayal that Gideon felt deserved death. He was just sorry that his Queen had to have the shadow of that brutal death cast on her innocent conscience. He recalled a time just last spring when Maialen had come across an injured rabbit in the gardens. It had torn a gash along its hind quarters trying to squeeze beneath the fence that circled her garden. Maialen had taken the rabbit to her chambers and made it a tiny bed from one of her best and softest gowns and every day had brought it morsels of food and tenderly dressed its wound. Then she had ordered every fence in the royal gardens to be removed so that no other creature would be hurt by them and everything could share in the beauty. She was too gentle a soul for the rest of them, Gideon thought while absently rubbing the claw marks Orabelle had left on his arm. Too gentle by far.

"I should have held her too," Maialen had sobbed when he had first brought her back to her chambers. "I should have stopped her. I knew she would kill him and I should have tried harder!"

Gideon had patted her hair awkwardly as she had curled her body around itself, her knees pressed to her chest and her face buried in her knees. "It wasn't your fault."

"But it happened here, in my kingdom. I let it happen. What if I am not meant to be a Keeper, Gideon? I have had the Emerald for one day and look what has happened."

"You couldn't have done anything else," Gideon assured her, inwardly berating himself for the feebleness of the remark. "What they did had nothing to do with you."

"It happened in Kymir. It was my sister. It had everything to do with me!" she argued. She sniffed loudly and lifted her head to stare across the room with watery green eyes. "Where is Astraeus?"

Gideon had hesitated, not wanting to tell her that the Air King had yet to ask after her. "He did not want to disturb you just yet and there were pressing matters to attend to. Because of all that happened," he lied.

Maialen had nodded her head. "And Orabelle?"

Gideon told her how Orabelle had sailed for Lehar as soon as she had awakened and Maialen had nodded once more then tucked her face back into her knees. He had risen and left her alone not knowing what else he could do for her.

He began to walk away from the room, feeling inadequate for his lack of words, when Loagaire's lush figure ascended the stairway to block his path. She looked over his shoulder at the door to Maialen's chambers.

"How fares our new Queen of Kymir?" she asked.

"She is no concern of yours," Gideon replied gruffly. He attempted to step around her but she threw out her arm to prevent his escape.

"Not so fast, Guardian," Loagaire purred, her full mouth tilting up into a smile. "First of all, you should remember who you speak to. I am not a servant to be brushed aside, I am Verucan royalty. Perhaps all of you Guardians have grown a little too... arrogant."

"I do not like the suggestion in your words," Gideon rebuked.

She laughed. "I am merely cautioning you. As you have seen today there are some who are not as forgiving to insult as I am."

"Let me pass."

"Now, now, Guardian. Do not be upset with me. I only want to see how our darling little Maialen fares. Chronus is quite worried about her. It must be hard for the child to have seen what she did, to have the first use of her power tainted by such violence."

Gideon wanted nothing more than to get away from the woman but he would not allow her to disturb his Queen. Maialen did not need false sympathy and lies at a time like this. "She will be fine soon. She merely grieves the losses."

"Of course she does, poor thing. It must be especially difficult seeing as how she was her sister's unwilling accomplice in the murder of your fellow Guardian," Loagaire mused.

"Maialen is not responsible for anything that happened! And Raynor did not deserve the title of Guardian. He was nothing like us, he had no honor."

"Us? By us do you mean you and Favian? You do realize you are the only ones left as of now," she pointed out.

Gideon sighed, wondering how much of an offense she would take it for if he just picked her up and physically moved her out of his way.

Loagaire continued to speak as if the thought was just occurring to her. "Who do you suppose the Water Queen will choose as a replacement?"

"It is not any concern of mine," Gideon replied flatly.

"Isn't it? The besmirchment of one is to tarnish the reputation of you all. Think of how it would look if another incident like this were to occur. People will already begin to fear you after today, to fear the Keepers. They will whisper about what happened here, about the power that you few hold unchecked. You must see how crucial the selection of another Leharan Guardian is. Everyone believes that it will be Colwyn. He is, after all, the next in command. He is a logical choice. Though perhaps Orabelle chooses her Guardians based on other qualities."

"I would pass now, lady. Either move aside or I shall move you myself."

Loagaire laughed suggestively. "Perhaps I would enjoy that, Guardian."

She stepped to one side, dropping her arm and motioning for him to move by. As he did she whispered in his ear, "Be careful with your Queen."

"A threat?" Gideon growled in an equally low voice.

"Not at all, Guardian. A warning. You must see that what is happening around us will not end well. I only caution you, protect the girl."

Gideon moved on, leaving the woman alone in the hallway before his temper could get the best of him. The strain of the day was wearing on his nerves and he felt his head began to ache. Was she right, were all of the Guardians now in danger because of what had happened? Would people really begin to fear and mistrust them whereas before they had always been honored and revered? He pressed his large fists to his temples as he bounded down the stairway and out into the forest.

# 6

The hours melted into days and days turned into weeks. Since leaving Kymir on the night of Tal's death I had waited for the pain of his loss to ease, to feel like I was myself again. I was beginning to realize this would never happen. I was no longer whole. A piece of me had been torn out and laid to rest in the Southern Sea where I had entombed my beloved Guardian beneath the waves.

During the day I would perform my duties as the Queen of Lehar, burying my broken heart under the mundane tasks and decisions required of me. It was the nights that destroyed me. I would lie awake for hours longing for the warmth of his body next to mine. When the breeze wafted over my skin it was his touch that I yearned for. I would walk the beaches, looking out over the ocean and trying to understand how he could be so completely gone. Not a single moment of the night passed without the thought of him. There wasn't an hour of peace from the constant, awful ache in my chest. I wondered how many tears I had to cry before I started to forget. Many times I would wade out into the cool surf, the water rising up to my waist, and I would spread my hands out over the waves to feel close to him.

The Sirens were often near me on these nights, walking up and down the sparkling sand forlornly. They would wade into the water with me to dissolve into the sea, their sad songs echoing through the night. I would think of his voice, his hair, the color of his eyes, the feel of his laughter, the shape of his mouth. I would think of the thousand parts of him that I would never see again. Sometimes I would stare into the vast darkness of the sea and the urge to fall into its cool, calm depths would nearly overwhelm me. I longed for the sweet release from the pain.

I had not chosen another Guardian. The very thought repulsed me. Tal was my champion, my protector and I did not want another. I had made Colwyn acting Commander of the army but it was not a position I had granted him permanently. I was not in denial of Tal's loss as many people whispered, for I felt the horrible pain of it constantly. It was simply that I could not imagine finding anyone to take his place. I did not want anyone else to be near me. I had wrapped myself in a shroud of solitude and I was not yet ready to remove the lonely garment. I refused to see my family or to speak to anyone who had been at the festival that night. Maialen had sent me messages and tiny gifts wrapped in colored paper that were meant to cheer me up. I returned them, unopened. I was like a ghost, a great empty shell of a person that had filled with his loss, leaving no room for anything else.

I was wandering the beaches one night, on the southern coast of the island near that part of the sea where his body rested, when I heard a noise out over the water and saw light flickering on the horizon. I stopped walking as a dozen more tiny lights appeared. The lights were soft, creating misty halos as they bobbed up and down with the movement of the tides. The lights drew closer and I could see that they were lanterns swinging from the bows of small wooden rowboats. Dark figures broke their oars quietly through the waves and a steady, rhythmic hum reached my ears. The boats formed a circle in what was nearly the exact spot where Tal's body gone into the sea. As the boats drew nearer to each other the combined light from their lanterns bathed the people who rowed them in pale yellow. They were Tahitians. Their dark skin glowed like rich mahogany against their white robes. They were humming together, the sound growing louder as the last boat joined the circle, then it stopped abruptly and a deep, male voice began to chant. The women sang a gentle background to the chanting and began to toss flower petals into the air. They rained down on the water like pieces of a darkened rainbow falling from the sky. When they had finished the men lifted heavy little bags and began to pour golden sand across the surface of the sea so that it shimmered and swirled through the colorful petals.

The last echoes of their chanting carried across the waves as one by one the boats began to recede back into the night till only a single vessel remained. In it sat an enormous man, bigger than anyone I had ever seen. He shone darkly in the soft light of his lantern and he reached over the edge of the boat and laid his palm on the glassy surface of the water.

"Go in peace, my brother," he said. His heavy voice carried sorrowfully through the air. He sat back and picked up the long oar and began rowing away.

# 7

"How is the Queen?" Colwyn asked the man who was carefully polishing the gleaming silver blade of his sword. Brogan glanced up at him and shrugged. The Captain looked tired and there were dark smudges under his eyes and a sweep of shadow across his jaw that was out of character for a man who was usually fastidious about his grooming. His blonde hair was still carefully combed, cut short and parted perfectly so that it shaped his head like a helmet. Colwyn was overall a rather ordinary looking man except for the impeccable perfection he took with his appearance.

"Sleeping," Brogan answered him. "When she is awake she is the same."

"She wants to go to Tahitia. Do you know anything about this?" Colwyn asked as he pulled up a seat across from the other soldier and sat down, his stiff countenance conveying his disapproval. He did not trust the Tahitians, they were still too wrapped up in the ancient ways and believed in too many old legends for his liking.

"I do not," was Brogan's short reply.

Colwyn sighed and plucked at some invisible piece of debris on his sleeve. "Well, she does, and soon. It is the last thing we need right now. Who knows what barbaric things are happening on that island? Those people are not like us."

"They were part of our kingdom before the banishment, how different can they be in one lifetime?"

Colwyn paused, studying the other man. He did not want to appear that he was hostile towards the other islanders, only that they should be wary, but he felt that somehow he was offending the other Guard. "Look, you know what they say about them. And what some of their customs are. To become a warrior they have to kill a blood-drinker. Can you imagine seeking one of those creatures out and trying to kill it for sport? We are lucky that they have not brought retribution down on all of us for it. And then the incident with the Verucans? It was better that they were banished before they could start a war."

Brogan set the sword he had been tending to away from him and ignored Colwyn's remarks. He liked the man and respected him as the Captain of the Guard, but he did not care to debate policy with him tonight.

"The Queen saw some Tahitians the other night on one of her walks. I was following her as you instructed me to and I stayed far enough behind that I wouldn't disturb her. I could not see or hear much aside from some people in boats singing. I believe it was some sort of tribute to Tal."

Colwyn rubbed the stubble on his chin. "Why would the Tahitians be paying tribute to him?"

"There have been many Guardians from Tahitia. It could be tradition among them."

"Why didn't you tell me before now?" Colwyn wanted to know. "You are supposed to report to me."

Brogan pulled his sword back to him and began to resume his careful ritual of cleaning the bright blade. "You ordered me to watch over her to make sure she was safe. She was not in any danger so there was nothing to report."

"The Tahitians are banished because they are dangerous. You should have reported the incident," Colwyn repeated sternly.

"You are my superior and as such I follow your orders but I am not comfortable spying on my Queen," Brogan said quietly. He continued to use the cloth to rub every speck of dirt and grime from the hilt of his sword as if they were having an ordinary conversation but there was a line of tension in his shoulders.

"I only want to protect her."

"I know that."

"You seem to be implying something else."

Brogan shook his head. "I imply nothing. We are the Leharan Guard, sworn to protect this Kingdom and its ruler. For generations the men of my family have been members of this Guard. They have carried this very sword into countless battles and one day I shall have a son and this sword will be his. It is not a duty that I take lightly but I am also your friend, Colwyn. If you would like to speak to me as a friend and hear my opinion then please, sit and speak."

Colwyn started to rise then lowered himself back into the chair across from Brogan. "What is it you would like to say to me then, friend?"

"We all know that you want to be Guardian. I can't imagine anyone else who would be better suited than you," Brogan began.

"Thank you," Colwyn inclined his head.

"But you are not him. You cannot take his place with her."

Colwyn stiffened. "Again, you are making implications without being clear."

"Then I will speak clearly. We all know what they were to each other, the Queen and her Guardian. I fear that you want to take his place, not just as her next Guardian, but in her heart. I am only telling you that it will not be so."

Colwyn scoffed. "You are saying nonsense, Brogan. I have no such thoughts and I do not think that I am worthy of replacing Tal, no man is, but if given the chance I will do my best to honor him and live up to his legacy."

"He was the best of us, wasn't he?" Brogan asked with a grin. "I would give anything to wield a sword with the skill he possessed."

"Keep practicing, my friend," Colwyn said, rising fully from his chair this time. He left Brogan and walked through the fort, staring down at the coralstone that gleamed beneath his boots. Brogan was wrong, he had no intention of replacing Tal. He wanted to be Guardian, yes, but he told himself it was only so that he could better protect his Queen. A wave of guilt passed through him at the lie. He did want to protect Orabelle but the truth was that he craved the prestige of that coveted title. He wanted to walk by her side, proud and strong, the best of all men in the four realms. He wanted to be acknowledged as the greatest warrior, the bravest and wisest of the Leharans, the man chosen by the Queen herself. He wanted to see the fear in their enemies' eyes when he approached, the wariness when his hand lingered near his sword. Instead of bowing to them, he would greet Gideon and Favian as their equal.

Colwyn found himself staring up at the beached ship that Orabelle had made her home. The soft curtains of her darkened windows billowed in the warm breeze. He would prove to her that he could be her Guardian, that he alone was worthy of the title. One day soon she would put away her grief and recognize him as the leader of the Leharan army and the one man she could not live without.

# 8

Tahitia was just as I remembered it. I had been there with my mother when I was child though I had stayed on the ship while she had visited the island. I remembered the swirl of her skirts and her cloud of pale hair floating around her as she had descended the long pier, her steps lengthening to match the stride of her own Guardian as he walked beside her. They had disappeared into the crowd of eager faces awaiting them and I had surveyed the unfamiliar island with youthful curiosity. I had been fascinated by the groups of skilled fisherman casting their wide nets into the waist deep water with rhythmic grace and had peered over the edge of the bow for hours watching them. Now I walked down the long pier from my ship following the path my mother had taken so long ago. I stepped onto the warm golden sand, taking in the unchanged island around me. The fisherman had watched our ship as it approached with our pale blue banners of peace undulating in the breeze. They now peered at me curiously, their eyes suspicious. Their dark golden skin gleamed with the sheen of sweat and they wore cloths that wrapped around their waist and tucked under their legs. They were stringing up their catch for the day, preparing to take them to be cleaned. I faced them, staring at each of them in turn.

"I am Orabelle," I announced and waited for them to be appropriately impressed. The fisherman glanced at each other skeptically and shifted on their feet.

"Yes, we know who you are. Are you expecting us to bow to you now?" the man asked scornfully, waving a fish in my direction.

I could sense the guards grow tense behind me. I looked the man up and down, tilting my head to one side. The Tahitians were warriors they would not respect weakness but I also could not afford to offend them.

"I could make you bow," I told him, "But that is not what I am here for."

"What exactly are you here for?"

"There's a man I'm looking for. I don't know his name but he knew my Guardian." I felt the familiar shadow fall over my heart at the mention of Tal and I forced my face to remain expressionless.

"There is no one here on Tahitia who did not know your Guardian."

"Who would call him brother?"

"There is only one who can do that. I know who you are looking for. His name is Damian. Walk down the beach for a while and you will find him. Or he will find you."

I turned and started off in the direction he had pointed.

"Lady Orabelle," Colwyn called out, catching up to me and laying a hand on my arm. I looked down at his hand and he immediately let go. "My Queen, I do not think that you should go wandering around this island. These are not people to be trusted."

"Why is that?" I asked him, "because my father says so? It was his council that banished the Tahitians, for reasons that are both vague and unfair to me. There is a new council now and this island was once part of the Water Kingdom. I will decide its fate."

Colwyn nodded. "I understand but I am worried that these people will not. They are known to be a violent race and judging from the reactions of those men on the beach they are not inclined to be friendly towards us. I think that the Guard should go ahead to make sure that it will be safe for you."

"No," I rejected bluntly.

"I am trying to protect you–"

"Right now you are merely hindering me, Colwyn, and wasting time."

His jaw clenched. "I am doing what I am sworn to do. Is it too much to ask that you cooperate just a little? The last thing we need is another incident like the one in Kymir!"

My eyes flashed white and I felt anger burn across my skin. "Do not forget who you are speaking to."

Colwyn hesitated. "My Queen, nobody blames you for what happened, but it would help matters if you would be reasonable in these situations."

I felt the sea behind me start to swell and the waves crashed hard against the shore. "What exactly are you implying?" I demanded through clenched teeth.

"I'm not implying anything but that you seem to have no concern for those whose only concern is you," he replied, lowering his head and avoiding my eyes.

I was breathing deeply, trying to control my temper as the ocean continued to churn and batter the shore. The rest of the Guard was stopped a few feet away, waiting uncertainly. The fishermen from the beach were gathering behind them. "You think his death is my fault?"

Colwyn continued to stare down at the ground.

"Answer me," I commanded. There was a soft keening that echoed across the waves as the Sirens rose from the sea. I heard the startled gasps from the fishermen and Colwyn's eyes were wide as he finally lifted his head to look at me.

"Isn't that what you think?" he asked reluctantly.

I felt my own eyes go dark as the anger flooded out of me, leaving behind nothing but the overwhelming sorrow. The waves receded and the sea became calm. I whispered softly so that only he could hear me. "Yes."

"Orabelle, my Queen, forgive me," he began, dropping to one knee.

"Enough," I interrupted, swallowing the knot in my throat and shoving down the pain that rose like a tidal wave inside me. My voice was steady when I spoke. "Stand up. I understand your concerns, but do not question my orders again in front of others. I will tolerate it this time because perhaps you are right. It is not a mistake that will be allowed again."

He stood and bowed. "Of course, I apologize, my Queen."

"Take half the Guard and go find me this Damian."

A deep baritone voice resonated from the gathered crowd. "There is no need to look for me. I am here."

I spun around and recognized the tall figure making his way towards me, the other fishermen moving aside to let him pass. It was the man from the boat. He was even bigger than I had thought, heavily muscled and towering over me at nearly seven feet tall. His hair hung down his back in long dreadlocks and huge hooks pierced his ear lobes. He had a net slung over one massive shoulder and carried a long spear in his left hand. He wore loose pants cut off at the knees and no shirt. His face was strong and dominated by large, dark round eyes.

"Damian," I bowed my head slightly, "I am Orabelle, Queen of Lehar."

"Your reputation precedes you, Queen," he said, taking my hand and bowing deeply in return. His voice was heavy and rich and so much like Tal's that I felt my throat tighten yet again.

"I would like to speak with you. Alone," I requested immediately.

He looked at the guards and back at the crowd gathered behind him. He chuckled softly. "Now I think that would take some doing. Perhaps we can offer you some refreshment in our village? It would be a great honor to us and I believe that once your men and my people are accustomed to each other we may find it easier to talk."

"Very well," I agreed. He was right, we had drawn quite a large group of spectators to the beach and judging from their curious expressions they would not be inclined to just go back to their daily routines and ignore us. I also did not wish to offend the fierce islanders, for it was my hope that I could bring them back into the Water Kingdom as my allies.

Damian grinned and clapped his large hands. "You heard the Queen!" he yelled, "Run up to the village and tell them we are coming!"

Several nearby children darted into the palm trees with undulating cries of excitement. I looked at Colwyn, allowing him to decide how we would proceed. He smiled warmly at me then looked away awkwardly when I did not return the smile. He cleared his throat. "You three, go ahead. I will walk with Orabelle and you two follow behind us."

"May I have the honor of escorting the Queen?" Damian asked, offering me his arm. I took it, feeling frail in comparison to his enormous strength. Colwyn gave him an unfriendly look then nodded curtly, falling into step behind us as we started up the path through the trees. The Sirens walked gracefully on either side of the captain, occasionally brushing against him and causing him to shudder, much to their amusement.

The coconut palms that ringed the beach quickly gave way to thicker vegetation and the air was heavy and damp. Over the path hung a canopy of trees so thick that it was almost as if we were walking through a tunnel. Flowers bloomed everywhere and dripped from the limbs above our heads. The path wound through the forest for nearly half a mile before we came upon a huge wall of wooden spikes nearly twice the height of Damian. A gate stood open and was crowded on either side with children who had bright colorful flowers tucked in their hair and shells adorning their wrists and ankles. They carried baskets of flower petals which they tossed across the ground happily as we entered the village. The sirens petted them, cooing, and plucked at the flowers in their hair. The children laughed, ducking and showering the sea creatures with petals.

"They are not afraid of the Sirens," I murmured to Damian. "Most people are."

"We are not a common people, our children are not raised to fear," he told me with pride in his voice.

I looked around curiously as we entered the village. It was composed of three circles of huts radiating outward from a central open space. The open space was quickly filling with people and a fire pit was being built in the center. Men were dragging heavy wooden benches to line the spaces of the clearing and women were bringing steaming bowls of food, baskets of fruits and jugs of liquids. They were all dressed in loose, easy clothing, covered with flowers and shells.

Damian led us to the edge of the circle and stopped. He pointed to two long benches. "Those are for you and your Guard. But please do not sit yet. I will be back in a moment," he said, releasing my arm and hurrying away.

"My Queen, what exactly are we doing?" Colwyn wanted to know.

"What do you mean?" I asked him.

"This! All this, what is this?" he waved at the clearing.

One of the guards, the young man named Kaden, leaned over and clapped him on the back. "Colwyn, it appears that we are having a party!" he exclaimed happily.

I looked at them, seeing the expectant look in their eyes. Perhaps we all needed to relax some. When Tal had been alive there had been dancing and songs and games. Since his death I had not had the strength to even smile, let alone to encourage my people to. "He's right, I think we have a party in our honor," I told them, "Try to enjoy yourselves."

"But stay alert! Do not get drunk!" Colwyn ordered hastily as Kaden let out a whoop. A pretty Tahitian woman near the men giggled and offered them fruit. Colwyn sighed and shook his head. "It's going to be a long day."

"Perhaps you should try and enjoy yourself as well," I suggested.

"I am not here for the festivities, and I don't think you are either. I am not questioning your orders but do you really believe this is wise, being here with these people?"

I took a deep breath. The warm, damp air filled my lungs and I felt a peacefulness flow over me that I recognized. This place was a part of me, I could feel it. These were my people. "Yes, Colwyn, I am sure. And the Guard, they are just men. Soldiers, warriors, yes, but still men. You have all suffered his loss too. Let them have a moment of ease. We all need it."

"It would be good to see you smile again, my Queen."

I met his eyes and his look was too personal for my taste. I turned away, uncomfortable, and saw Damian approaching. He no longer carried the net or spear and the wicked hooks through his ears had been replaced with blue jewels. He wore a longer pair of loose pants that were a rich cobalt blue, but still no shirt. He carried a folded cloth in his arms which he held out to me proudly.

"A queen should not have to sit uncomfortably. I have brought this for you. It belongs to my family," he offered, spreading the cloth over the bench.

"It's beautiful." I ran my hand over the bright colors.

"It is the sea during the spring, when the sun is bright and the colors are purest. My mother, Cossiana, made it herself," he explained. "Please, sit. I will bring us something to drink."

I sat patiently as he hurried off again, returning with a clay jug and two goblets. He poured a dark amber liquid into them and passed one to me. "Do not gulp it, little Queen, its rather strong. Small sips."

I froze, my fingers inches from the offered cup. "What did you call me?"

He looked at me quizzically. "I referred to you as the Queen that you are."

"You said little Queen."

"Ahh. I am sorry, Lady Orabelle. It was Tal's name for you. I should not have used it," he apologized, his face softening with sympathy.

It was my turn to be confused. "You know his name for me? How-"

"Later, please. It is a story that needs to be told but not just yet. Later we will talk," he promised with a glance back at Colwyn who sat behind us watching with contempt, one hand on the hilt of his sword.

I nodded and took the cup from him, taking a small sip. "It's delicious!" I exclaimed.

"Ah, you like it! Good. It's something we make special here on Tahitia. Just remember small sips. And now if it would please you, Queen, there are many who would like to meet you."

"And I shall be glad to meet them. But first there are things that I need to know. Not about... him...but about the banishment. I was a child when it all happened and I have asked my father and the other elders but no one seems able to give me an answer that I find satisfactory. I know only that a ship of Veruca was attacked by your people and that many were killed. I would like to know your side of it."

He leaned back slightly, his eyes moving over the other villagers as they continued to bustle about. "I too was a child.

I have heard the story enough times that I could tell you, but again I would ask you to wait."

"I came here for answers, Damian," I said pointedly.

He sighed. "I know that. And you will have them when the time is right."

"Very well," I consented, once again not wanting to offend the islanders whose customs I was unfamiliar with. Perhaps Damian thought I was being impolite with my abruptness. "But I will not be put off forever."

He laughed. "Yes, that I believe."

The next few hours I spent greeting the villagers. They seemed divided between those that were wary and suspicious of me and my motives for being there and those who embraced me warmly, glad that they had a chance to be restored to the Water Keeper's favor. Damian sat beside me protectively, introducing each of them in turn and hurrying them on when they lingered too long, explaining who they all were and their roles in the village. Finally it seemed that I had met everyone there was to meet. I stood stretching the muscles of my legs while the afternoon sun hung low and heavy in the sky and the air stirred with the first cool brush of the oncoming night.

"We shall eat now," Damian announced. "And after that the children will sing, then the elders will tell stories and then there will be dancing. Would that suit you?"

"And if it does not then I am sure you will calmly tell me why it should," I said with a shrug. A group of girls began bringing out bowls of food and passing them around. As we ate the children of the village gathered around the fire pit and began to sing. They sang happy, joyful songs about the beauty of the sea and songs about the great Tahitian warriors of the past. I listened respectfully, closing my eyes and letting the air caress my skin. I thought of how much Tal would have enjoyed this day, these people, and my heart ached with his loss.

"You are sad," Damian said quietly. I opened my eyes and looked at him. He was staring down at me, his face drawn with worry.

"I was remembering."

"Sometimes remembering is good, if we remember not to get lost in the memory."

I searched his dark eyes. "How does one find their way out if they are already lost there?"

"They have to begin to forget. Now the sun is setting and the elders will tell stories."

I focused on the center of the circle where an old man hobbled forward, leaning heavily on a wooden walking stick. He cleared his throat and began to speak and his voice was surprisingly clear, carrying easily across the clearing.

"There are many stories that our people tell," he began. "There are many legends that we believe. The Samains of old foretold many things."

"Samains?" I whispered to Damian.

"Our storytellers. Record keepers if you will. Some of them have also been seers, able to foretell the future," he explained quickly.

I focused back on the old man who was pacing around the fire, making sure that everyone's attention was on him as he orated. He stopped in front of me. "Tonight, a special story for the Queen who has bestowed such great honor upon us. There is a legend, a story that we have told for years, of the Solvrei."

The Tahitians murmured expectantly and made encouraging noises. Beside me, Damian sat up straighter, the muscles of his shoulders tightening though his face remained carefully blank. I leaned toward him to ask a question and he shook his head saying, "Now is the time you should be listening."

The sun was dipping low in the horizon and the fire behind him grew brighter. "A long, long time ago the elements were strewn across the land. There were no Keepers and the people roamed restlessly, lost. The gods in the heavens had forsaken them for they had been vile, wicked people, and had destroyed the gifts the gods had bestowed upon them. They lived this way for many years, hungry and homeless. Finally, one of the gods felt sorry for them. He wanted to come to them and help them. The other gods said no and they tried to dissuade him. They said that men were evil and could not be helped. But the one god insisted. He believed that men could change, they could be taught. He convinced the others to give men another chance, an opportunity to repair the world they had destroyed. The gods relented and they came down to Imbria and divided the people into the four realms. They gave them each an element and helped them to choose a Keeper for their element. They were then charged with the task of mastering their elements, of creating with them, of making the world beautiful again. The Edicts were written and for many years men strived hard to do as they had been charged. They flourished and the lands of Imbria flourished. Kymir grew thick with trees and the earth bloomed, Samirra rose up from the land and produced fruitful farms, Verucan was rich in metals and industry, and the Islands were one with the bountiful sea. However, there was one group of men that the gods had left alone. These were the blood-drinkers, the tribes of the Fomorians. Their evil was so great that they were left to themselves, banished to the underworlds to be a lesson to the rest of the land on what can become of a person. But time passed, people forgot the lessons they had learned and began to fight among themselves. Jealousy, hatred, greed and power all began to resurface among men. The gods chastised the one who had believed in man. They called him a fool and they told him to destroy all men, to be rid of them forever.

Again, he pleaded our cause. He offered to go down to the world and live among the men, to find out what there was that was worth saving among the people. So this god disguised himself as a man and came down to Imbria. He lived among the people for many years and began to think and feel as one of them. Eventually he fell in love. The other gods were displeased by this for they wanted him to come back to them. They gave him a choice. He must leave the woman and return to his rightful place, or he must become mortal and remain in our world forever. To their shock, he remained, sacrificing his immortal life and a son was born to him. The boy would become the one that was chosen to unite the elements and to rule the people as one. He would be the first Keeper of all four elements. He would be the Solvrei, the one who would bring peace to men. But there were many that opposed this idea. They hated even the stories of the Solvrei and wanted that power for themselves. From the moment the boy was conceived there were those who tried to destroy him and all that he stood for. They used deception, corruption and trickery. They bribed and coerced and threatened. Their fear and their greed drove them to into a great war, which created a rift in the elements. Only the Solvrei could reunite them. If he failed, the gods would have no more pity for men and would destroy them completely. They were already angered by the murder of the boy's father, killed while in mortal form, who had been very favored among them, despite his compassion for the lesser races. They only gave the boy a chance to save his world because of his father who had been one of them, the one who was named for the rain."

The old man stopped talking and gazed at me. I could feel the eyes of all the Tahitians and a shiver went down my spine like icy fingers trailing along my back. I looked at Damian who was staring down at his folded hands. I snapped at him irritably, "I did not come here to listen to made up stories and silliness. What is going on?"

"That story has been around longer than you, Queen," Damian said to his hands. "And it was meant for you to hear."

"I came here to learn about..." my voice trailed off and I couldn't say his name. Tal whose name meant rain.

"Tal. You came to learn about him. To me he was a friend, a brother, but some of our elders believe there was more to his story. My parents found him one night when he was a boy, wandering around lost in a rainstorm. My father had to go outside in the storm to repair part of the roof that had blown off. He spotted the boy out in the forest and chased after him, bringing him home. That's how he got his name. They named him because they found him in the rain. They thought that he was from Lehar but no one claimed to be missing a child and the boy wouldn't speak. He didn't speak for months. Just watched everything around him. When he finally began to talk he never spoke of where he had come from or how he had come to be on Tahitia, wandering around that night in the rain. I asked him often if he remembered and all he would ever say was that he had been lost. Did you know that as children we began to train for service to the Queens and Kings of Lehar? We were once the favored of the Leharan royalty. Only Tahitians were chosen as the Guardians of the Water Keepers, for we were the strongest, bravest, noblest of the island peoples."

"Not modest, however," I remarked, raising an eyebrow.

He smiled broadly. "No, we are not modest. We are a proud people. We trained and Tal was the best of us. Fought like nothing we had ever seen. The banishment occurred and still we continued to train, thinking it temporary and the Council would come to its senses. After a few years we realized that was not to happen. My parents made an offer to a family on Lehar to take Tal and claim him as one of theirs so that he could have a life that was not bound by the shores of this island."

"You must have seen him again. He came back didn't he?" I asked.

"Yes, he came back often. He would tell us stories of his life, of what was happening in the world, of you. He loved to talk about you, Lady Orabelle. Even before I saw you today I knew every feature of your face, every strand of your hair, that was how much he spoke of you. He called you his little Queen. That was why I said it earlier. I am used to thinking of you that way."

I took a heavy swallow from my cup and let the warm liquid spread through me before murmuring softly, "Had he let me I would have given up everything for him."

"That was not the way things were meant to be," Damian said.

"Meant to be? Are you speaking of your old legends? You cannot possibly expect me to believe that story. Tal was no god, he was a man. A great man, but still a man. And you seem to be missing a key element of your story. We don't have a son," I pointed out.

"Can you be sure of that?" he asked, looking at my stomach. I stopped short, and tried to remember when I had last had a cycle. I had been so consumed with my own grief that I hadn't noticed. I felt the blood rush to my head. The thought of being pregnant with Tal's child was one that I had never even imagined and a storm of emotions rushed over me.

"I can't remember," I whispered. My head felt light and I was dizzy. The goblet fell from my fingers and rolled across the ground and I feared that I would faint. Damian caught me and tried to steady me but my legs wouldn't seem to work. "Get me out of here. Some place quiet,"

"Can you walk?"

I shook my head and he lifted me easily, carrying me out of the circle. He had taken me past the first circle of houses when Colwyn stepped in front of us, sword drawn.

"Let her go!" he ordered, his face flushed.

"She is ill, I am taking her to lie down. To my mother's house," Damian explained carefully.

Colwyn sneered at him. "I know what you are doing! Release her, now! Or banishment will be the least of your people's worries."

"You threaten me?" Damian's voice had gone cold.

"Stop this!" I ordered, struggling to clear my head. "Colwyn, I am fine. Damian, please put me down."

He set me gently on my feet and patted my back. "I was not going to hurt you."

"Do not touch her again!" Colwyn yelled, brandishing his sword.

"I do not want to fight you," Damian warned, bracing his feet wide in a defensive stance.

I sighed, exasperated. "There will be no fighting! I command you both to stop this at once!"

Damian relaxed slightly and tried once again to reason with the other man. "My mother is a healer. I was taking the Queen to her. I meant her no harm."

"And why would I believe you?" Colwyn continued to snarl. "You, whose people were so treacherous that you had to be isolated from the rest of Imbria."

"My people were banished because of a lie! Because Chronus did not want the truth to be known and there were those among us that would have stood against him and exposed his lies!"

I whirled to face Damian. "What? What are you talking about?"

He glared at Colwyn. "I would not suggest that you hear it in front of this man."

"I am her protector, not you!"

"That is her choice, not yours."

Colwyn scoffed. "You think that you can do better than me? I am Captain of the Leharan Guard!"

"But you are not her Guardian. And you never will be because you are not good enough," Damian taunted, his round eyes narrowed to slits.

Colwyn let out a cry of rage and swung his sword. Damian lunged inside the circle of the weapon and slammed his massive fist into the other man's gut. He struck his forearm heavily with the side of his other hand sending the sword flying as he grabbed Colwyn by the throat and lifted him off the ground.

"Now," he said calmly, "I could snap your neck if I wanted."

Colwyn kicked his legs violently, his face turning purple.

"No," I cried, stepping forward. Damian released him suddenly and Colwyn collapsed in a heap on the ground, gasping.

"I am sorry," Damian told both of us and dropped to his knees. Colwyn looked at him as if he were mad and continued to take large gulps of air, his color gradually returning to normal.

"It is late. We should go. Colwyn, when you are able to stand, please get the men and tell them we are leaving." I stepped over him and walked to pick up his sword, handing it back to him as he pushed himself to his feet. He took it from me and hesitated, looking from me to Damian who was still kneeling, his head bent so that his long dreadlocks hid his face. "I will be fine," I assured Colwyn. "Wait for me at the gate."

He nodded and walked away, glancing over his shoulder frequently. I waited till he was finally out of sight then I laid a hand on Damian's arm. "Why do you kneel still?"

"I have asked for your forgiveness, I will wait here till you have given it."

"And if I don't?"

He didn't answer but continued to stare at the ground. I watched him for a long while, thinking. I needed a Guardian, someone that I could trust. I felt a connection to Damian because of Tal and he had no ties to anyone else on Imbria outside of his island. I also needed to learn what he knew about my father and the banishment. Knowledge like that would be useful to me in the Council, especially if I was pregnant. That was not going to be news that Chronus nor Blaise would take well. Maialen would support me but I would have to find a way to sever the strength of Chronus' hold on her. Astraeus was an idiot, he would do whatever seemed popular among the others and he would most likely follow Maialen. She was the key to gaining control of the council. If Damian knew something that would damage Chronus in her eyes, then I needed him.

"Come back with me, Damian."

He finally lifted his head, his dark eyes boring into mine. "What?"

"Come back with me. As my Guardian," I repeated. It was impetuous and probably foolish but I didn't care.

"I am not Tal."

"I know only too well the truth of that. But I have no one else. If it is true that I am carrying his child then I will need a Guardian now more than ever. There are things that must be done and I have wallowed in my own grief long enough. You say this is what you were trained to do, what your people pride themselves on. Then come with me and the banishment ends. For you and for all the Tahitians."

Damian was skeptical, cautious. "The Council will not allow it."

I laughed. "The Council, I predict, will not allow a lot of things that I am going to do. They have been corrupted by my father and manipulated by his lust for power for years. I will see that it changes, or I will refuse to be part of it. What council can there be without all the four of the elements?"

"You would stand against the Council, against the other Keepers, for me? For us? That is foolish, little Queen."

I shook my head. "No, not for you. They will be angry about you, yes, and they will not be happy that I have brought Tahitia back into my protection. My father will try and prevent it, however he can. But very soon they will have much bigger problems to worry over than your small island. I need you, Damian, and your warriors, because I plan to kill Blaise and to destroy Veruca."

# 9

Blaise slung himself into the large, ornately carved wooden chair of the Earth Keepers, his booted feet resting atop the smooth white granite of the council table. He shook his bright red curls away from his face and grinned at Chronus, running his hands over the smooth curves of mahogany, etched and carved to resemble the gnarled roots of a tree.

"Comfortable chair you have here. It might be a bit too big for that pretty little daughter of yours."

Chronus looked down his nose with a baleful glare and adjusted the heavy gold cuffs on his wrists. "Don't be childish."

Blaise laughed and swung his feet down, sitting upright. "Must be hard to have to give it all up, the power, the privilege....the chair. What will you do with yourself now? Gardening, perhaps? I have heard that some Keepers go mad after losing their powers. Just look at Astus. Although I think he was well on his way to madness before he gave up the Sapphire. Feeling any twinges after giving Maialen the Emerald?"

"You are not amusing me, boy."

The humor faded from the Fire Keeper, leaving him smoldering. "I didn't come here to amuse you, old man. I assume that you wanted to meet with me to discuss your other, less obedient daughter. The one you promised me but have not been able to deliver."

"You were the one that made me have her Guardian murdered!" Chronus snapped angrily. "You damned fool!"

Blaise slammed his fist down on the table and shouted, his voice echoing in the chamber, "What choice did I have but to come to you? Was I to let her run away with another man? To let her flaunt him in my face, making a laughingstock of me?! And I did not tell you to murder him in front of her, nor to use my Guardian to do it! Now she thinks it was me that ordered it!"

"Yes, you fool, she does and you will continue to let her think so! You should have done what you were told to do and been patient and not pestered me with your whining if you don't like my methods. If you hadn't been so damned petulant about the whole thing we would not be in this mess. With him alive we could have controlled her! She'd have done practically anything to keep him safe. Now what do we have as leverage? Nothing! And that is your fault."

"My fault? I would not have had him bludgeoned in front of her!"

Chronus made a disgusted noise and moved away from the table to pace the room. "You have made a mess of things with your foolish sentiment. She is too powerful already. And now that she's shut herself away on that cursed island of hers we have no idea what she is doing!"

"So what do you suggest we do?"

"Kill her." Chronus spoke in clipped tones, as if they were discussing crops and not his eldest daughter. He was curious to see what the young king's reaction would be to his latest proposal. Blaise had never been squeamish when it came to death but Chronus was beginning to see that his fascination with Orabelle ran deeper than he had first perceived.

"No!" Blaise jumped from the seat and grabbed the older man by the front of his robes. "You promised her to me and I want her!"

"You're being a fool!" Chronus said, shoving his hands away and smoothing down the rich fabric. "She doesn't love you."

"Love?" Blaise scoffed. "She doesn't have to love me as long as she belongs to me."

"You should kill her now while you have the chance! She has no Guardian, she is grieving, she is weak. She is vulnerable now!"

Blaise raised an eyebrow and a smile spread across his face, his rage quieting like a dying fire. He flung himself back onto the Earth Keeper's chair, grinning. "Ahhhh, I see. I should kill her now? I should? Perhaps I should choose a new Guardian so you can bribe them also, so that you may sit back and keep your hands clean? Ha! Such a doting father I wonder why she detests you?"

"She is not my daughter, she is a witch!"

"I want her," Blaise insisted. "I will not kill her and neither will you."

"I do not take orders from you, boy."

"Oh? And suppose I tell your darling Maialen all about this conversation? Imagine how she'd feel knowing dear old daddy murdered a Guardian and wants to murder a Queen who happens to be her beloved sister? Or perhaps with Orabelle dead I could have Maialen instead. After all, you promised me a daughter and I will have one."

"Maialen is not for you!" Chronus protested quickly. "I have heard rumors of your ... tastes."

Blaise leered. "I wouldn't hurt her. Much."

Chronus stared at him with unconcealed disgust. "No. Stay away from Maialen."

"Then give me Orabelle."

"Just remember that I warned you against this. We would all be better off with her dead. But since you insist on having her, we need to find a way to get her here. You can't very well storm Lehar and take her."

"If there were a Council meeting she would have to come here," Blaise said.

Chronus rubbed his chin thoughtfully. "True, but there must be a reason for calling an emergency meeting of the Council. One that she would not question. Then once she is here we can insist on the marriage between the two of you going forward."

"And how will you insist on it? You no longer have authority at Council, old man."

"I will if you and the others decide that I should oversee the Council, as High Regent. I would have the deciding vote between the four of you."

Blaise laughed. "And why would any of us do that?"

"Because you are all young and inexperienced. You will decide that it is wise to have someone with experience, with knowledge of the proceedings, to guide you and help to make the best decisions for Imbria," Chronus explained.

"Oh that is rich!" Blaise said, laughing again. "For Imbria! Ha! The problem is that Orabelle does have significant experience with Council. She will see through your ruse and she will never agree to it."

"She doesn't have to. A three to one vote will give me what I want and there will be nothing she can do about it."

"You still have no reason for a meeting in the first place," Blaise pointed out.

"You could choose a new Guardian, the Council must meet to confirm that choice."

"No," Blaise said hotly with a flash of temper. "You, old man, have shown me that it is not in my best interest to put so much trust into someone so close to me."

"If the Fomor tribe, the blood-drinkers, were to attack someone, a noble or someone important, something that would be quite horrific, then Orabelle would have to leave her precious island for Council," Chronus mused.

"The blood-drinkers haven't attacked anyone in years."

"And I think we both know why. It would not be difficult for you to arrange, considering your connections with them."

Blaise watched Chronus carefully, still smiling broadly though his eyes had narrowed. "I have no idea what you mean, old man, but yes I do think that such an attack would effectively bring our Water Queen out of mourning. Now, if the Fomor do decide to do this, where would be the most strategic place for their attack? Obviously Veruca is not an option and Lehar is across the sea. Besides, we do not want to provoke your darling daughter further."

"I do not want them near Kymir," Chronus said with finality.

"Of course not. That leaves Samirra, which should work out quite nicely. Astraeus will need someone to tell him what to do and that will help with your idea of leading the Council. I assume that you can coerce Maialen into going along with your clever little election plan."

Chronus nodded. "Of course Maialen will agree. Especially if they are attacking her fiancé's kingdom. Then with the Council in session and me as the overseer I will order Orabelle to go through with the marriage to you. She will have no choice, she cannot risk breaking away from the Council and upsetting the balance of power. But I still think you are a fool, and one that is likely to wake up to a knife at his throat on the wedding night."

Blaise stood and clapped the older man on the back. "I'm a light sleeper," he said with a wink and strode out the doorway.

# 10

*We were on the high cliffs that overlooked the sea on the western side of Lehar, the sky above bloated and grey with unfallen rain. I stood looking up at him, my hair loose from the braids that confined it and floating around me like a ghostly white shadow. He was dressed for battle, his silver armor gleaming, and there were tears on my face and he smiled down at me gently.*

*"Do not cry my little Queen," he murmured, his velvet voice wrapping around me, heavier than the thick sky and pressing down on me so I could barely breathe. The tears fell faster, scalding my cheeks. He reached out and brushed his thumb across my face.*

*"Please don't go," I begged. "Stay here with me."*

*"I would if I could, Orabelle. You know that."*

*I shook my head. "I don't believe you."*

*He sighed. "You are my life, my soul. We are never truly apart. Part of me lives in you now. You have to be strong."*

*"I don't want to be strong!" I cried, "I want you!"*

*"I have to go now. Please don't cry anymore. You have to make things right for our child," he said and leaned down so that his lips brushed mine.*

*"Please! Please don't go, Tal!" I sobbed as he backed away towards the edge of the cliff. I lunged after him, trying to keep him from walking to certain death.*

I woke with a start, throwing myself from the bed. I hit the floor heavily and knelt there, breathing hard, hot tears burning my eyes. I screamed, banging the floor with my fists, the loss of him ripping me apart yet again.

"Queen Orabelle!" Damian shouted, bursting into the room. "Are you in trouble? What happened?"

I shrieked again and continued to beat on the floor. "He's gone! He left me and he's gone and I could not stop him!"

Damian crossed the room and grabbed me around the waist, lifting me and pinning my arms. "Stop," he said, his deep voice calm and steady, "Stop this, you will only hurt yourself."

I wailed again and my cry was joined by the Sirens out on the beach, their mournful keening rolling out across the waves. Damian set me on my feet and shook me roughly.

"Stop it!" he ordered.

I blinked through my tears and tried to focus on his face, pushing down the enormous weight of grief that threatened to overwhelm me. I choked back a sob and stood, breathing heavily.

"I'm sorry," I gasped, my voice dry and hoarse.

"I did not mean to be harsh with you, my Queen, but there is a messenger here from Kymir. He insists on speaking to you directly and says it is urgent. He is waiting down at the beach," he told me, still watching me carefully.

I rubbed my eyes and took a deep breath. "Let me get dressed."

He nodded and went to wait outside the door. I changed quickly and splashed water on my face. The reflection in the mirror stared back at me with hollow eyes that were red-rimmed and smudged with dark circles. My hand passed absently over the gentle swell of my stomach, a gesture that had become habit for me since I had realized that I was pregnant. I took a last deep breath and turned away from the image of the lost girl in the mirror, forcing myself to clear my head.

I walked out, Damian falling into step beside me, another new habit we had acquired in the weeks since he had returned with me. "The Sirens did not alert me to any ships coming. What is this about? Something is wrong?" I asked him.

"The messenger came with a Samirran on an eagle. I fear this is going to be bad news, my Queen. He insisted on speaking only to you, saying that your sister had given him direct orders."

"Is something wrong with Maialen?" I demanded, my stomach turning at the thought.

"No, he said she is safe, but that was all he would say."

I nodded, the fear subsiding. We strode quickly down to the beach where the messenger waited, surrounded by several of my Guards. He looked nervous and strained, his eyes darting across the sea. Behind them was the lithe form of the Samirran rider, soothing the shining feathers of the massive eagle that had carried them here.

"You have a message for me," I said coming to stand before them.

"What is he doing here?" the Kymirran man demanded, gesturing towards Damian.

My eyes flashed angrily. "I am Queen here, you do not question me. If you have a message then deliver it now!"

He frowned deeply at Damian and from the cut of his eyes I knew that he did not approve. As if I cared what one of my sister's messengers thought.

"Very well," he said stiffly, "Your sister has sent me to deliver you a summons to Council. The Fomor Tribe has attacked Samirra. The Earth Queen was there but she managed to escape unharmed. The Council is meeting immediately, as soon as you arrive in Kymir."

"Maialen was there? How? What happened?"

"I do not know more. I was only sent with that message."

"Very well." I turned to Damian. "We leave immediately. I want three war ships armed and ready to go. We will be ready to protect Kymir."

The messenger looked relieved, despite his obvious doubts over Damian's presence. "Thank you. We welcome your assistance, Queen Orabelle."

I left Colwyn on Lehar to make sure our own kingdom remained safe and we sailed out within the hour, the men having moved quickly, grateful to have something to occupy them. I stood leaning against the rail of the ship, the salty air cooling my skin and Damian beside me, his huge spear in one hand and two curved swords on his hips.

"And so it begins," I said to him with a small smile.

"It begins," he repeated.

"The blood-drinkers haven't attacked anyone in years. And it was even longer than that since they attacked one of our kingdoms. The random merchant ship that strayed off course or a group of travelers who wandered into the wrong cave is one thing, but this? It doesn't feel right."

"I think there is much going on that we are not aware of, my Queen. I have asked some of the soldiers to go through the city upon our arrival and see what they hear from the Kymirrans. Rumors usually have a foundation in the truth."

I nodded, watching the waves, trying not to think of the last time I had been in Kymir. The night of the festival and of Tal's brutal death. I needed to be focused on the Council, to convince the others to end the banishment without stirring up too much hostility. I needed to control the hate I felt welling in me at just the thought of sitting at a table with Blaise and seeing my father in all his smugness. The only thing I was looking forward to was seeing Maialen.

"Damian," I said, turning to face him. The sun glinted off the silver tip of his spear and bathed his skin in light so that he seemed to radiate power. His stance was strong and firm and I felt a surge of pride that he was my Guardian. "You once said that the banishment was to cover my father's lie. I have not questioned you, but is it something that I should now know?"

He watched me carefully. "It is not something I wish to tell you."

"Why?"

"You have felt enough pain recently. It is in the past. If the banishment ends then perhaps there is no need to bring it to the present. Chronus is no longer part of the Council, he holds no threat to us. It is my wish to leave it alone, buried where it belongs. If the need arises, if they refuse to do as you ask, then it may be necessary to tell you. But only then."

"Very well. Though I think that anything involving my father will be knowledge that I may one day need. He does not trust me, nor I him. He has always hated me," I said bitterly.

"There are some people whose love would do you more harm than good. I worry for your sister."

"Maialen is too innocent. Her goodness is her greatest asset and her biggest fault."

"You will protect her as best you can, but you must realize that she is your equal now, Orabelle. She is the Keeper of Earth, she must stand on her own," Damian warned.

"And if she falls then I must watch her fall? You know I can't do that."

Damian did not reply but merely gazed out over the sea. The ships were making good time and the wind was strong behind us. I wondered if Astraeus was helping us along. He must be eager for the advice of the Council, to have others to rely on. He was a good leader at face value: charismatic, strong, brave. But when it came to politics and making decisions that would have serious consequences, he was lost. Between his ineptness and Maialen's unfailing belief in everyone, I worried for them. They would be wonderful if left to themselves to rule but with those like Blaise, Loagaire, Damek and my father clawing for their power, what would happen to them?

# 11

As the shoreline of Kymir came into sight I felt my chest tighten. It was so unchanged, like the past few months had never happened. I saw that the forest was heavily guarded and archers lined the docks. A group clustered together at the end of the pier, the familiar figure of my sister among them. The ship pulled in against the dock and our eyes met and I could see the haunted look on her face. She was pale and drawn, twisting her hands in agitation. A mottled purple bruise ran along one cheek and her lip was swollen with little black marks, like a seam on her dress, where her teeth had cut into it.

She broke into a run as soon as I stepped off the ship, throwing herself against me and burying her face in my neck. I stroked her long chestnut hair and held her tightly as she trembled. "What happened, Maialen?" I asked softly, pulling away so she could look at me.

"It was so horrible, Orabelle! I can't! I can't talk about it!" she protested vehemently.

"You don't have to, Maialen. We can talk later when you've calmed down. Are you hurt?"

She shook her head and tears filled her eyes. She tried to speak and the words seemed to choke her. Finally she managed to gasp out, "It's Gideon! He's hurt and no one has been able to help him!"

"Hurt how?" I wanted to know.

"One of them, one of those monsters bit him, tore a piece of him off and ate it! It was ... oh Orabelle, you can't imagine what it was like! I could hear it chewing. They were snapping and biting and clawing and they looked human and I just couldn't seem to... I couldn't grasp how they could be people!" Maialen cried, her voice rising shrilly.

I took her hand in mine. "Sshhh. You must remain calm, Maialen, they can't hurt us now. What happened to Gideon? Finish telling me about Gideon."

She gulped and her eyes were wild. "They bit him. One of them did. And it won't heal. It's awful and festering and we have tried everything but he just seems to be getting worse. He doesn't know where he is or what's happening and he has these nightmares and he screams. I don't know what to do!"

Damian stepped forward. "I think that I can help."

Maialen's wide green eyes grew even larger as she stared at Damian. "Orabelle," she whispered, "What have you done now?"

I laughed mirthlessly. "Maialen, this is Damian, my Guardian. He is a Tahitian. At Council today I will formally request that their banishment ends."

"What? How?" she stammered.

Damian cleared his throat and interrupted. "As I have already said I think that I can help your Guardian, Queen Maialen."

Hope flooded across her face and she forgot completely that she had been taught to distrust his kind. "You can?"

"Well, not me exactly but my mother. She is a great healer and she knows much of the Fomorians and the poison in their bite. She has seen it before and I think she could heal the man."

Maialen whirled around to face me. "Orabelle is that true? Is he telling the truth?"

"He would not lie," I assured her.

"Then please, please, bring her here! Please!" Maialen begged, grasping Damian's huge hand in hers. He looked to me.

I nodded. "I will send a ship for her. It will take at least another day if they sail through the night. Can he... will he be able to wait that long?"

Once again her face paled and her eyes filled with tears. "Oh, Orabelle, I don't know! Please just send them now! Get her now!"

"Damian," I prompted and he jogged over to the captain of the ship, giving him orders.

"Thank you! Thank you so much! I'll try anything, I'll do anything to save him. I can't imagine losing him, Orabelle, I don't know what I would do without him, without my Guardian." Maialen stopped talking abruptly and her face flushed. I stood expressionless, trying to swallow my own grief.

"Oh, no," she whispered, "I am so sorry, Orabelle! I didn't think... I wasn't thinking..."

I shrugged, knowing that I could lie but that my eyes had darkened till they were almost black, showing the depth of my sorrow to everyone around us. "You are worried for your Guardian, that is enough for now, do not worry about me too, little sister. I am fine. "

"Come; let us go to my house. Gideon is there, maybe you can talk to him? He doesn't seem to know what is going on but..." Maialen's voice trailed off. I smiled reassuringly and took her hand again, letting her lead me through the trees. Damian walked proudly behind us and everyone who saw him gaped and whispered frantically to each other.

"Father should hear about this in the next few minutes I would guess," I remarked ruefully.

Maialen gave me a small smile. "News travels fast here. Especially concerning our family."

We had nearly reached her house in the trees when my eyes wandered over towards the garden where Tal had died, despite my silent and repetitive order for them not to. I knew the exact place, I could not forget it, but the path through the trees that led there was gone and a thick tangle of shrubs and vines hid everything from view. I stopped and Maialen followed my gaze.

"I never wanted to set foot on that ground again," she explained gently. I did not respond and we turned away and went into the house. Maialen led me to the room where Gideon was sleeping. The smell nearly choked me as I passed through the doorway. It was thick and putrid and reeked of rotting flesh. I opened my mouth, forcing myself not to breathe through my nose. Something about the smell was slightly familiar, like some horrible nightmare I had long forgotten. Gideon was lying in the bed, the sheets twisted around him and soaked in sweat. His skin was an odd color, tinged with grey and the bandage that covered his shoulder seeped with fresh blood.

I hesitated in the doorway, the sense of Deja vu' growing stronger as I gazed upon his wrecked body. Whatever it was tugged at the edges of my memory, just out of reach. Maialen crossed the room to kneel at the side of the bed, smoothing his damp hair away from his forehead.

"Gideon, Orabelle is here," she said. "She has come to the Council, and oh, how I wish you were awake so you could see, but she has a new Guardian. And, of course, it is one that is sure to cause quite a bit of distress! I will let her tell you."

She looked up and waved me over. I took a step toward the bed and felt panic rise uncontrollably in my chest. Every instinct in my body was shouting at me to run from the room. I glanced back at Damian helplessly. He had moved to the side of the room and was watching me intently, his body taut with readiness as he sensed my panic.

Maialen stood up from the side of the bed. "What is it, Orabelle?"

"Orabelle," my father's voice boomed garishly through the sickly air as he appeared in the doorway frowning. He stopped short at the sight of Damian and the color appeared to drain from his face and then pour back in bright scarlet. He appeared so enraged I thought he would choke on his ire.

"So it's true! You have defied Council and brought this man here? As your Guardian?!"

I would have shouted back at him but I stopped short, my mouth open, staring wide eyed at his scalded face. The panic was worse, my fingers numb with it, only this time a memory came with it. The smell, the grey skin, my father yelling, his cheeks stained dark red with anger. I remembered Ursula lying in her bed wasting away and I backed away from him and whispered in horror, "Mother."

Chronus's eyes narrowed to slits and he reached for me, but Damian's huge form stepped between us. My father backed away quickly, his lip curled as if even being that close to Damian was too unsavory to contemplate.

"What did you do?" I demanded of Chronus, my head whipping back and forth between him and Gideon, seeing neither of them, only my mother, wasting away.

"Orabelle, be silent! You are only trying to stir up more trouble!" Chronus hissed. Maialen was standing beside me now and she laid a hand on my arm.

"Please, can we leave here? This is not the place to be fighting," she pleaded and ushered me out of the room. I stared at Chronus as we passed him, my mind reeling. My mother's illness had had the same look, the same smell, hers just hadn't been as strong. Had she been bitten by a blood-drinker? And if so, how would it have happened? And if the Tahitians knew how to heal it, then why had they been banished when they could have saved her? The questions battered my mind as I followed Maialen through her chambers.

"What was going on back there?" she asked me fretfully.

"Nothing," I assured her, trying to regain my composure. Whatever was going on, it was not something that I wanted to share with Maialen at that moment. Reminding her of our mother's loss while her Guardian lay suffering a similar fate would just be cruel. "I just wasn't prepared to see him like that."

"You have never been squeamish, Orabelle," she said pointedly. Of course my sister could tell I was lying to her.

"It's nothing, Maialen," I repeated firmly. "Come, let us go to Council."

"Yes, it is almost time," she agreed with a sigh, giving me a last searching look.

We made our way across the outer clearing to where Damian stood waiting beside the heavy doors that led to the Council Chamber. The doors had been meticulously carved with a seal, the patterns of the four elements, all entwined to represent the unity that was the purpose of the Council. Long, curving lines represented water flowing like a stream around a burning sun. Surrounding that was a wreath of flowers and the outermost circle was the swirling clouds of the air. I let my eyes linger on the visage and wondered how it came to pass that the four of us were chosen to hold such power. If we had been born in a different time and the fate of Imbria had been left in the hands of others, would our lives have been better? My fingertips brushed over the seal and I walked down the stairs into the large underground chamber where the Council was held. The room was already crowded with regents and advisors clustered in groups, arguing loudly amongst themselves. We approached the marble table where the Keepers had sat for generations, their four chairs spaced evenly around it. Damian moved to stand off to the side, close to me but still out of the way. I stopped as I reached the table.

"There are five chairs," I said to Maialen.

"Before you arrived we asked father to sit with us in Council. We don't have any experience with this and he wants to help," Maialen explained, her eyes pleading with me to not be angry.

"You cannot be serious about this! On what authority will he sit here?" I demanded to know.

"As a High Regent, an overseer of the Council. He will help us with-"

"There is no such thing!" I exploded, cutting her off. "Now he is just making up titles to give himself?"

The room was growing quiet as attention began to settle on us. Maialen's eyes swept the crowd and she gave me a stern look. "He is just going to help us, Orabelle. There is no need to overreact."

I was about to ask her if she had gone mad when a flash of red caught my eye. Blaise approached the table, a wide smile of his face. He was dressed in the polished black battle uniform of the Verucans, his ruddy skin healthy and his blood-red hair shining in contrast to the dark armor. It struck me as odd that someone so handsome could be so completely vile.

He walked up to me slowly, the noise of the room quieting to a hum as more turned to watch what was unfolding at the table. His grin broadened as he paused to look Damian up and down. He turned his amber gaze back to me and I fought the urge to strike him, to slap the smile from his face.

"Orabelle," he said, "you are beautiful as always."

I swallowed hard and inclined my head slightly for the benefit of those around us. "Blaise. You look well."

He took my hand in his and pressed his lips to it. "I was hoping for a more enthusiastic greeting."

My eyes flashed pale white and I felt my face redden. "Oh believe me, it is not the greeting I wish to give you, Fire King, but only the one that is appropriate in front of these people."

He lifted an eyebrow. "Do not tease me, Water Queen, with thoughts of what would happen were we alone."

I turned away in disgust just as Astraeus and Chronus entered the chamber, followed by Favian, the Samirran's wiry Guardian. The Air Keeper looked tired and his face was lined with stress. Maialen moved to greet him, clasping his hand in hers and murmuring something to him. He looked up at me and nodded in greeting then gestured to the table.

"Shall we begin?" Astraeus suggested, sliding into his seat. Maialen sat next to him and Blaise and I faced each other on opposite sides. My father had conveniently placed his own chair at the head of the table and he now stood behind it clearing his throat.

"People of Imbria," Chronus boomed, his voice echoing loudly through the chamber, "The Council has decided, by their majority vote, that I shall act as their overseer and High Regent of Imbria. With this authority I call this session to order."

Across the table Blaise rolled his eyes. Chronus did not seem to notice but continued on pompously, thanking the various regents and nobles who were present. I stopped listening, my thoughts returning to Gideon and my mother. I was sure that it was the same affliction and if my father had willingly sent away the only people that could have saved Ursula, then he had effectively killed her. Though I had no way to prove it. Before I could do anything I would have to see if Cossiana could save Gideon. If he died, then I would have no grounds to accuse my father of anything.

"Orabelle," Chronus's sharp voice caught my attention. "We demand to know what you are doing by defying the Council's edict and bringing this man out of Tahitia."

"I have chosen Damian as my Guardian and the Tahitians are my people. They are part of the Leharan kingdom and I want the banishment lifted," I stated defiantly.

One of the regents from Samirra spoke up, "This is good! They are the best warriors and we need them to fight the Fomor Tribe!"

Several others murmured assent and nodded. I continued, "These people have been punished long enough. Those like Damian were merely children and the events that occurred had nothing to do with them. They have committed no crime. Let them be back under my protection and my supervision."

Chronus was frowning deeply. "The Tahitians committed a very serious offense against the Verucans. They attacked them, destroying one of their ships and killing everyone on board."

"An attack which they claim began on the Verucan side."

"Of course they say that. Orabelle, do not be naive," Chronus lectured.

My temper flared and I snapped at him, "Verucans also attacked me and one of my ships several years ago and that was forgiven."

"We are not here to discuss that offense. Do not stray from the topic at hand in your attempt to dilute the seriousness of this matter."

"The Tahitians have shown no hostility nor have they ever gone against the terms of their punishment. They have behaved honorably all these years. I do not see why a people, who were mere children at the time and have shown no ill will since, should continue to serve out the sentence of Council members that no longer hold power. We are the Keepers now, it is our decision to make, not yours."

My father's eyes narrowed to menacing slits at the insult I had thrown at him. Before Chronus could reply Blaise held up a hand to stop him.

"Orabelle does have a valid point. I believe that because the incident leading to this matter began with Lehar and Verucan, that we should be the ones to decide," Blaise said, smiling at me. "I agree with Orabelle."

"No! The Council decides as a Council. You cannot pick and choose who makes what decisions!" Chronus argued.

"Then we shall vote on it," Maialen spoke up. "And I agree with them also."

"As do I," Astraeus offered.

Chronus was seething as he sat back in his chair. "Very well. You have decided and the banishment ends."

I glanced at Damian who was grinning unabashedly. The banishment was over and he could bring the news of their restored honor back to his people and I knew that he was proud. Favian leaned over to grasp his shoulder in comradery and several others offered their congratulations.

"I would like to discuss Samirra now," Astraeus said. "We have done nothing to provoke an attack from the Fomori. They have never been so bold as to come to our towns, and never with such wanton destruction and violence. This was not merely a raid for 'food' as they seem to think of us, this was a bloody massacre."

I turned to Maialen. She was holding Astraeus's hand tightly and staring down at her lap. "You were there," I said to her, "I know you don't want to speak of it, but if you saw or heard something that could help us understand then we need to know."

"Your sister has been through enough, Orabelle, leave her be," Chronus said, glaring at me.

"No father, she is right," Maialen interrupted. "I have been reliving it in my mind anyway, perhaps telling it to someone else will help. I was in Samirra to see the land and become familiar with its people before the wedding. I... I want to be a good Queen to them as well as to Kymir. I wanted to visit some of the villages. Astraeus told me that I should wait until he was able to accompany me but I thought that the sooner the people came to know me, the more they would accept me. I wanted to go ahead without him and of course I had Gideon with me so I was not worried."

She paused, taking a deep breath and letting it out slowly. Then she told us of what had happened in the village. She had gone there on horseback with Gideon. It had been late afternoon and they already visited several other of the outlying villages of Samirra. This was their last stop before they headed back to the palace. As they approached people came out from their homes and jogged in from working the fields to greet them. They smiled and chatted with the villagers, who offered them gifts and fed their horses apples as they rode by. Then Maialen had heard screaming and a woman came running down the path, her dress torn and bloody. She had been hysterical, throwing herself in front of Gideon's horse and trying to clamor onto it with him. She had knocked Gideon from his mount in her hysteria and the horse had run, spooked, as more people came screaming from the edge of the village. There had been an awful smell, indescribable except that Maialen told them it was the smell of evil. She had tried to dismount to help Gideon but he had shouted for her to stay on her horse, pulling his axe from the leather straps that held it across his back. That was when they saw them. There was a large group of them, more than ten, huge and frightening with glowing eyes and sharp teeth. They were growling like dogs and there was blood running down their faces. They were attacking everyone without prejudice, even the children. Maialen had watched in horror as people were slaughtered, screaming and begging for help. Her horse had panicked and reared, its nostrils flaring at the evil stench of the attackers and she had been thrown to the ground just as they converged on Gideon, his axe swinging fatally through them. Maialen had gotten to her feet, dazed, then she was knocked back to the ground by the fleeing villagers. She rolled to the side to avoid being trampled and one of the beasts had spotted her, breaking away from the group and hissing at her. It had snarled, biting the air and laughing as she screamed. Gideon whipped around at the sound from her and as he did, one of them used his distraction to leap onto him, tearing at his arm with its teeth. He had shouted at Maialen to use her power and she had clutched at the green jewel around her neck frantically, having forgotten that it was there. The ground shook and began to crumble away beneath the creatures and several of them tumbled into the gaping hole in the dirt. The rest backed away warily, including the one who had been intent on attacking her. They were staring at her hatefully and she held out the amulet, shouting at them to go away. One of them said something in a language she could not understand and they began to lope back the way they had come, their long strides somewhere between a man and a wolf's. She had then run to Gideon, forgetting about the hole in the ground until she heard the things in it screeching as it closed around them, the earth settling back to the way it had been before Maialen had called for it to change and burying them alive.

"I am sorry," Maialen said softly. "I should have been better with my element."

"The Earth Element was not made to fight, dear daughter" Chronus told her. "There is nothing to be sorry for. Without you the destruction would have been much worse, I am sure."

"You said that one of them spoke. You have no idea what it said?" I asked her gently.

She covered her face with her hands and once again breathed deeply. When she lowered them her eyes were damp. "No. Its voice was strange, different from ours. They were no words that I had ever heard before. It might have been the ancient language but I was never as adept at learning it as you, Orabelle."

Astraeus patted her hand and turned to the rest of us expectantly. "What do you think?"

"If they didn't take any of the bodies with them, then it appears as though they were there to purposely inspire fear," Blaise mused. "Almost like a warning."

"A warning against what?" Astraeus demanded.

The Fire King shrugged. "How would I know. It is you they seem to have a problem with, Samirran. Are you sure you have done nothing to provoke them?"

"We have done nothing! I have already told you that!"

"Let us remain calm," Chronus said, spreading his hands in a gesture of arbitration. "Maialen are you alright?"

She nodded. "I am just so worried for Gideon. And for all those people who are living out there unprotected."

"Astraeus, perhaps you should invite your people to move into the larger of your towns until we find out more about what is happening," I suggested. "It may also be wise of you to supply some of these villagers with adequate weapons to defend themselves."

"If they do not work their crops, there will be nothing to trade for these weapons," he pointed out.

"I am sure that you and Blaise can come to some sort of arrangement. I am only telling you that in a vast land such as yours, it will be easier to defend people if you have them gathered together. Obviously your army is not great enough to cover the entire northern boundaries. It is easier to defend a town than it is dozens of tiny villages. If you like, only bring in those that are nearest to the mountains or any caves. We know the Fomori dwell beneath us, they are in the most danger."

Astraeus sighed as if I had deliberately placed a great burden on him. "I will see if it can be managed. In the meantime, perhaps we should think about the idea of destroying these things altogether."

"Yes, that is the desirable outcome," Chronus agreed. "However, we need to know more about them before we can go after them. We should set up scouting parties to ride north and see what they can find."

"I'm sure you will have many volunteers for that endeavor," I said sarcastically. "There must be something in your great library. I cannot fathom that during the age of exploration no one thought to enter a labrynth of tunnels that runs beneath all of Imbria."

Astraeus shook his head. "Unless they never returned alive. But I will try to find out more. If I can discover their routes perhaps we can ambush them the next time they come to attack us."

"Excellent plan. Please inform me as soon as you have collected this knowledge and we can begin," Chronus said in a voice that indicated the subject was closed for the time being. He turned to me. "There is one more matter to discuss. Your impending marriage."

My eyes flew open wide and I felt my stomach churn. So this was why Blaise had been so willing to side with me about the Tahitians. They had both known this would be coming. By making it a matter of Council they were leaving me no choice.

"Perhaps now is not the time for this, father," Maialen suggested quietly.

"Nonsense! She has grieved long enough, it has been months. She has chosen a new Guardian," Chronus pointed out. "She will do as was decided for her and she will marry Blaise. The sooner the better."

"Better for who?" I snapped.

"For you!" he retorted, "and for your two kingdoms. What better way to welcome the Tahitians back to us than with this marriage, which promotes peace between your two realms."

The other regents began to nod in agreement. I realized that they had tricked me, that they had known and had planned to give Tahitia back to me all along so that they could use it against me now.

"Father, please," Maialen began.

"There is no reason why she cannot marry him!" Chronus insisted.

"He is right. There is no reason for her not to, it will only benefit them both," Astraeus said.

Maialen's mouth dropped open and she whirled to face her fiancé. "She doesn't love him!"

"What does that have to do with it? We are all doing what is best for Imbria," Astraeus shrugged. A look of hurt washed over Maialen's face and she struggled to hide it.

I looked across the table at Blaise who was staring back, his amber eyes burning into me, ignoring everything else. I felt a fresh wave of hatred welling up and I wanted more than anything to shove a knife deep into his heart. I imagined the blade sinking through his flesh, splintering the bone, piercing his black heart as the fire in his eyes grew dark.

A smile played on Blaise's lips. "Perhaps we should marry now? Everyone is already here and assembled."

"No!" Maialen burst out, "there must be a wedding! After all the horrible things that have happened we should have a celebration. It will be a good way to reintroduce the Tahitian people as well. We can have our weddings together, as we had planned!"

She gave me a hopeful look and I understood that she was trying to do anything she could to keep me from Blaise. At least this way I would have some time. The problem that not even Maialen knew was that my pregnancy was going to be very obvious soon. I must have been nearing six months and the thick, flowing gowns I wore still hid it effectively but in a few more weeks I expected that there would be no hiding it. I had hoped to be safely away on Lehar till the child was born and not in the middle of my own wedding festivities with half of Imbria there as witnesses.

"I will agree to the marriage," I said with feigned lightness, "though I will request that the wedding is postponed till the new year. This has been an unlucky time for us and I think it would be best to celebrate these new beginnings with a new year."

Blaise lifted an eyebrow, his eyes still never leaving me and the mocking smile still playing at his lips. "I will agree to that, but on the condition that the banishment of the Tahitians continue until we are married. Consider their freedom to be my wedding gift."

"But you already agreed! The Council has decided!"

"I agreed to lift the banishment, I did not agree that it would be immediate. You must learn to compromise, darling."

"Damian is my Guardian! I need him with me," I argued through clenched teeth. My fists were balled on the table, knuckles white as I struggled to hold my rising temper at bay.

Blaise inclined his head slightly. "Of course, my bride, you may keep your Guardian. It is the rest of them I am referring to."

"But the healer... Orabelle is sending for a Tahitian to try and help Gideon," Maialen murmured.

"Ahhhhhh," Blaise sighed, leaning back and lacing his fingers behind his head. "Now that is a problem."

I wanted to reach across the table and tear his hair out. He and Chronus were manipulating me too easily. They had anticipated everything I would do.

I unclenched my hands, laying them flat on the cool surface of the table. "Perhaps there is an arrangement that can be made regarding the healer."

"Now that I think about it, there might be," Blaise mused thoughtfully, as if the idea had just occurred to him. "The healer will be here tomorrow I assume. The time that the Tahitians are here, you, my dear Queen, must spend with me."

"You cannot be serious. That is completely ridiculous and I have a kingdom to look after," I argued.

He shrugged. "I am sure that the Leharans can manage a few days without your presence. For poor Gideon's sake."

"Fine, I will agree," I practically spat out, not even bothering to hide my distaste. I refused to look at my father, I could not bear to see his gloating triumph in that moment.

"I believe that would be fair. If she is to be their queen it will do her good to acquaint herself with the Verucans," Astraeus agreed, oblivious to the game being played around him and clearly feeling generous that he was bestowing his great wisdom upon us. Maialen looked at me desperately and I gave her a small nod.

"I agree then," she sighed.

# 12

I stood on the pier with Damian, waiting for the sleek shape of the Leharan ship to appear on the horizon. It was still dark outside and though the first brushes of dawn had painted pale grey streaks across the sky, the chill of night still lingered at the edges of the shore.

"Do you really believe that your mother can heal Gideon?" I asked, shivering as a cool wind blew, rustling the leaves in the trees behind us.

"Yes," he replied. "Cossiana is the best healer among our people. She would often be called away when we were children to tend to the royal families across Imbria."

"Did she ever come to see my mother?"

Damian looked down at me, his round black eyes solemn. "Yes, she has told me that she did."

"But she couldn't help her?"

"No, they were sent away before she could."

I nodded silently, breathing in the night air. I was becoming more and more convinced that my father had deliberately kept people from my mother who could have saved her. The question I couldn't begin to fathom was why. He had not tried to steal her power, he had not wanted to be with someone else. Instead he had let her linger on for years, watching as she wasted slowly away, almost as if he had been punishing her.

"Orabelle," Damian said, rolling his heavy spear between his hands, "I do not like the idea of you going to Veruca with the Fire King."

I sighed. "Neither do I, but I was foolish and I allowed them to manipulate me."

"What do you think he intends? I do not understand why he would agree to the wedding being postponed for months and exchange his leverage for a few nights with you now."

"Blaise is a strategist," I told him, "He has some sort of plan. All I know for certain is that I feel like I am walking into the lion's den."

"I will be with you. I will not let anything happen to you," he vowed.

"Damian, you aren't going with me."

He stared at me as if I were mad. "Of course I am going with you, my Queen, I am your Guardian!"

I shook my head. "I have already lost one Guardian to him, I fear that he may do something to you in order to hurt me."

"But who will protect you?" he wanted to know. "And what if he learns of the child?"

I shuddered at the thought, wrapping my arms tighter around myself. "I would rip his heart out and feed it to the Fomori myself before I will let him hurt my child."

"You are very strong, my Queen, but you will be in Veruca, where his power is the greatest. The sea there is not your sea. It is black and thick and does not flow as normal water should. You will be separated from everything that gives you strength."

"Veruca is an awful place but there is still water there, no matter how tepid, and I can draw on it. Please, Damian, if you want to help me then make sure Cossiana heals Gideon as quickly as she can. It is his life that I am saving and as soon as he is well again then Blaise will have to let me go."

"I can see the ship now," he said, pointing out to sea. I had already known it was there because the Sirens were on board, making sure the old woman arrived safely.

"Then I shall go and say goodbye to Maialen. Watch over her for me, Damian."

He reached for my arm as I turned to go. "Do not do this. Do not go there alone."

"I am taking part of the Guard with me. I will be fine. What I need from you is to learn what you can here and to take care of my sister and Lehar while I am gone."

"You are not invincible, Orabelle. If he wants to he will find ways to hurt you," Damian warned.

"If not for my child I would gladly slit his throat before dawn today, but I cannot take the chance before the baby is born. I have to make sure that the place as my heir is secure, that my child will not be ostracized with me for my actions. So I will wait and I will play at the Fire King's games and I will find his weakness and one day soon, Damian, I promise that I will kill him for what he has done to me."

"I only ask that I be there to see him die."

# 13

The mountains of Veruca towered above us as I stepped onto the hard land. The shore was littered with fragments of shiny, black volcanic rock that bled into the waves causing the water to churn darkly. It was like smoke trapped beneath the glassy surface, contaminated and impure and a shiver of revulsion crawled across my skin. I took a deep breath and the air felt heavy and hot in my lungs. It smelled slightly of sulpher and smoke and all around us plumes of steam hissed up from cracks in the rock, as if the entire mountain was exhaling its angry breath. Along the cliffs that bordered the harbor a tall black wall, ten feet high, rose intimidatingly, stretching as far as the eye could see.

"This way," Blaise ordered, taking my elbow and steering me toward a huge iron door carved into the base of the mountain.

"There is no need for you to touch me," I snapped and pulled my arm from his grasp, though I continued to walk beside him to the doorway which swung open slowly, revealing a long, dark tunnel.

"You will have to get used to it soon enough," he replied with a grin, his eyes raking over me.

I glared at him. "I will do everything that I possibly can to make sure that never happens."

"You have agreed to the marriage, Orabelle. Short of killing yourself there really isn't much you can do."

"Perhaps even that alternative is more pleasing to me than the thought of being with you," I retorted.

Blaise laughed, reaching to take a torch from one of his soldiers who stood waiting at the tunnel. "Don't be so dramatic. If you were going to kill yourself you'd have done it already."

I wanted to scratch his eyes out but I forced myself to remain calm. He was baiting me, enjoying my anger. Blaise loved to taunt, to see the reaction he could ignite with his sharp wit and I did not want to give him that satisfaction. I ignored him as we walked through the smooth black tunnel of rock. I glanced back over my shoulder at the members of my Guard walking behind me. They looked as uncomfortable as I felt. We were used to open air, ocean breezes and the wide expanse of the sea. This place felt as if it was closing in on us like a tomb. Finally, I could see the orange glow of daylight ahead of us as the tunnel sloped upward and opened into Veruca. The massive city was built into a huge valley between the lines of the mountain, carved into the black rock itself. There was a constant clamor echoing throughout that rose from the mines and the smelting and the blacksmiths. The Fire Keeper's castle towered over everything, an enormous giant cut directly from the cliff around it with huge black spires rising up into the sky, piercing the yellowed clouds.

As we walked towards the castle the rough-skinned people of Veruca began to turn and stare. I studied them as we passed, noting the dirtiness and the poor quality of their homespun clothing. I also noticed that they did not smile at Blaise, nor greet him warmly as the Leharans did me. They seemed to avoid looking at him and instead focused on me and the Guard with barely concealed hostility.

"After you, my dear," Blaise said, sweeping an arm toward the entrance to the castle gates, which stood open in anticipation of our arrival. I moved past him and entered a huge stone chamber lit all around with torches and bare of any other adornment.

"How inviting," I muttered sarcastically.

Blaise laughed. "Do not worry, my dear, it gets better."

The chamber had four doorways evenly spaced around it. I was led through one of them and up a long stairway. At the next level, the rooms were much more lived in, the walls draped with tapestries and the floors cushioned by heavy rugs. There was a long table with sturdy chairs and enormous brass candelabras. We passed this, moving on to another doorway that led us to a set of rooms.

"These are my personal rooms," Blaise told me. "You will be staying in here, beside mine."

He led me into a room with a high bed covered in pale blankets. Tapestries depicting the cool seas of Lehar hung from the walls and there was a long table with a cushioned bench. The table held a vase of shells and a large glass urn of water, along with various other feminine objects, including a brush and a mirror that were silver inlaid with pearl.

I looked at Blaise. "What....what is all of this?"

"It is for you." He flashed me another grin, as if to say that it was some sort of silly joke between us. "I did what I could to make it more comfortable for you to be here, away from your island."

I was confused. "You did this for me?"

He shrugged and moved around the room, running his finger over the edges of things. "I am not completely uncaring, Orabelle."

I felt my temper rise. "You only care about what you want. Do not think that a few tokens and trinkets like these will make me forget what you really are."

His amber eyes burned though his face remained pleasant, his smile still easy on his lips. "And what am I then?

"A murderer," I stated bluntly, lifting my chin and staring back at him.

"Then I should be a fitting match for an adulteress."

My own eyes whitened with rage. "Do not ever speak to me that way again," I warned him, my voice low.

He crossed the room, grabbing me by my wrists and pulling me near so that I could feel his breath hot on my face. "Or what? What will you do to me, Orabelle? Kill me? Ha! Your father would love that! He'd have his hands on your kingdom in no time and you know it. He is waiting for any opportunity to destroy you."

"And you aren't? You are both cowards and pigs!" I spat.

He was standing so close that all I could see was the brightness of his eyes. "I brought you here to save you! Your dearest daddy wanted you dead and I am the one that refused!"

"What are you talking about?" I demanded.

His grin broadened. "That's right, lovely, your father asked me to kill you before the Council meeting. I'm afraid he will try on his own which is the reason I brought you here where I can protect you."

"I do not need your protection, I do not belong to you!"

"Not yet, but soon enough you will and I don't want you damaged in any way or dead before I have you."

"Let go of me!"

He dropped my wrists and took a step back. "Do you not believe me?"

"I believe you. But it doesn't change anything between us. You want to protect me like you would a prized possession, you want to own me. You want me to belong to you even though I never will. I will never come to you willingly, I will never touch you with anything but disgust and hate. I will never love you," I swore.

He laughed. "Always this ridiculous notion of love. I care not if you love me. You are right about one thing, though, I do want you and you *will* belong to me."

He turned abruptly and strode through the doorway, leaving me alone. I stared after him, thinking of what he had said. If Blaise was telling the truth then Chronus wanted me dead and sooner rather than later. My own father wanted to kill me and he had asked the man he was forcing me to marry to do it.

I passed a hand over my stomach. I was sure that Chronus knew nothing of the child yet and if he was already was planning to murder me, he would only try harder on learning that I would soon have an heir. He would most likely want to be rid of the child as well, something more easily accomplished while I was pregnant, but it could also be possible that he would have no qualms killing the baby after it was born. They had all betrayed me, manipulated me, used me, and now they sought to kill me as well. For no reason other than I hadn't been exactly what they wanted me to be. For nothing but their pride and their greed and their selfishness. I was the Water Keeper, Queen of Lehar, the strongest and most powerful Water Queen there had ever been. I would not be treated like their pawn. I would not bow down to them, I would not cower to them and be afraid.

The anger burned across my skin, tearing through me. I flung my hand towards the urn of water, shattering it as the liquid swirled up into the air. I threw it across the room, sending the contents of the table scattering and smashing them against the stone floor. There was a shout from the doorway and I spun around, flinging the water before me like driving rain, each drop piercing with the intensity of my hate.

"My Queen, no! It's me, Kaden!" the man in the doorway shouted, raising his arms in front of his face.

The water fell in harmless droplets to puddle on the floor. I was breathing heavily, the anger flowing out of me as Kaden, one of the soldiers of my Guard I had chosen to accompany me, slowly lowered his hands. He was still wearing his full armor though he had removed the helmet and his pale blonde hair was tied back from his face. He looked down at the liquid that seeped into the stone, then back up at me. "I heard a commotion, I thought you might be in trouble," he explained.

"I'm sorry, I am fine now. Thank you," I told him.

He glanced around at the debris strewn across the floor, pieces of glass glinting in the torch light. "Didn't care for your room?"

A small smile tugged at the corners of my lips. I lifted my chin and said haughtily, "No, it was not to my liking."

He grinned. "Can't say I care much for this place either. Feels like a tomb. All this rock. I don't know how people live here."

"It's what they know," I said with a shrug.

"I will be happy to be back in Lehar and away from this place as soon as possible. By the way, did you know that the Fire King still has no Guardian?"

I raised an eyebrow. "I did not notice, but you are right, he had no Guardian at Council. I have been too distracted lately I seem to be missing a lot of things."

"That's what I'm here for, my Queen!" Kaden said happily. "I will learn all I can about this place and report back to you."

"Just be careful, I don't think Blaise would be too happy to find you snooping around."

He nodded. "I can be extremely discreet. And women are the same everywhere, they love to talk! No offense meant of course."

"None taken," I smiled. "Go on then and I will stop breaking things here."

He laughed and bowed, backing out of the room. He was right, I did need to learn as much as I could while we were here and standing around smashing things was not helping. I walked to the doorway and looked down the corridor. The door to the

Guard's room stood open but the others were shut, including the one that Blaise had pointed out as his chamber. I moved quietly past it in case he was inside and made my way to the far end of the hallway. It ended in a heavy iron door with two massive bars across it to keep it from being opened from the other side. I ran my hands over the cool metal.

"And what are you hiding in here?" I murmured out loud. I hefted one of the bars up but could not lift it at all, even a fraction. The bars were obviously meant to keep something out, heavy enough so that it must have taken several men to place them. I walked back to my room and waved a finger over the water that had puddled on the floor. Some of it had already seeped into the stone but there was enough that I could use it to lift the bars. I held it between my hands, tiny rivers flowing between my fingers and over my skin as it swirled around itself. I carried it back to the doorway and let it fall, then pulled it upward underneath the first bar. The column of water rose, lifting the heavy piece of metal and then spreading outward so that the bar was lowered quietly to the ground. I did the same thing with the second bar then stepped over them and tugged at the door. It swung open on well-oiled hinges to reveal a stairway carved into the rock that descended down under the mountain into darkness. I grabbed a torch from a sconce and began to climb down the steps. They seemed to go on forever, darkness surrounding me on all sides, save for my small circle of torchlight. Finally the stairs ended in a narrow room with tunnels running off from the opposite ends. They were nearly identical so I chose one and started down it, winding through a labyrinth of corridors and tunnels but repeating the same pattern of turns to that I would be able to easily find my way back.

The further I walked underneath the mountain, the more I noticed the lack of water around me. I could not feel my element at all, everything was smooth rock and stone, the air hot and dry. My throat grew parched and my skin was flushed. I was taking deep breaths but my lungs didn't seem to be able to draw in enough air. I felt as if the mountain was closing in on me, crushing me under a ton of hot, dry rock. I needed to get out of there, to find water.

I was starting to turn around to go back when I heard a noise from the tunnel ahead of me. It was a scraping sound, like something being dragged across the ground. I walked toward it and listened again but instead of the noise, the smell hit me. The tunnel reeked so strongly of decay and rotting flesh that I nearly gagged on it. I doubled over, hand pressed to my mouth as waves of nausea rolled through me. I began to back out of the hallway, trying not to breathe through my nose, though every breath I took raked painfully over my dry throat. The scraping sound had stopped but there were other noises coming from the dark, one that sounded like a hiss. It seemed to be growing closer and I moved faster, keeping my eyes trained in the direction of the sound. The smell was also growing worse instead of easing. It smelled like Gideon had when I had last seen him, wasting away in his bed, like my mother had when she had passed me the Pearl. Only this was stronger and more repulsive.

Terror welled up inside me and I couldn't think of anything but the awful smell and of watching the people I loved die. This was the odor of death. Suddenly there was a flash of movement in the darkness and a long, low sound like a growl. Then I saw it.

I screamed and fled, running as fast as I could. I could hear it behind me, hissing and growling, the thing that was part man and part beast. It was one of the blood-drinkers, a man of the Fomor Tribe. He was huge, with dull grey skin that looked thick like hide and hair that hung long and tangled from his head. The eyes were bright and yellow, standing out sharply against the grey of its face. His mouth had gaped open at me, revealing fanged teeth stained pink with blood, saliva dripping off them as it snarled. The rest of its features were completely human, so that it would look almost normal if it weren't snapping and biting.

I could hear him coming after me and I frantically tried to call my element but there was no water anywhere and nothing that I could use to channel my power. I screamed again, in frustration this time, the sound tearing at my throat. I turned a corner, trying to remember the pattern I had kept, when my torch went out and I was swallowed in blackness. I cursed aloud and groped along the corridor wall, trying to find the next tunnel. Suddenly the smell of decay rolled over me again, assaulting my senses and I could hear the thing breathing. It was in the room with me. I kept feeling my way down the wall, forcing myself not to run, fleeing. If I did I would more than likely fall over something or run straight into a wall and knock myself unconscious, leaving a very easy snack for the thing that was after me.

"Who are you?" it hissed in a serpentine voice. Maialen was right and it spoke in the ancient language of the gods and kings who had come long before.

I remained silent and kept searching and finally I found the curve of a new tunnel. I backed into the corridor, the dead torch held in front of me like a club. If it ran towards me perhaps I could at least injure it with a good solid blow to the head.

It sniffed the air. "You smell....different than what we are used to."

I could see the yellow glowing eyes as it crept nearer. I tried to control the panic that threatened to overwhelm me.

"Where are you from?" it asked, in a voice that it obviously thought would be soothing but which sent shivers up my spine. "Wait, wait, I know it now.... you are Leharan, that is why you smell so sweet. We do not often get your kind to feed from. But there is something else."

It was nearly in front of me and I stepped out of the shadows, swinging the torch at its head with all my strength. It started to turn at the last second so that instead of a solid blow to the face as I had hoped I caught it on the side of the head. The thing stumbled sideways and I thought it would fall but it righted itself, clapping a hand over the ear I had hit and howling with rage. I swung again but this time it was prepared and it struck out, knocking the torch from my grasp with such force that pain shot through my wrist and up my arm. It lunged at me and I brought my knee up into its groin, hoping that it was human enough for the technique to be effective. The thing groaned and dropped to its knees and I whirled around to flee down the tunnel. I had taken one step when I fell painfully to the ground, the air knocked from my lungs, leaving me gasping for breath and writhing on the hard rock. It had grabbed the hem of my dress and was clawing at my legs, pulling me back towards it. I shrieked again, kicking wildly at its snapping jaws.

"Orabelle!"

I heard my name echo from somewhere nearby.

"Here! I'm here, help me!" I shouted as one of the blood-drinker's hands grabbed my thigh. My fingers scraped across the floor, leaving small trails of blood as it yanked me underneath its body so that it straddled my legs, pinning me to the ground.

"Orabelle?" the beast asked curiously, lowering its head so that its foul breath hissed in my ear. It breathed in deeply, nuzzling my neck. "The Water Queen. Now I know."

"Let go of me!! I will kill every one of your kind!" I cried, struggling vainly to escape the gaping jaws that were lowering towards my neck.

It laughed, the sound like a hideous parody of human laughter. "You are in no position to kill anyone, Water Queen."

"No, but I am."

There was a startled cry then the thing collapsed on top of me heavily and the odor of death poured out of it in a dark sticky fluid.

"Orabelle," the voice belonged to Blaise. "Be still."

"Get this thing off of me! Now! Please!"

"I'll get it off you, but I can't see and you could be hurt," he said impatiently and I could hear that he was moving away.

"No, please! Blaise, don't leave me!" I could feel the thick stuff flowing out of it and spreading around me in a putrid puddle. My stomach heaved. "Just get it off me!"

"I'm not leaving," he promised. The hot edge of his power sparked through the air and a red-orange glow began to creep over me. I blinked rapidly, adjusting my eyes to the light. I could see the black puddle that spread around me and the long smears of blood where I had been dragged. My fingernails had been mostly ripped off and my hands throbbed with pain.

"I'm going to move him now," Blaise said, setting the torch he had created down on the ground beside me. Suddenly the weight bearing down on me was gone and I scrambled to my knees and away from the heinous creature, scooting my back up against the wall. Blaise dropped the thing unceremoniously onto its side and it hit the ground with a thud, its head hanging at an odd angle. He had slit its throat so deeply that he had nearly decapitated it. The wide slash of torn flesh broke through the last of my reserve and I turned to one side and retched violently.

"Are you hurt?" Blaise asked, coming to kneel beside me and holding my hair carefully back from my face as I continued to be sick. Finally the retching stopped and I knelt, panting and shaking. I shook my head.

"No, I'm not hurt," I said, looking down at the black ooze that stained my clothes and skin. "But I need to get this off me."

"Can you walk?"

I nodded. He paused as if not sure whether he believed me or not, then helped me to my feet. He took my arm and began to lead me through the tunnels. I barely noticed which way were going, only that he never had to hesitate. He knew the tunnels well.

"How did that thing get down here? And how did you know where I was?" I asked after my breathing had returned to something close to normal.

"These tunnels are ancient, even I don't know the extent of them and how far they go. But some of them must lead to the Fomori. That thing must have been lost down there for a while and eventually ended up here. As for you, I saw the doorway unbarred, and you weren't in your rooms. It wasn't hard for me to figure out where you had gone. Then I heard you screaming and I ran towards the sound," he explained with a shrug.

"And you killed it."

"Yes." He stopped walking and faced me. "I killed it. It's dead now, Orabelle. It can't hurt you."

"But why did you kill it? Wouldn't it have been easier for you, for everyone, to just let it have me? It would have saved you all so much trouble." I couldn't keep the bitterness out of my voice.

"I told you before, I do not want you dead," he reminded me quietly, his amber eyes searching my face. He reached out to touch me and I stepped back, away from him. A shadow passed over his features and his hand dropped to his side. "I saved your life, Orabelle, and still this is what I get?"

"You saved a life that you already ruined."

He stared at me a long moment before he finally turned and started walking again. I stayed close behind him and he did not speak again even as we passed back through the iron doorway where a troop of his soldiers waited. They slammed the door shut behind us with a heavy clang.

# 14

Damek shaded his dark eyes from the bright glare of the sun. The harsh light glinted off the turquoise water and bounced along the golden sand of the beach to reflect off the coralstone walls of the Leharan fort in undulating waves. He squinted uncomfortably, longing to be back in the shade of the Kymir forest. He hated the southern islands with their unbearable, sticky heat and sharp colors. Chronus had sent him here and he had gone obediently to do as he was told, hoping to get his task accomplished quickly so that he could get off the wretched island as soon as possible. He did not want to disappoint Chronus and would do anything he asked of him but this was pushing his limits. He also worried about leaving his beloved master with that wretched whore, Loagaire. Damek preferred to keep an eye on Chronus's many indiscretions, not allowing them to get too close. He was the only person that Chronus really needed, the only one who had always taken care of him and been by his side. That red-headed tramp was more clever than the others and no matter how many times Damek warned him to send her away, Chronus ignored his advice.

"Regent Damek, what brings you to Lehar?" Colwyn asked with a slight bow.

Damek frowned. "I have been waiting here for some time," he pointed out, waving a hand at the shore. "Does Leharan courtesy not extend to those of Kymir?"

"I am sorry to have kept you waiting, Regent," Colwyn's reply was bland.

Damek felt a twinge of irritation. He nodded curtly, following the other man through the courtyard of the fortress and into a room that was thankfully out of the stifling heat. Sweat was already running down his forehead and his dark robes seemed to absorb the very heat from the air around him. He looked at Colwyn who seemed perfectly at ease in the light armor of the Leharan Guard. His frown deepened.

Colwyn called for refreshments then motioned for Damek to take a seat in one of the two chairs that stood along one wall, separated by a low table. The Guard passed him a glass of cold juice that Damek sipped carefully, despite his thirst. It was bitter and tart, just as he'd expected. Everything about this place was distasteful.

"You asked to meet with me, Damek. What is it that you want to discuss?" Colwyn asked bluntly taking a long swallow from his own cup.

Damek adjusted his robes, inwardly fuming at the lack of manners. It was no wonder to him that the Leharans wanted the Tahitians back, they were the only people on Imbria who were even less refined than they were. "Chronus has sent me to speak with you."

"Concerning what matter?"

Damek shifted his thin limbs again. The man's bluntness really was extremely annoying. Perhaps it was too much sun that made them all so disagreeable. Or the influence of their current ruler. Orabelle had never been known for her manners.

"He wishes to know that things are being taken care of in the Queen's absence."

Colwyn smiled. "The Queen has only been gone a few days. There is no reason for her father to be concerned. She has left me in charge here and I am perfectly capable of looking after things till she returns.

"Yes, yes, of course you are," Damek said reassuringly, his voice dropping into the sycophantic tone that he used when manipulating people to get his way. "So capable, in fact, that it was quite a surprise that you were not chosen as Orabelle's new Guardian."

Colwyn stiffened slightly. "I respect the Queen's decision."

"Yes, I am sure that you do. You are a noble man. But that doesn't mean that it was the best decision. We are worried that her grief may be clouding her judgment on matters."

"So that is the real reason you are here," Colwyn said flatly.

"I am merely here to inquire as to the state of my lord's daughter. He is worried for her. She is being careless. Ever since that fool, Tal, was murdered she has -"

"Stop!" Colwyn interrupted roughly, rising from his chair. "You will not speak that way of him here, not on Lehar!"

Inwardly, Damek seethed. Tal was a fool and so was this one. A whole nation of fools that followed a foolish whore Queen. He forced a smile. "No, no, no, you are correct. I apologize to you, I did not mean to speak ill of your former commander. Merely, that his death was foolish. Surely you cannot argue with that?"

"You mean his murder?"

"Please, Captain, sit down. Yes, his murder was foolish, a waste. One that I fear will have many more consequences than you can foresee. The Queen, as I have said, is not thinking clearly. And we fear that the Tahitian man has tainted her thinking even more. Even Tal was wise enough to leave them where they were. Surely he would not have advocated that man as his replacement?"

Colwyn sat down slowly. "I cannot speak for the dead."

"No, you cannot. But the living is who we are worried for. Orabelle should have chosen you as her Guardian. What could she possibly want with those people? She is ostracizing herself in the Council and Leharans will be the ones to suffer. What happens when the banishment ends? Damian will bring his people here, they will take your places and you will be useless," Damek said, warming to his task. He could see by the tic in the man's jaw that his words were having an effect. He went on, "We know that you are being treated unfairly, that it is Orabelle who is making the mistakes, but the rest of the world looks on and says, there must be something wrong with the Captain, a reason why she would not choose him. She has made you look weak. She has insulted you, choosing barbarians over her own people."

"If you have a purpose here, Regent, you had better get to it," Colwyn ordered coldly.

Damek leaned closer to him, "We can make you a Guardian. We will grant you the respect that you deserve."

"And just how will you do that?"

"Things cannot continue as they are. Surely you see that. There are going to be problems, especially with Veruca, if Orabelle continues the path she is on. But you, Captain, you can help us and help your people. Lehar is strong but you need the rest of Imbria. Where will you get the silver for your swords if not from Veruca? The wood for your ships if not from Kymir? You have many resources here but how long would they last if you were forced to use them up, isolated from everyone else? What about herbs, medicines that come from the high kingdom of Samirra? Orabelle is creating a dangerous disturbance in the Council and she is breaking traditions that have kept us at peace for years."

"Orabelle will protect Lehar."

"She is not in the state of mind to protect anyone and you should know that," Damek said impatiently. He was so close to breaking the man, he just needed to find the right thing to say, the one phrase that would sway the soldier.

"I will not betray her, and if you suggest it again, there will be consequences," Colwyn warned.

"We do not ask you to betray her! We need you to help us save her before she does irreparable damage to herself or to Lehar! We do not wish to harm her, merely to have an insight into what is going on with her so that we can guide her, help her make the right decisions. Such as choosing a new Guardian. You."

Colwyn sat silently, his brow furrowed.

Damek kept speaking, "If she had chosen you then Chronus would have no objections, there would be no concern. We are merely offering to help you to set things right for her. She is a woman and she has suffered. She needs you."

Colwyn drew in a sharp breath and Damek saw the flash of emotion. So that was the key. This one wanted to be a hero.

"What exactly is it that you are asking me for? You say you want to help her, that I can help her, but you are talking in circles."

Damek smiled at him in encouragement. "We only want knowledge. Knowledge that will be used to benefit all of us. Orabelle may not see it now, but she needs you more than ever. She needs you to look out for her, to protect her interests. One day soon she will thank you for it, she will see that you did what was best for her and then she will be grateful."

Colwyn nodded his head. "It has always been my greatest duty to protect my Queen."

Damek felt a rush of elation. He knew that he had the Captain. They really were a kingdom of fools.

# 15

I woke from the nightmare, a scream caught in my throat. My hands clutched at the linen sheet that covered me and I could feel that the bandages had come off. My fingers throbbed with pain where I had reopened the cuts on them and I felt blood running down my wrists. The room was completely dark and I closed my eyes briefly as terror welled up inside me, the remnants of my nightmare haunting the black room. I slid out of the bed, pushing aside the blood stained shroud of linen and breathing deeply to assure myself that if they were here I would be able to smell them. Just the memory of the blood-drinker's stench made my stomach turn, though I had not eaten. I had bathed in the hot springs, scrubbing my skin till it was raw. My hair I had to unbraid and wash over and over till the foul black ooze was gone and finally it was white again, curling wildly around my face and falling in thick wavy clouds down my back.

I felt along the edge of the bed then made my way to where I thought the doorway would be. There had been a candle lit when I had fallen into the bed but that had burned out sometime in the night. I found the cool metal of the door hinges and grasped at the knob, wincing at the pain. My fingers slipped off the handle and I cursed softly, wiping the blood on my nightdress. I was going to be quite a sight if anyone met me.

I opened the door and cursed again, the hallway being just as dark as my room. I sniffed the air, peering through the blackness. There was nothing. I hesitated and then heard a voice coming from the room next to mine. Blaise. I waited but heard nothing more. He must have raised his voice for me to have heard him. I slid across the wall and pressed my ear to the door. The voices were heavy and muffled but I could make out some of what they were saying.

"He attacked her, I did not have a choice. Tell him that! He was about to tear her damned throat out!"

"Did he know who she was?"

"I called her name. He may have known."

"Carushka should have his people under control. This is his fault, not yours."

"That does not mean he won't be angry. He will use this as an opportunity to extract something else from me. "

The next response was spoken low and I couldn't understand it. I pressed harder to the door and heard a curt exchange of goodbyes. I whirled around and groped for my doorway, not finding it as a sliver of light cut across the hallway from Blaise's room. I retreated down the hall, huddling in the darkness. A man I didn't recognize walked out, Blaise close behind him with a small torch. At the end of the hall he handed the light to the man who kept going and the Fire King turned to go back into his room. He paused just outside it, staring hard at the wooden door.

I realized I had left a smear of blood when I had pressed close, trying to listen. He touched his finger to the spot and rubbed it against his thumb. He lifted his hand and I felt a hot rush of power as a flame grew in the air above his palm, lighting the corridor. I had no time to make it back to my room and nowhere to hide, so I slid to my knees on the hard floor and began to rock back and forth, hugging myself tightly.

He saw me, turning his wrist so that the flame stayed where it was as he walked to me. "Orabelle? What are you doing out here?" he demanded, a sharp edge to his voice. I wiped a hand over my face, pretending to brush away tears and leaving a trail of blood that I hope looked pitiful. I ignored him and continued rocking back and forth, making soft crying noises.

Blaise knelt in front of me, grabbing my face roughly. "What are you doing?" he asked again, forcing me to look at him. Then his eyes moved over my wild hair and bloodstained clothes and he relaxed his grip and slid his hands across my cheeks. I forced myself not to jerk away from his touch but let him stroke the hair back from my face. He picked up my torn hands and sighed.

"I had a nightmare," I whispered, not having to fake the fear that crept into my voice. "I woke up and I couldn't see. My bandages came off and I could feel the blood. I kept seeing it, that creature, climbing up my legs."

"It is dead now," he said.

"They aren't all dead."

He gave me one of his careless grins. "Then you should stay close to me. Come, let us get you cleaned up."

I allowed him to help me stand, careful to not get too close to him so that he wouldn't feel the swell of my stomach. Without the heavy cloth of my gowns it was more noticeable. I kept my arms around myself, pretending to shiver as he took me into his room. He snatched the covering off the bed and draped it over my shoulders and I let the folds fall over me. There was a basin of water in one corner of the room and he motioned me towards it. I bent over it and plunged my hands into the cool liquid, feeling calm flow over me like a wave.

"You look so at peace with your element," he commented, watching me as I let the water swirl around my hands, easing the stinging of the cuts.

"Don't you feel better when you are around fire?" I asked.

"Not like that. I don't feel peace. I feel power. Sometimes anger. It grows in me with the flames until I feel like I will burn myself up if I don't destroy something. It feels good, but not like what you feel. I see your face and your smile and I don't know what that's like." Blaise was speaking quietly, his head to one side as he looked at me. He seemed to be struggling with himself.

"Perhaps that is just the nature of your element. Fire consumes, it burns, it destroys. Even when it is gives off light or warms our rooms, it is still dangerous and a thing to be feared. It will hurt us if we get too close."

"Is that why you don't want to marry me?"

I looked up, startled. His face hadn't changed but I could see emotion in his eyes. For a moment I almost felt sorry for him, then I remembered the broken body on the forest floor, the ache that never left me and the tiny pressure of the child inside me. I would not allow myself to feel pity for Blaise no matter how lonely or tormented he was. I looked away.

"Orabelle," he began, crossing the room and standing in front of me. "I don't mean to be this way. I am not the monster you think that I am. Just tell me what you want. Tell me what I can do."

"You can let me go."

He shoved his hands through his hair and closed his eyes. When he opened them they burned even brighter than before. He took me by the shoulders and I could feel the heat of him even through the blanket. "I can't!"

"Yes, you can!" I cried. "I don't love you and I never will! Why do you want that? Why do you torture yourself wanting that?"

His grip tightened on my shoulders. "I don't know! I can't help it! You... you have no idea what it is like for me when I see you. When I touch you. I want to protect you but at the same time I want to destroy you. I want to crush you, to break you, to make you beg and yet I would kill any man who would hurt you. Just seeing you like this makes me want to go into the tunnels and hunt down every one of those beasts and at the same time I want to throw you to the ground, to wrap my hands around your neck and see your fear in your eyes."

He jerked me against him and kissed me roughly. I put my hands frantically between us, trying to push him away so he couldn't press against me. I started to call my element and he felt it and shoved me back.

"No, Orabelle. I will not fight you. Go, now."

I hesitated, breathing hard. I should have killed him then, in his moment of weakness. Poured the water down his throat so he choked on it. Drowned him in it. He hates himself for what fire does to him, I would gladly help him be free of it. Just a few more months and then the child would be born. Then I would be free to kill him.

"Get out of here!" he shouted, the torches flaring brightly and flames dancing across the stone ceiling in a glowing arc. I turned and fled the room.

Back in my own room I climbed onto the bed in the empty darkness and pulled the bloodied sheets around me. Tears spilled down my face and I held my stomach with one hand while I rubbed at my mouth with the other, trying to wipe away the taste of him. There were noises coming from his room and it sounded as if he were tearing the place apart. I thought of my own outburst earlier when I had done exactly that and the tears fell harder. Was I doomed to be like him? An angry, hate-filled shadow of a person?

"No," I whispered softly. "I won't be like him. I have you now."

I ran my hand gently back and forth over my belly and the tears dried up and I smiled as I closed my eyes. In the room next to mine there was a last, loud, anguished cry and then silence. I fell into a dreamless sleep, comforted by the child within me.

That morning I stepped from my room, dressed and with my unruly hair tied back as best I could without the Sirens to help. I nearly tripped over Kaden, who was lying across the threshold.

I looked down at him, one eyebrow raised. He smiled up at me, clear blue eyes shining pleasantly. "Good morning, my Queen!"

"Please get off the floor," I said, moving so that he could rise to his feet.

He brushed himself off and looked at me apologetically. "I didn't intend to fall asleep. The King, he woke me up late last night. Said you had been having a nightmare about the thing in the tunnel and I should stay outside the door in case you needed anything."

"Thank you. Where is the Fire King? Is he still in his room?" I asked. I gestured at his curly hair which was sticking up ridiculously. He tugged on it, making it worse.

"No, he left last night, after he came and woke me."

"Left?" I repeated, surprised.

Kaden nodded. "Yes, he left. Had a messenger he was sending out and at the last minute he decided to go with him." He lowered his voice and looked around. "I think we need to talk. You wanted me to ask around. Well, the things I'm hearing are not good."

"I don't think anywhere in this castle is safe. Perhaps we could walk outside? I could use some fresh air."

"The air isn't really any fresher out there," he muttered.

"We will be home soon," I assured him.

"But if the King is gone, can't we just leave?"

I thought about it. "No, I made an agreement and until the healer is back on Tahitia I have to stay here. I am not giving Blaise anything that he can use against me. Come, lets walk and you can tell me what you have learned. But first, please, make yourself presentable. You look as if you slept in a doorway."

He laughed and bowed, running into his room. When he returned his hair was damp and the blonde curls fell perfectly in place. I smiled appreciatively. We left the castle and moved through the valley, Kaden walking silently beside me. He was unusually quiet, especially for him and I began to worry that his news was worse than I expected. Eventually we stopped next to an open face of rock so that anyone approaching would be seen long before they reached us.

"My Queen, I would not stand to accuse the Fire King of any crime, I am only repeating to you the rumors that I have been hearing. I have seen the fear in these people's eyes. I do not want to believe it, but... "

"Please just tell me," I prompted him, trying not to show my impatience.

"The people here, some of them say that Blaise.... that he....." he trailed off and his face was lined with worry.

"Kaden, just tell me!" I ordered.

"They say he deals with the blood-drinkers."

"I don't understand what you mean?" A shudder passed through me at the mention of the beasts from below and I had another flashback of snapping teeth looming over my neck.

"He trades with them. He gives them his own people as food. It is a punishment he uses for those who disobey the laws here."

My eyes widened. "That cannot be true."

"I don't want to believe it either."

"No, it can't-" I stopped abruptly, the conversation I had heard through the muffled door of Blaise's room coming back to me. He had been talking about the blood-drinkers. About having to kill one of them. "Tell me, have you heard the name Carushka?"

He shook his head. "No, but there is a girl here, her father was one of the people that have been fed to them. Ironically, the man was condemned for stealing food for their family. She may be willing to tell you more, if you'd like to talk to her?"

"Stealing food?"

"Yes. Apparently the Verucans give almost all that they have in tithes to Blaise, his soldiers and those in the royal castle. The rest live in poverty to work the mines for scraps."

"Where is this girl?" I wanted to know.

"She is an assistant at a weapon smith's forge. I can take you there now."

I followed him to a hollow carved from the mountain, surprised that no one stopped us along the way. I had been prepared for a confrontation as I had assumed Blaise would have ordered me confined to the castle. It was what I would have done were I in his place. Perhaps the freedom he was allowing me was a gesture of good faith on his part, or he had simply left in a rage and not considered it. Either way I counted myself lucky that I could come and go as I pleased. I did not worry about the Verucan commoners, most of them seemed too overwhelmed with fear to even look at me.

Black smoked billowed out from the hollow and the orange glow of the forges inside radiated heat. The clamor of metal was loud. We ducked inside and Kaden talked briefly to a bearded man with scarred hands. The man nodded and disappeared into the smoky interior, returning with a thin, willowy girl with long, auburn hair who trailed behind him, her huge brown eyes darting everywhere. She looked at me and her reddened face flushed even more as she dropped her eyes to the floor.

Kaden took her arm and bent to whisper something to her. She looked up at him, then at me. I waited as she approached. She was older than I had expected from her tiny child's body. Her face was already showing signs of strain and I guessed she must be at least sixteen or seventeen.

"Alita, this is Queen Orabelle," Kaden told her.

"I know who she is," the girl, Alita, said quietly. She curtsied clumsily, the movements awkward in her tattered clothes.

"May I speak with you?" I asked her, inclining my head in greeting.

Kaden spoke for her. "Alita's home is just around the corner. We can go there, I gave the smith a silver piece to let her have a break."

Alita's home was a tiny cave with a broken chair and three dirty mats lying on the floor. There was a fire pit in one corner with a large black pot next to it and a pile of old clothes.

"I don't really have anywhere for you to sit," she said, looking around, her face flushing again.

"The ground suits me just fine," I told her, settling myself on the hard rock next to one of the mats. She sat warily across from me and Kaden moved to the cave opening to stand watch. "Who do you live here with?"

"My two younger brothers. They are in the school, training to work the forges. "

"That is hard work for young children," I pointed out.

She shrugged, "It is better for them than the mines."

"I want to talk to you about your father," I began carefully, not wanting to upset her.

She glanced back at Kaden.

"Why do you care?" she asked me.

"Alita, if there is something going on here that involves the Fomor Tribe then I need to know about it."

"That is not an answer," she retorted stubbornly.

"If you don't want to talk to me then this is a waste of time. I will go." I started to stand and she stopped me.

"No, wait. You want to know what I told Kaden?"

"That and more, if you know more."

"My father was a servant in the castle. He wasn't anyone important, he was in charge of keeping the torches lit and replacing them if they burnt out. Because that was his job, he was able to go a lot of places that other people could not. And often times, the lighting of the torches needed to be done when there were important things going on, so he would get to watch or to listen. He was very good at his job and they hardly even noticed him when he came and went. He would tell us fantastic stories of the people he met and saw and the things they talked about. We thought a lot of times he made it up, just to entertain us, but we didn't care."

"So he overheard something about the blood-drinkers?" I prompted, trying to get her to focus on the information I wanted.

"Yes. Several times he came home and told us of the scary beast men from the underworld who came through the tunnels. At first we thought it was a joke. He would say that they came to take away the bad children who misbehaved, so we must be good. Then one day I realized that he wasn't just joking. But the beast men didn't just take away the bad children, they took away anyone they could. Father started to have bad dreams about them. He came home one time and he was shaking so badly. I asked him what had happened and he said that they had given the beast men a girl about my age. He had listened to her scream as they dragged her down the tunnels, taunting her. He said her screams just went on and on. That was when I noticed that my friend Katia went missing. I think that she was the one they took. My father had begged me to be good, to stay out of trouble so that nothing like that would happen to me."

Alita paused and looked down at her hands. Kaden was watching her from the entrance, his face impassive, which I knew meant he was angry. I myself was growing more and more furious by the second. Surely this could not be true. That this had been happening and no one had known about it seemed inconceivable.

The girl continued, "Sometimes Father would bring things home from the castle. He always told us that stealing was wrong, and when he would arrive here with extra bread, or cheese, or one time with a whole slab of meat, he would tell us that it was because he had done such a good job that day. I knew he was lying but I pretended to believe him because I didn't want him to stop bringing things home for us. One day he got caught. The soldiers came for him, and they took him and we never saw him again. I can't help but imagine him being dragged away down the tunnels, screaming and screaming for help."

Her lip was trembling and I was afraid she would start to cry. I moved to sit next to her and took her hand, holding it tightly. "I need to ask a few more things, Alita. Did your father ever mention the name Carushka?"

She nodded. "I remember it because it was one of his favorite stories. It was from years ago, when the old King still lived."

"So this was going on before Blaise was ruling Veruca?"

"Yes, for years before. Carushka came to the castle himself to meet with the old King and his general, who as you know, became the new King. It caused quite a stir, this band of beast men showing up under the castle. Apparently they all sat down in a room together and my father says they were in there for hours. When they came out, Father was lighting the torches in the hallway and he said Carushka stopped and looked at him. Father said he was the biggest creature he had ever seen, with glowing yellow eyes and teeth like a wild cat, and that he smelled of death. Father said he was the most frightening of them all because in his yellow eyes you could see so much knowledge. Carushka sniffed at Father and laughed when father was afraid. He told him, 'Do not be afraid, I have not come for you.' Father said he nearly died of fright."

"Carushka, is he the leader of the Fomor Tribe?"

"Yes, that is what my father thought."

"Alita," I said, still gripping her hand tightly, "why has no one ever said anything? Why have none of you told the Council?"

"They have told, but no one will listen. They say that we are thieves and liars. They don't believe it and then those who tried to tell are punished."

"Aren't you afraid of being punished?" I wanted to know.

"No," she said, a hint of a smile moving across her lips for the first time. "Kaden told me that you will take me with you. I don't have to be afraid."

My eyes flew to the doorway where Kaden stood, looking back at me. He was right, of course, we couldn't leave her here. However, there was no way Blaise would just let me take her, especially if he really had fed her father to the blood-drinkers. I stood, letting her hands fall back into her lap.

"Alita, I will do everything I can to help you," I promised. The girl showed the same ghostly smile and once again glanced back at Kaden. He gave her a nod and her cheeks reddened.

"Thank you. I should get back to work now. Queen Orabelle," she paused, her fingers toying with the frayed fabric of her shirt, "You are truly a great lady."

It was my turn to flush and I saw Kaden lift his head proudly. We left the dirty little cave and Alita scampered off in the direction of the smith.

"This will not go over well," I said to Kaden as we watched her tiny figure disappear around a corner.

He looked uncomfortable. "I did not mean to put you in such a position, my Queen. I just did not see how we could leave her. Forgive me."

"There is nothing to forgive. You did the right thing. Though a little warning would have been nice. I don't suppose you have a plan in mind?" I asked hopefully.

He smiled. "As a matter of fact, I do!"

I rolled my eyes. "Of course you do. And I am quite sure it will be completely impossible and very dangerous and you will have yet another harrowing story of bravery to tell around the fort."

He gave a short laugh, then his face clouded. "That may be but this is one instance that I care not for bragging rights."

I knew how he felt. My own conscience was tearing at me. I could not fight without risking my child, which meant I would have to walk away, leaving these people in the hands of evil. I was trading the life of one for who knew how many others that would die a hideous death in the next few months. But at the very least I would take the girl with me.

"There is one more thing," Kaden added, avoiding looking at me.

"What is it?"

"She wants to bring her two young brothers with her."

I groaned aloud. "Oh well, of course she does."

That evening I walked along the high wall surrounding the city. It glowed with fiery red light beneath me, like a gaping mouth ringed with sharp black teeth, jaws open wide to swallow me up. I looked away from the despair I felt for the Verucan people and out over the sea. The black waters churned by the shore, frothy gray waves battering the rocks. I closed my eyes and reached out my hands and called to the Sirens. I would need their unquestioning help for Kaden's plan. I had not brought them to this place with me, for I knew they hated it and it made them restless and unhappy. Hopefully, they would not have to be here long.

They answered my call and I could hear their soft keening waiting for me. All we needed now was to hear the news of Gideon. Kaden and the other Guard took turns on watch, staring up at the sky for hours, waiting for one of Astraeus's great birds to bring us word that we could leave. We all feared that Blaise would try to keep the news from reaching us, another ploy to move us into the position that he wanted us. As I watched the dark water I wondered what it would be like, those final moments between us. I would kill him, that much I was sure of, especially after what I had learned today. Though now, my desire for revenge was not my only motivation. I had the people of Veruca to save. The girls like Alita and her poor friend Katia. I could not imagine being dragged away by those creatures while the one who was your sworn protector looked on and did nothing. Yes, Blaise would need to die. Very soon.

"You're in a lovely mood tonight," I muttered to myself. I leaned on the edge of the wall, feeling my loneliness wrap around me like a dark cloak. My thoughts went to Tal and I remembered the times before when I would stand, staring over the sea, and he would come to me, silent and proud and tall, the hint of his smile at the corner of his mouth. I thought of his silver hair that shone in the moonlight. His grey eyes that saw into my soul. The ache within me was worse tonight than it had been since those first weeks without him. I realized then that I also missed Damian. He had become my friend as well as my Guardian and it was times like this that I needed him. I turned away from the sea and began the long walk back to the city. I could stand on my own, I would keep going, but it was so much harder to do without having the people I loved around me.

# 16

Maialen lifted her head and yawned, stretching her arms out to ease the knots in her shoulders. She rose from the chair that she had slept curled in and moved to the window, pushing back the curtains to let in the sunlight that filtered through the trees. Her body ached from exhaustion and she had not had a decent night's sleep since the attack in Samirra. Every time she was away from Gideon's side she was racked by dreams of his dying, of waking up and not being able to find him. And so she had given up trying to sleep and instead kept her constant vigil in the chair at his bed side. She had watched day and night as the Tahitian woman had ground herbs and boiled roots and flowers, pounded strange berries into poultices and mixed foul smelling concoctions to pour down the Guardian's throat. Maialen had assisted her whenever she could, coming to enjoy spending time with the older woman whose melodic voice told wonderful stories as she worked.

Maialen was not aware of the dark smudges under her eyes or the unkempt mess of hair on her head as she smiled cheerfully and began her morning ritual of greeting the unresponsive Guardian who lay wasting away in the bed.

"It's a lovely day, Gideon. I wish you were awake to see it. It would be a good morning for a hunt. I'm sure you would come back with a feast for us! I am having a new bow made for me and I cannot wait for you to see it," she babbled on as she began to tidy up, plucking at the cheerful vases of colorful flowers she had placed around the room. "Cossiana should be here soon with your morning herbs and our breakfast. I am sure if I ask her very nicely she will be happy to sit with us and tell us another story."

"Those herbs taste awful." The grumbling baritone voice caused her to spin around, knocking the flower vase she was arranging to the ground with a crash. Her mouth hung open and she stared at Gideon as if seeing a ghost. He smiled thinly at her with pale, cracked lips and she thought her heart would burst with joy.

"Gideon!" she screeched and flung herself on top of him, hugging him fiercely. She began to sob happily as she clutched at him and he tried to ease her off of his injured side. He couldn't feel his arm except for a slight tingling sensation near his fingertips.

"My Queen, you look tired," he told her.

"Yes and it is all your fault!" she accused, laughing happily as she bounded off the bed and skipped to the doorway. She flung it open, calling out, "He's awake! Gideon is awake!"

There were noises from down the hall and Gideon was startled to see a huge, dark skinned Tahitian man fill the doorway. He tried to sit up, calling out to Maialen to get away from the man. She looked back at him in confusion then laughed, shaking her head.

"Oh, Gideon, I had forgotten how long you have been asleep. This is Damian, Orabelle's new Guardian."

"Her..." Gideon's voice trailed off. "Orabelle is here?"

"No. She is in Veruca, waiting for you to be healed by Damian's mother," Maialen said quickly as if it explained everything. Gideon felt his head swim and he closed his eyes, wishing that he could fall back asleep for just a little longer.

"How do you feel?" the Tahitian man asked him.

"Thirsty," Gideon confessed with a cough.

"Of course you are, I'll be right back!" Maialen cried, hurrying out the door to fetch him something to eat and drink.

The Tahitian man approached the bed and looked down at Gideon with black eyes that were unforgiving. "I asked you how you feel but I was not concerned with your thirst. If you are healed then I need to know right away."

Gideon's head was aching and his throat burned but the awful blackness that had been surrounding him since he was bitten was gone. The pain that had coursed through his body constantly had abated and there was only a dull throbbing at the site of the injury. "I believe that I am healing. Why is it of such importance to you?"

Damian's eyes flashed and his hands tightened into fists. "Orabelle has bartered her life for yours. You owe her a great debt. If you are healed then I can go for her."

"What do you mean? Please, Guardian, explain yourself," Gideon said in frustration.

"My mother, a Tahitian, healed you. The Council would not allow her to come because we are a banished people. The Water Queen agreed to go to Veruca in exchange for them allowing my mother to be here. She has to remain there until you are either dead or healed so surely you can understand my urgency when I asked you if you were well."

"Orabelle did that for me?"

Damian glanced at the doorway. Maialen's exuberant footsteps were bounding down the hall. "I believe it was also for her sister, not just for you."

"Look, father! He is awake! I told you!" Maialen exclaimed as Chronus followed her into the room.

The older man nodded and looked anything but pleased. "How wonderful. You, Tahitian, take your healer back to her island immediately."

Gideon could feel the tension in the room and he wondered what else had been happening while he had been lost in his tormented nightmares. Damian had narrowed his dark round eyes at Chronus's words and there was no mistaking the animosity between the two men. Even Maialen noticed and her smile slipped from her face.

"I will send Cossiana back but I will not be escorting her. I am going to Veruca to retrieve the Queen," Damian stated firmly.

"You do not give orders in Kymir," Chronus warned.

"You are correct," Damian said, turning to Maialen. "With your permission, Queen of Kymir, I would like to send word to Orabelle and to leave immediately for Veruca. I would request that the Kymirrans escort Cossiana back to Tahitia as a tribute to the great gift she has bestowed on you by healing this man."

Gideon suppressed his amusement as Chronus purpled with indignation. They would have to keep an eye on this Tahitian for he was a clever one. He had just made it impossible for the old man to argue with him.

"Yes, of course. I will send one of Astraeus's eagles at once," Maialen said, bowing. "And I would like to personally see both you and your mother safely out of the harbor. Her services as a healer will be greatly rewarded."

"We do not seek rewards," Damian answered curtly and strode from the room.

"Only your sister would wish to be around someone like that!" Chronus ranted at the empty doorway.

"Only my sister offered herself to save Gideon," Maialen said softly.

"Do not mistake Orabelle's intentions. She didn't do this for you or for him. She did this for herself so that we would be indebted to them."

Maialen's eyes were damp as she looked up at Chronus pleadingly. "Can you not ever see any good in her, father?"

"Perhaps if there were some there to see then I could," he snapped. Maialen looked away from him and he sighed, forcing himself to be kind. "I am glad that your Guardian is well, my daughter. Tend to him and to yourself and leave your sister and her scheming to me."

He kissed her forehead and she sat down on the edge of the bed, helping Gideon to drink from the cup of cool water she had brought up for him. "Gideon, do you think that any of them will ever stop hating each other?"

"When it comes to your family, my Queen, I never know what to think."

# 17

It was two days later, just after dawn, that Kaden came running down the beach yelling my name. I had grown even more melancholy as I waited for news, wondering of the fates of all of us. I had taken to standing on the rocky beach most of the day, the Sirens plaiting my hair in a long thick braid, then undoing it and braiding again. They were agitated and ready to be back in the cool blue seas of Lehar. We were all ready to leave this dark place.

"Orabelle!" he exclaimed, out of breath as he reached me. "The message has come, an eagle rider brought it this morning! Gideon lives and the old woman has gone home. Damian is on his way with the fastest ship!"

The sirens cooed happily and I felt the heavy weight ease from my chest. We would be going home soon. "Have you told Alita?"

"Not yet. The ship will be here by nightfall! I wanted to tell you the news first," he said in a breathless rush.

"Make sure that she knows the plan. We will leave as soon as the ship gets here. I will not spend one more second in this place than I have to," I vowed. I felt happiness rise in me and I couldn't help the smile that spread across my face.

Kaden grinned back at me. "I have been going over everything with her so many times that she is thoroughly tired of me. She will be prepared."

"I do not think she will ever grow tired of you," I commented.

He winked at me. "I have that effect on women."

"You can laugh it off but I have seen you look at her."

He shrugged. "She is kind and caring and brave and strong. Any man would be lucky to have her as a wife."

I raised an eyebrow. "A wife?"

He waved me off, laughing again. "Don't tell anyone I said that!"

"Your secret is safe with me. Go now, make sure everything is ready. Tell her I will stop by to see her soon."

He gave a quick salute and turned to jog back down the beach. I noticed that he too seemed to have a weight lifted from him. I prayed that Blaise would not return before we left and that everything would go according to the plan.

I left the Sirens at the beach and made my way very slowly back to the city, relishing the fact that this was the last time I would be forced to do so. If I ever came back it was going to be of my own will, to free these people from the rule of a monster, not to be at the mercy of one.

I walked through Veruca looking at the faces of those around me. Their gazes were less hostile now, they were used to seeing me walk through the town. A few of them even greeted me cautiously though their salutations were tinged with fear. It made me grateful for my own people who embraced me with warmth and affection and I longed for my beloved island.

I came around to the little cave where Alita and the boys, Aron and Akrin, lived. Kaden was still there, talking animatedly to Alita who gazed up at him in adoration. I cleared my throat and she looked over his shoulder at me, her face lighting up. She bounded over, throwing herself against me and hugging me tightly. I was startled and stood stupidly for a minute before patting her back awkwardly. She pulled back and the smile slowly faded from her face. Her hand moved down to sweep across the swell of my stomach. I caught her wrist before she could speak and gave her a hard look.

"Is it... the King's?" she asked fearfully, in a voice that was barely a whisper.

"No. Please, keep quiet."

She nodded and stepped away from me. Aron, the youngest of the siblings was barely five years old. He waved at me and stuck his head under the thin sleeping mat, giggling. I looked around for Akrin, the middle child, who was eleven and a nervous boy, constantly jumping at the smallest noises.

"Akrin is at the forge already. Aron wanted to stay home so we said that he was ill. He doesn't understand most of what they say anyway," Alita explained, tickling the feet that stuck out under the mat. He laughed wildly, squirming further under the cover.

"Are you sure, Alita, that you want to do this? You know that you can probably never come back," I warned.

She stopped tickling the little boy and looked up at me, her eyes old in her child-like face. "What do I have to come back to? Nightmares, fear, hunger? I will never come back here. I will die first."

"Very well. Kaden has told you that it is to be tonight?"

"Yes, he has told me everything. The boys are also ready."

"Then we will go. I will see you at midnight," I said and moved to leave. Kaden fell into step behind me.

"Orabelle?" Alita called quietly as we reached the entrance. I turned to her. She held Aron tightly in her thin arms, his cheek pressed against hers. "Thank you."

I did not respond, but walked out of the cave quickly.

"You are doing a good thing," Kaden said quietly.

"Yes but it is so little. What of all the others we are leaving behind?"

"My Queen, you must do what you can, when you can. We will come back for them. For all of them that want to go and with the power of the other nations behind us."

I smiled at him. "When did you become so wise?"

He grunted, "I think I have spent too much time with Damian!"

The day seemed to drag on forever as I waited impatiently for the fall of night. Blaise had not returned and for that I was immensely grateful. The hours stretched on till finally the muted light of the sun began to fade. I went down to the beach and waited, watching the Sirens running up and down the shore, scanning the horizon. When they finally shrieked happily, their cries echoing across the waves, darkness had fallen completely. The torches that flanked the entrance to Veruca had been lit and burned malevolently behind us. Kaden and the other Guard clapped each other on the back, pointing out to sea as the sleek dark shape of the ship appeared. I concentrated my power, using the sea to carry the ship towards us as fast as I could. I stopped it before it ran onto the sand and could just make out the small boat that lowered from the side to retrieve us. The group of Verucan soldiers who had escorted us watched in stony-faced silence and I half expected them to try and stop us.

"Damian!" I exclaimed as he stepped from the little boat into the shallow black waters. He waded up to me and I threw my arms around him and hugged him tightly, thankful to at last feel the comfort of his presence. He smelled of home, of the sea and the sun and his dark skin carried the warmth of the islands.

"You are fine?" he asked worriedly, taking my face in his hands.

"Yes, yes. Let us leave this place, though. Now."

"Very well. Ah Kaden! Good to see you!" Damian said, punching the other man on the shoulder.

"I never thought I would be so happy to see your ugly face!" Kaden joked, taking a mock swing at Damian who ducked it easily and laughed.

"Let us go, please," I repeated, glancing warily at the waiting Verucans. Their black armor shone darkly in the rising moonlight and although I knew they were just boys and men, there seemed to be an otherwordly malevolence clinging to them. I shuddered, ready to be away from this place as soon as possible.

Damian gave me a searching look. "Of course, my Queen. This has been hard on you. Come." He took my hand and led me to the edge of the water where he lifted me easily and carried me to the small boat. The Guards piled in, everyone talking at once. I sat back quietly, watching the beach and the soldiers. They made no move to interrupt our departure and even helped to give the boat a shove to speed us along.

"Damian," I interrupted, touching his arm once we were far enough out to not be heard. "We are not leaving for Lehar just yet."

He looked at me, waiting for an explanation. I told him briefly of what had gone on, and of the plan to take the ship around the edge of the cliff that created the harbor and wait there for the Sirens to carry Alita and the boys to us.

"It is dangerous for them," he said as we boarded the larger ship.

"We saw no other way without attracting attention," Kaden told him.

"Yes, I see that. But we should be able to bring the small boat around, staying in the shadows of the cliff, so that we can at least watch over them if anything happens," Damian suggested. He squinted into the moonlit night to watch the soldiers on the beach filing back through the tunnel. They seemed to unaware that anything was amiss.

Kaden nodded. "That would make me feel better than just waiting here to see if they make it."

"I will go with you," Damian offered.

We sailed the ship quietly around the bend of the cliff and held it there. As midnight approached the men climbed into the small boat. I stopped Kaden as he swung one leg over the side. His face was pinched with worry.

"She will be fine," I assured him.

He nodded and as the boat lowered into the black waves I settled myself on the deck and reached out to the Sirens, watching the shore through their eyes as they waited in the water. It seemed an eternity before the first small shape appeared through the great doorway, squeezing through the narrowest opening of the door. It was Alita, Aron clasping her hand. Akrin stepped out behind them, looking around nervously and rubbing his arms in agitation. Alita scanned the beach quickly, her eyes moving over the high wall where the Verucan soldiers patrolled. All was quiet. She pulled Aron along, hurrying towards the sea. The Sirens began to rise up out of the water and she gasped at the sight of them reforming in front of her. Aron huddled behind her, his eyes huge. Akrin made a noise and she turned to him, whispering something quietly. He shook his head, trembling. She let go of Aron and walked to him, taking his arm to pull him with her. He struggled, shaking his head.

"Come on, Akrin, just go with her," I murmured aloud.

He shook her off and backed up a step just as the huge door swung open, banging against the rock with a boom that reverberated through the dark night. I stood up on the ship and gasped as soldiers flooded out through the doorway. Alita looked around in alarm and the Sirens wailed at her, trying to urge her to run to them.

"You there!" one of the black armored soldiers shouted. "What are you doing out here?"

Akrin turned and ran towards the soldiers. I heard his small, terrified voice through the Sirens' ears. "We are here!"

"Akrin!" Alita called. "What are you doing?"

"It's okay, sister," he said, moving behind the line of soldiers as they spread out. "They've come to take us back. I told them I didn't want to go and they said we didn't have to, that they would take care of us."

"You told them?" she shrieked. "Why? When?"

"Earlier today. I don't want to go away, I'm afraid of the water!" Akrin answered, his voice wavering. "I thought you'd be happy. They want us to stay."

"They will kill us!" she screamed at him. He began to cry.

"No, they are here to help us!" he insisted.

The soldier interrupted them. "Come with us, girl."

"No! I will not be food for those beasts!" Alita spat at him. She whirled around to see the Sirens waiting, beckoning to them. "Aron, go!"

The little boy was confused but he began to run towards the Sirens as he had been told. One of the soldiers lifted his bow and fitted an arrow, pointing it at the child.

"No!" I shouted. At the same time I heard Alita's screams of panic and Damian's war cry rise up from the shadows. Kaden dove into the water and thrashed toward the shore while Damian pulled back his huge spear and let it fly. The hiss of an arrow whistled through the air just before the soldier flew back, the spear piercing his chest. I watched in horror as the little boy, Aron, crumpled to the ground. Alita was running at the soldiers, their huge battle maces raised as they waited for her approach. Kaden was close behind her but he wouldn't catch her before she ran to her death.

I let out a long wail that was echoed and magnified by the Sirens till the sound of it filled the night. The ocean rose up in a huge black wave and I flung it angrily at the soldiers. They scattered, their cries mixing with Alita's as the Sirens fell upon them with the wave. I wove my hands through the air before me, the movements harsh and purposeful. I covered the Verucan men with the water, holding them under it while they gasped for air. The Sirens grasped the first soldiers they reached by their throats, lifting them from the dark water and twisting their necks before dropping them back into the sea.

"Kaden, get the girl!" Damian shouted. Kaden grabbed Alita around the waist and dragged her past the raging water and the struggling men. She was screaming for Aron. He shoved her in the direction of the boat.

"Swim!" Kaden ordered her. "I will get him."

He turned back to the beach and I could feel his bloodlust. The Sirens were tearing through the soldiers quickly but there were a few still left alive. He pulled his sword from the sheath and strode up to the nearest one. I let the water recede so that he could have his revenge. The man lay gasping for breath, coughing the black sea from his lungs. Kaden swung his sword in a wide arc, severing the man's head. He then turned to the next one who was trying to crawl away on hands and knees. One of the Sirens grabbed the man, her barbed arms holding him to the ground. Kaden drove the sword through his heart.

There was a loud beating of drums. More soldiers would be coming. Damian heard it also and yelled, "We must go, now!"

Kaden stabbed his sword down once more twisting it in a man's gut before jerking it out. He kicked the Verucan harshly in the face then ran down to where the boy lay on the sand. Akrin was crying and fled wailing down the tunnel to the city. Kaden picked Aron up carefully and set him in the arms of the Siren who was standing nearest, her barbed tentacles smoothed over so that she cradled him harmlessly. She moved into the water, and I knew through her that the boy was already gone. Alita had reached Damian and he pulled her into the boat as the other Siren dragged Kaden through the water to us.

Soldiers were streaming out from the entrance and I watched as those with arrows lifted their bows.

I laughed out loud, lifting my arms and once again a great wave rose up, pouring over them. I fed my hate and my anger into the wave. Their ranks broke apart as they scrambled to try and retreat back through the tunnel. The wave followed them, filling the tunnel with water so there was no escape.

"Orabelle! Get us out of here!" Damian cried, breaking my concentration. I shoved him away, intent on killing all of them.

"Orabelle!" he shouted at me. "We must go, now!"

I blinked and the water flowed out of the tunnel. The others were back on the ship. I turned my power away from the beach reluctantly and used it to push the ship out to sea. When we were far enough away I collapsed on the deck, drained. Damian was there, kneeling beside me.

"Are you alright?" he asked me.

"Yes," I panted, trying to fight off the dizziness. "I am fine."

I looked across the deck at the tearful girl who clutched the little body to her. Kaden stood beside her, blood splattered across him and matting his hair, his face impassive. I closed my eyes and tried to stop the sob that threatened me as I thought of the little boy giggling under the mat that morning.

"What have I done?" I asked Damian.

"This was not our doing. That is an evil place that makes evil people. To kill a child... you are right, Orabelle. Veruca and its King need to be destroyed. I fear this is the beginning of a war."

# 18

The dawn light melted softly across the deep blue ocean. Everyone was gathered on the deck forming a half circle around the tiny body. I had helped Alita to wrap him carefully in a shimmering white cloth cut from one of my own gowns. She sat beside the boy, patting his little arm through the fabric as tears flowed from her red-rimmed eyes. Kaden was behind her, his face still set in stern lines. He had cleaned the blood from his pale hair and it was tied back neatly, his armor gleaming in the growing light. As I looked upon his face sadness filled me at the thought of the shadow he would now carry in his eyes.

Damian moved forward and placed a hand on Kaden's shoulder. "It is time."

Kaden nodded and carefully pulled Alita back from the boy before lifting the little body in his arms. She sobbed brokenly. He stepped to the edge of the rail where the Sirens waited, gazing up at him from the waves.

"We give this child to the sea, take him in your embrace and comfort his soul," Kaden said softly. The Sirens took the child from him, their voices lifting in song as they paid tribute to the dead. I sang also, my voice mingling with theirs. The others joined in as the sun rose along with our song, the pink rays warming the cool air.

I lifted my hand, clutching a handful of cloth that I had cut into the shape of flowers, since we had none on the ship. I scattered them into the wind as the Sirens sank into the deep, taking the boy with them. Alita wailed pitifully, watching the tiny silk flowers as they fell into the ocean.

"The gods keep him with their own," Damian murmured.

"Sleep well, brave little boy," another of the guard whispered.

"You will not be forgotten," I swore.

"Be at peace."

The others gave their farewells as the flowers faded among the waves. I moved to Alita and took her hand in mine. She looked at me, her features raw with grief.

"I am so sorry," I said to her.

She clutched at me, burying her face in my neck as she cried. Finally she lifted her head and her eyes met mine. "I will be indebted to you forever."

"No," I protested, shaking my head.

"Yes, I will. You have risked everything for us. You are a Queen, we are nothing to you, we are not even of your kingdom, and yet here you stand, apologizing to me for the havoc I have certainly brought upon you. Upon all of you." She turned her teary gaze on the others. "You have all risked your lives for me, for my brothers. I can never repay you."

Kaden pulled her from me and she leaned against him as he wrapped his arms around her. She continued to look at me. "I saw what you did. What all of you did for me. I never thought there was such bravery, such selflessness. You all came to save me. You avenged my brother. And I am no one, I am nothing!"

Kaden tightened his arms around her. "You are not nothing, Alita."

"You are the brave one," Damian said. "How could we not be so when we saw you?"

Alita gave him a teary smile. "May I sleep now? I am so tired."

"Of course. Kaden, take her to my rooms," I offered. He nodded and led her gently away, her dark head resting on his arm and his pale yellow hair falling over her shoulder as he whispered something to her. The others began to move away as well, going back to their duties on the ship.

"We should be home in a few hours," Damian said to me when everyone had gone.

"Home," I repeated. "I feel like I have been gone for a lifetime."

"Much has happened. You have seen enough sadness for many lifetimes, my Queen."

I moved my hand across my belly, feeling the baby stirring inside me. "Seeing that child, Damian, seeing him die, it makes me worry more for this baby. They will want it dead. I could not bear it..."

"As long as there is breath in me that child will not be harmed," Damian vowed fervently.

"You know what I have to do. The only thing that will save him."

He sighed and looked over the sea. "Do you really feel it must be so?"

"How can I not? How can I keep him safe from people like that? All my power is nothing when compared to a brief second of evil. How can I stop the blow from a weapon that I can't see coming? Who would have thought they would turn their arrows on a helpless child?" I demanded.

"I have no answers to comfort you, Orabelle."

"I do not expect answers." I faced him, my eyes darkening till they were nearly black. "I only want a promise. Promise to take him away from me, even if I tell you not to. Promise me that you will keep him safe, keep him away from me. Me, who seems to bring only death to those around me."

"Orabelle-"

"Promise me, Damian! Swear to me that you will take him away and never tell me where he is!" I commanded.

He lowered his head. "I promise."

"Thank you. I am afraid I will not be strong enough to give him up, but I trust you to keep your word, no matter what the cost to me."

"I will keep my word."

We arrived at the shores of Lehar as the sun crested the top of the sky. People were crowded along the coastline awaiting our arrival. I felt my heart ache as I watched them. These were my people. I could never imagine turning on them the way Blaise had turned on the Verucans, trading their pain and suffering for my own personal gain.

I moved through the crowd, Damian at my side, while Kaden and the others waited on the ship for the excitement to die down. I wanted Alita brought in quietly, without being seen by too many. The longer I could keep her presence here unknown, the less blame that Blaise could direct at me for what had happened in Veruca. It had been dark and no one had actually seen me. I could argue that my ship had already left and I knew nothing of what they were talking about. Everyone would know it to be a lie, but they would not be able to prove anything if the girls whereabouts were not known. At least until my child was born. Everything lately seemed to depend upon that.

"My Queen!" Colwyn interrupted my thoughts. I looked up to see him standing before me. "It is good to see you returned safely to us."

"Colwyn, thank you. How were things here during my absence?"

"Everything has been fine, my Queen," he announced proudly.

"Very good. You have done well. Please, assemble the Guard at the fort. I would like to have a meeting within the hour."

"But you look exhausted, surely you need to rest?"

"No," I said firmly. "There are things that must be discussed immediately. These are not trivial matters, Colwyn."

"What has happened?" he asked anxiously, looking from me to Damian.

"Too much, I am afraid. I will fill you in as soon as you are all assembled."

He bowed and moved away, giving orders to the men near him. The Guard was quickly assembled around the long table in the strategy room of the fort. I walked in and they stood, bowing as one.

"Please, sit," I told them, too tired for formalities. I had not slept at all on the ship and still felt drained from the use of my powers.

I told them briefly of what had happened in Veruca and of the pact between the Fire Kings and the Fomori. There were exclamations of disbelief, loud curses and cries for war. I quieted them all with a wave of my hand.

"We cannot allow these actions to go unpunished," I said to them, my eyes moving to every man in the room, "but war is a bloody and violent instrument that too often claims the lives of the innocent. If we were to move against the Verucans now I have no doubt that we would defeat them but our losses will be great. If the other Kingdoms stand with us there will be less need for bloodshed and fewer casualties of Leharans."

"Surely they will stand with us!" one man spoke up.

"We must have proof of this evil. The others will not want to fight, they will not want to believe what we are saying," I explained.

"How do we convince them?"

I hesitated momentarily, knowing my response would not be well received. "The only thing I can think of is to go the Fomor Tribe myself."

"What?!" Damian shouted, rising from his chair. "Absolutely not!"

The others were also voicing their dissent. I waved a hand at them again. "They have obviously met with humans before and refrained from eating them. If they can make a pact with Blaise, perhaps there is something else that we can offer them to betray him."

"He offers them sacrifices of his own people! What can we offer in the face of that?" Colwyn asked pointedly.

"You will not go!" Damian insisted once more.

"I will go. And you will go with me. Along with any of you who volunteer. I will not force you."

"Once again I ask you, my Queen, what can we offer them?" Colwyn wanted to know, his voice rising above the others.

"I do not yet know. They are creatures that have been hidden away in caves and beneath the land for a long time but if the stories are true they were once human like us. There must be some way. If their numbers are dying off they may be desperate. And if there is nothing they want from us, we can always take one by force, though it will be harder to get a confession."

"I will gladly volunteer for that task," Kaden said from the end of the table where he had been sitting quietly.

I inclined my head to him. "Then if it comes to that, it is yours."

"How will you find them?" one of the men asked, and I was glad to have a practical question to answer.

"Well, I obviously cannot go back to Veruca. But there is someone here who knows how to find them." I looked pointedly at Damian. "We all have heard the tradition for the warriors of Tahitia. You must kill a Fomor."

"I will not help you," he refused with a definitive shake of his head, black eyes flashing in defiance.

"You will or I will go to Tahitia and find someone else who can."

"This is a foolish idea!" Damian bellowed, banging the table. "Half those men never came back from that journey!"

"You did."

His eyes narrowed to slits. "You will not want to make this miserable journey, my Queen. There is a reason that this is the ultimate test of strength for my people."

"I have to try! I cannot waste anyone else's life when there is a chance that I could spare them!"

"By throwing away your own? Trusting yourself to those demons that we know nothing about?"

"We must have some kind of proof for the Council!" I said adamantly.

"She is right, they will not want to believe it, so they will not listen to her. She will need proof. And there could be a chance that she can stop whatever bloodshed comes next," Colwyn agreed. "When are you planning to go?"

"The beginning of the next year, before the Council is to meet to lift the banishment and consecrate my marriage. Until that time, there will be no outside ships allowed in Lehar. Trading vessels will be kept offshore and supervised personally by all of you. There will be no ships leaving the island without a detachment from the army. We will act as a kingdom at war, though the war has yet to begin. If what Blaise has told me is true and my father intends to kill me, we will not make it easy for him."

"What reason will we give for not letting the other ships in?"

I shrugged. "We will give no reason. We tell them nothing. There will be no lies and we cannot yet say the truth. If you are questioned, you say those are the orders of the Queen. I will deal with the other rulers."

"What if the Fire King moves against us?"

"He must cross an ocean to get here. Do not think that I will let that happen."

Kaden smiled bitterly. "After the wave you brought down on Veruca, I should not think they will be too enthusiastic about attacking us."

"Damian, Colwyn, please assign everyone to these tasks and make sure my orders are followed. If there is nothing further to discuss now, I will take my leave of you."

I left the room and as I walked through the hallway dizziness swept over me and I stumbled, nearly fainting. My head was pounding and I pressed my hands to my temples. I was too weak. I had used too much of my power at once but the baby was making it worse. It was draining my energy from me more and more each day.

"Orabelle." Damian walked up beside me and offered his arm. I took it gratefully, letting him support my weight as we walked. "You really are a stubborn woman, you know."

"I know," I consented with a tiny smile.

# 19

Blaise stormed into the castle and strode through the great stone entryway, ignoring the pleadings of several people who tried to speak to him. He brushed them off, heading straight for the dining hall where the soldiers were having their meal. At first the men did not seem to notice him. He stood quietly just inside the room, his amber eyes scanning quickly over the long table. They were eating boisterously, faces and beards dripping with fat from the lamb as they talked loudly to each other, laughing and joking. Eventually, their voices died down as they began to realize that the King had entered the room. Silence fell as Blaise walked slowly up to the table and picked up a piece of meat from one man's plate.

"Eating well, I see," he remarked casually. The soldiers stared down at their food. Blaise dropped the meat back down on the table and lifted a glass of wine. "And drinking. Would there be a cause to celebrate?"

The men were silent, no one daring to look up. He waited, then flung the goblet with all his force against the opposite wall. "Answer me!"

"No, sire, there is no cause to celebrate," one man answered. Blaise grabbed the man by his hair and shoved his face towards one of the candles that lit the table. The flame grew and the man struggled vainly to lean away from it.

"Then tell me why it appears that you are celebrating! Eating here like kings when you have knowingly failed me!" he demanded, the flame of the candle swelling brighter. The man began to whimper as his skin darkened and blistered, his eyes watering. Blaise released him suddenly and shoved him aside so that he fell from his chair and hit the ground. "Someone had better answer me."

"It was the Queen, she attacked us on the beach! It had to be her, Sire. There was a huge wave and those things of hers, those sea witches, were there," another man stammered.

"That is not an explanation," Blaise said balefully, walking slowly around the table. He stopped behind Caranor, the highest ranking of the men in the room. "Caranor, perhaps you would care to explain to me why I have eleven dead soldiers and a dead brat's blood on my beach."

Caranor swallowed hard, his face carefully blank. "Sire, we were trying to stop a girl from leaving. Her brother had come to us that day, telling us that they were going to sneak off with the Leharans. I sent a group of men to stop them and the girl went crazy. There was a huge wave and then those things, the ones that killed Raynor, started attacking them."

"And where was the Water Queen during all of this?"

"I don't know. She had left on her ship and we thought she had gone but they must have waited around the cliffs for the girl. One of her Guard was there on the beach and he also attacked us. I sent reinforcements but they all nearly drowned. By the time the water receded everyone had vanished."

"Vanished?" Blaise asked lifting his eyebrow. "Is that the way you say that you let someone escape you? That one helpless girl and one man were too much for you? And the Queen herself was not even there?"

"No, Sire. But there was so much water and it was dark. We could hardly see past the beach," Caranor said hastily.

"Who was this girl? Why did they want her?" Blaise wanted to know.

"She was nobody. A weapon smith's assistant. I don't know why they wanted her."

Blaise slammed his fist onto the table, rattling the plates. "There must be some reason! And you fools are too incompetent to have found it out! The Queen would not risk one of her Guard for no reason!"

Caranor flinched. "Sire, I swear it was just a common girl and her two brothers!"

"Her two brothers? I will assume one is the dead boy that I have already heard about. The other I suppose you let vanish as well?"

"No, the one who warned us, he is here in Veruca. He ran back to the city when the fighting started."

"Bring him to me. Now!" Blaise commanded, kicking the chair out from underneath Caranor. The soldier scrambled hastily off the floor and went to find the boy.

"Will we be retaliating against the Leharans?" one soldier asked.

"Because you did so well against one of them, you'd like to face more?" Blaise asked with disgust. "No, we will not be retaliating. The less said of this incident, the better."

"But if the Queen-"

Blaise cut him off with a sharp gesture. "The Queen is up to something. I need to find out what that is before we do anything. I know Orabelle, she will not be telling anyone of what happened. To do so would admit that she attacked us on our own land and she would be in violation of the Council's laws. "

Caranor returned a short while later pushing the boy into the room ahead of him. "Here he is, Sire."

Blaise studied the child thoughtfully. He was small and nervous, his hands constantly fidgeting with his grubby clothes and rubbing his arms. He kept his eyes on the ground, not looking up once as Blaise circled around him.

"What is your name?" Blaise asked, dropping to one knee and forcing the child to look at him.

"Akrin," the boy squeaked.

"Well, Akrin, I need to talk to you about your sister."

His eyes went wide. "They told me she was dead!"

Blaise shrugged. "She may be. But I think she is alive. Why don't you sit and have something to eat then you can tell me all about what happened."

Akrin stared hungrily at the heaping plates of food, practically salivating. He nodded.

"The rest of you get out!" Blaise ordered. The men jumped up and began to hurry from the room. As Caranor tried to move past him, Blaise grabbed his shoulder. "Not you, Caranor. As ranking officer what happened was your fault. You will wait here while I talk to the boy, then I will deal with you."

The soldier's face paled and he looked pleadingly at the other men. They ignored him, leaving as quickly as they could. He stood beside the table while the boy and the King ate, praying that his punishment would not be that which he had often helped to inflict on others. Just the thought of the foul creatures coming for him through the dark tunnels was enough to make his blood run cold.

# 20

Alita held up a long trail of lace for me to view. "What do you think of it?"

"It's beautiful," I replied, raising an eyebrow. "What is it for?"

She shrugged and wrapped the lace around her little body, twirling herself in it. It had been nearly two months since I had brought her to Lehar with me. For the first month she had rarely smiled and had spent most of her time out by the sea, mourning the loss of her brothers. Kaden would often go and sit near her and they would share the silence for hours at a time. Eventually, as my belly grew larger, I came to need her help. I still wanted to keep the child a secret and so Alita had agreed to pretend that she was pregnant, sauntering around with a pillow stuffed under her dress and claiming to be a mourning widow. I, for the most part, stayed away from everyone. I made appearances on the balcony of the citadel and waved at the Lehrans below, my own protruding belly obscured from sight. When Damian's mother, Cossiana, came to check on me it was under the ruse that she was tending to Alita. The poor girl seemed to find some amusement in the whole charade and eventually her sadness had begun to recede slowly so that there were moments like this when the shadow was gone from her eyes and she could laugh again.

"Perhaps for your wedding gown!" she teased, giving me a look to make sure that I knew she was being playful.

"That is not the slightest bit amusing," I said flatly and she laughed. "I will be wearing something awful and unflattering and black."

"You would be beautiful in anything, Orabelle."

I smirked. "Hmph. Perhaps you should be thinking more about *your* wedding gown?"

Her face turned bright red. "I don't know what you're talking about."

"Really? You have no idea that my poor, dear Kaden is so hopelessly devoted to you that he has become completely useless to me as a Guard? I have been thinking of demoting him to deck hand on one of the ships till he can get his head straight."

Her mouth fell open in surprise. "Is he really being that terrible?"

"No!" I assured her. "Now I am teasing. Kaden is one of my favorites. But you must know that he cares for you?"

"Yes...." she began, her already flushed face lowered so that she could hide behind her hair. "I mean, I had hoped so."

"He has not said anything?" I asked in surprise. She shook her head and I rolled my eyes. "Ridiculous. I shall have to speak with him."

"Oh, stop it!" she said, tossing the pile of lace at me. I swatted it away and as I did there was a sharp pain in my stomach and I felt the air catch in my lungs. Alita's eyes widened and she hurried over to me.

"Orabelle, what is it?"

There was another pain, this one worse than the last. I cried out, clutching my stomach, trying not to faint as my vision swam. Alita shouted for Damian and he burst into the room, his huge form filling the doorway.

He took one look at me and rushed over, placing his hand over mine on my belly. "It is too soon," he told me.

I nodded, gasping for air then crying out again as the pain ripped through me.

"What is wrong with her?" Alita asked Damian, her voice rising.

"You must stay calm, Alita. Do not be upset. Orabelle will be fine. I need you to send someone to find the healer and bring them back here. Quickly. We had hoped to have my mother here when the baby was born but she is early."

"You mean, she is having the baby?"

"I do not know for sure. Now go!" Damian ordered her. She kissed me quickly on the forehead and ran out the door, stuffing a pillow under the bodice of her dress. It was so ridiculous I would have laughed but for the pain that was tearing through me.

"Damian, "I panted, sweat running down my face and liquid trickling down my legs. "Something is wrong."

He frowned and lifted me up, carrying me to the bed where he set me gently. He grasped my hand as the pain came in waves that broke through my body. I screamed, writhing on the bed as he tried to hold me still.

Alita burst back into the room, her arms full of blankets and a large, steaming pot of water. "I sent the Guard Brogan for a healer and Kaden has gone to get your mother, Damian. He said sometimes these things take a very long time and we may need her since the baby is so early. I would have gone myself but I thought I could help you here."

Damian looked at her gratefully and waved her over. "Have you seen a birth before?"

"My mother. I saw her give birth to Aron. I was much younger and he was turned the wrong way..." her voice trailed off.

"She died, didn't she? During the birth?" I asked her through clenched teeth.

"That will not happen to you," Damian said firmly.

"You cannot just order me to be fine," I glared at him.

"Yes, I can," he retorted.

Alita set the pot of water carefully next to the bed and spread one of the blankets over me, tucking it up at my knees. She knelt there and then looked back up at Damian. "She is bleeding."

"The baby must come now," Damian said. He stroked the hair back from my face. "Orabelle, the next time it hurts, you will need to push."

"Excellent advice," I snapped sarcastically, then groaned as another wave of pain tore through me.

"Push!" he ordered.

"Push, Orabelle! Harder!" Alita chimed in.

I pushed as hard as I could and it felt as if my insides were being ripped out of me. Alita was making small noises of encouragement and if I could have sat up, I may have strangled her. I pushed, the pain nearly making me black out several times. There seemed to be no progress with the child and Alita was starting to panic when an old woman with wild grey hair that floated around her in an unruly tangle came hurrying into the room, followed by Brogan. He took one look at me and the bloody quilts and turned away, fleeing the room.

The old woman was named Rashana. She was one of the most respected healers and midwives on Lehar and she had attended to me several times over the years and so I was grateful for her presence. She glanced at me and my obvious impending birth and raised a bushy grey eyebrow.

"Well, isn't this a surprise! I thought you were the one with child," she said, glancing at Alita. The girl reached under her bodice and tossed the pillow onto the floor with a sheepish shrug. Rashana laughed loudly and shook her head. Then she smiled at me, felt my forehead, and squeezed Damian's bicep appreciatively.

"Good strong man, always useful to have around. I'm getting older, you know, hard for me to hold 'em down," Rashana said with a wink, still chortling to herself over my scandal. "And it never hurts to have a handsome man around, no matter what the occasion! Though I would say from the state of you, my Queen, that you already know that!"

"Rashana, please!" I interrupted, breathing heavily as I waited for the next pains to come.

She moved Alita gently aside and her mirth disappeared. "My Queen, the child must come soon. You are bleeding too much and soon you will be too weak to push. Damian, please, get behind her and let her lean against you so that you can hold her. Little girl, you sit here and when I tell you to, I want you to push down right here, understand?"

They did as she told them, Damian resting me against his chest and his arms bent through mine. The next pain came and Rashana yelled for us to push. I tried with all my strength but I could feel myself weakening. There were bright spots before my eyes and I felt the pain ebbing as I started to slip into unconsciousness.

"Ow!" I cried out as Rashana slapped me as hard as she could. "How dare you–"

"I didn't tell you to sleep, I told you to push!" she railed.

"You devil witch!" I shrieked at her angrily. She grinned at me and ordered me to push again.

"It's not working," Alita cried frantically to the old woman, trying to push her away.

"Get this one out of here!" Rashana ordered and Damian slid from beneath me and dragged Alita out as she collapsed in a fit of tears.

"Orabelle," Damian spoke softly in my ear as he returned to my side. "You need to use your power. Call it to you, it makes you stronger."

"I can't! I can't focus, it hurts too much!"

"You can, Orabelle! Or the baby will die and so will you! Do not be so weak!"

"Bastard," I snarled through clenched teeth but I started to do as he said. I called my element to me, feeling the moisture gather in the air around us. I called to the sea and the Sirens began to sing. I felt the power move through me, easing the pain, and I concentrated as hard as I could on the baby. Tal's child. I couldn't let the last part of him die. I was not weak, I was the most powerful ruler on Imbria. The power flowed towards the baby as water filled the room like still rain, the water of the sea, the lakes, the rivers, the sky. I called to all of it, giving it to the child.

A loud wail filled my ears, breaking my concentration. I blinked and looked down at Rashana. She was holding the baby in her arms, and I could only see part of the outline of the tiny golden body covered in blood as she wrapped them in a soft blanket. I felt tears on my face and Damian hugged me tightly.

"Orabelle, my dear." Rashana's voice was filled with apprehension. I pulled my gaze away from the baby and up to her withered face. "You are still bleeding."

"You must do something," Damian ordered her. He took her by the arm and moved her away from the bed towards the doorway.

She spoke quietly to him so that I couldn't hear and then she left the room, taking the child with her. Damian knelt beside the bed and held my hand. My eyes felt heavy and I longed to sleep but he stopped me, squeezing my hand. "You must stay awake a little longer. She is making you something to drink that may stop the bleeding."

My lips felt dry and my tongue swollen in my mouth so that I could barely form words. "I'll be fine, just need to sleep."

"Orabelle, no! Not yet!" he argued loudly.

"Damian, remember your promise," I whispered. He closed his eyes and rested his forehead on our joined hands.

"I remember."

It was Alita who returned with a cup that Rashana had sent her with and which she pressed against my lips. The liquid was thick and tasted awful. I choked, spitting it out. She turned her pleading gaze on Damian and he grabbed me firmly by the back of the neck and poured more down my throat as I gagged, trying in vain to push him away though I could barely move my arms. Finally, he seemed satisfied that I had swallowed enough of the foul stuff and moved away from me.

I did not remember falling asleep, nor anything that happened for the next several days. The first time I recalled opening my eyes after the baby had been born was to see my sister standing next to the bed, her finger pointing in Damian's face as she ranted at him. He stood silently looking past her, further infuriating her.

"Maialen," I spoke weakly and she spun around, her anger melting away as she threw herself down on the bed, wrapping me in her arms.

"Orabelle! You're awake!" she exclaimed happily. "You almost died, you know!"

"What is going on? Why are you yelling at Damian?" I asked.

"You have a lot of explaining to do this time, Orabelle," she said crossly. "You were with child?! And you never told me? Were you ever going to tell me? The only reason I came here was because I felt something...change. Through my element. It felt different and I knew something had happened to you."

"I'm sorry, Maialen. I tried to keep it a secret as long as I could. The baby is Tal's."

"Yes, I thought so. Everyone is going to be so angry!" she worried.

"Please, Maialen, you must not tell anyone. Do not tell our father. And why were you yelling at Damian? It is not often I get to see you angry," I smiled.

She flashed him a dark look, her big green eyes narrowed. "I really don't know how you spend so much time with him for he is truly quite unpleasant. I am angry because he refuses to let me see the baby. The child is my blood and he won't let me!"

My eyes flew to Damian and he gave me a slight nod. "I have kept my promise."

"You made him promise not to let me see the baby?" Maialen asked, her voice filled with hurt.

"No, no, little sister. It wasn't that."

"Then what?" she demanded.

Damian said, "Orabelle made me promise to take the child away from her."

"What?" Maialen cried. "Orabelle! I don't understand!"

"You said yourself they will be angry. There are things happening, Maialen, that you don't know about. The baby will be safer away from me," I told her, struggling with the knot in my throat.

"Oh, Orabelle, you can't mean that!"

"I mean it. I trust Damian."

"Orabelle, please, what is happening? I don't understand how you could-"

"Maialen, enough! The decision was mine and I have made it!" I interrupted her harshly.

"Is this about Blaise? Surely he wouldn't harm a little baby!"

"I have seen his soldiers slaughter a child. I know what he is capable of. Not everyone is as good as you want them to be, Maialen. You have no idea what he is and what he's done!" I practically shouted.

She stood and began to pace the room, wringing her hands. "Then tell me! I don't understand any of this! I come here to find that you had a child. A child, Orabelle! I find out that you have to been lying to me, to everyone, for months! Now you talk to me of slaughter and tell me what a monster Blaise is, but you aren't telling me why! I know that you are still hurt by what happened to Tal, but to give away your baby like that? Blaise has told us that Raynor acted alone, that he had never liked Tal and they had exchanged angry words at the festival and one thing had led to another and-"

"This has nothing to do with Tal!"

"Then tell me!" Maialen insisted.

"No, Maialen, for your sake, I can't. Not yet. Please, just listen to me."

"I am not a child any longer! And it has everything to do with Tal, he was the father!" she argued.

"Do not say his name again!" I was shouting at her now and sat upright, sweat beading my forehead and my breath quickening.

Damian placed a hand on my shoulder. "Orabelle, you must calm down, you are still very weak. Maialen, perhaps you should go for now."

She turned to him, her face flushing. "Do not presume to tell me what to do! I am the Queen of Kymir and she is my sister! I will yell at her as loudly as I please!"

"Look at her. She is not well, the last thing she needs is for you to upset her," he said patiently.

Maialen's lip trembled slightly as she looked from me to Damian. "I am not trying to upset her, but this... all of this..."

"Maialen," I began as I saw the shine of tears in her eyes. She turned from me and hurried out of the room, brushing past Damian with a hateful look.

He sighed. "Should I go after her?"

"No," I said, "let her calm down first."

"Would it be better if you told her what was going on?"

"I don't think so. She still trusts everyone, including my father and she will certainly go to him. I am convinced that he knows something of what is happening with the Fomori in Veruca, just as I am convinced that he let my mother die. I cannot tell her all of that. It would break her heart."

"You know that her heart will be broken eventually. She has to find out sometime."

"Yes, but not today. Let her keep her innocence just a little longer," I said, settling back into the pillows. "That's what you didn't want to tell me, isn't it?"

"I'm not sure what you mean."

"About the banishment. You didn't want to tell me that you believe Chronus set it up so that your people wouldn't be able to heal my mother."

Damian didn't answer but I did not need him to. He covered my forehead with a cool, damp cloth. "How are you feeling?"

"Tired, but alive," I replied, letting him change the subject. "So Rashana's nasty little potion worked?"

He smiled at me. "No, but it helped. Kaden arrived with my mother. She has taken care of you."

"Seems we are all very much indebted to that woman. Where is she?"

"I have sent her back. Once your fever broke I was able to take care of you myself. You should try and sleep now, my Queen."

I made a noise of disgust. "I have been sleeping for days. I want to get up."

"I'm sure you do," he laughed. "But not just yet. Please, for me, try and do as you are told for once."

I frowned at him but did not argue. I could see by his face that he had hardly slept. There were dark circles under his round eyes and lines of worry on his forehead. "You should get some rest yourself."

"I will, soon enough. I will check on your sister for you," he offered, walking to the doorway.

"Damian?" I called quietly after him.

He paused, looking down at the ground. "The child is safe, Orabelle. I have made sure of it."

My eyes were stung with unshed tears and the knot had risen again in my throat. "Thank you," I whispered.

My recovery took longer than I expected but I slowly built my strength back up. Maialen stayed with me for days, trying many times to talk about what had happened with the child. I stubbornly refused to tell her anything, ignoring her questions when she asked them. When she finally left to return to Kymir, she had asked me what she should say to everyone. I had shrugged and told her that it did not matter to me. She had not argued and instead hugged me tightly to her before leaving.

As much as I tried to pretend that I felt nothing, I spent hours each day thinking of the baby. I had not seen Alita since that night and I was comforted by the thought that they were together, though I missed her as well. It had been easier with Maialen there but when she had gone I felt more acutely the constant pain of all their absences. I never asked Damian about them. The less I knew, the easier it was for me to stay away but I couldn't help but wonder. If the eyes would be as grey as Tal's, or if they were blue like mine. I thought of the pale wisps of hair that I had seen in that brief moment and wished I could touch them. I ached to hold my child, just one time. There were moments that I would stop and close my eyes and pretend that the baby was there in my arms, that Alita was beside us, laughing and happy. Other times I would imagine Tal there, smiling down at our child with me. I could see the joy that I knew would fill his face. The only thing that saved me from drowning in my loneliness was knowing that one day this would all be over and I could have my child back with me. It was up to me to make that happen, to make things right.

# 21

The air in Samirra was cool and sharp as the crisp edge of winter blew through the mountains. The lush greens of the valleys and farms had already given way to the bright colors of autumn and were now beginning to fade to the muted browns that marked the end of the growing season. The low granite hills that mottled the Samirran landscape were sparse as the wind carried away the dying leaves from the scattering of trees. Astraeus stood silently on the balcony of his home, a magnificent white palace that dominated the cliffs near the sea and overlooked his bustling kingdom. The palace was an octagon built of blue-veined marble and was topped with an extravagant dome of copper. Four minarets flanked the corners of the three storied structures, each sporting a smaller version of the central dome. Open archways led to balconies that wrapped around the palace and were decorated with screens of intricate piecework. Each level boasted elaborate carvings and floral arabesques inlaid with gold and silver so that the entire palace glinted like a jewel in sunlight. Astraeus was staring out across the hilltops watching the enormous eagles that soared through the air majestically, his hands clasped behind him as the chilled wind tangled through his dark hair.

"Come in from there, Astraeus, you will surely catch a sickness!" his mother, Irielle, called from inside the palace. He took a deep breath and forced himself to smile, turning to face her.

"It is not yet winter, mother, I am in no danger of catching a chill," he said to her, taking a biscuit from the tray she had brought and settling himself on a plush chair.

She set the tray on a table and sat across from him, absently smoothing her dark hair back from her high forehead, though it was already impeccable. "Do not try that false smile on me, my son. What is it that troubles you?"

He sighed and tossed the biscuit back onto the tray uneaten then leaned back, lacing his fingers together behind his head. He stared at the ceiling, admiring the painted frescoes of clouds and birds swirling through the air. His mother cleared her throat, drawing his attention back to her.

"Is this about Maialen?" Irielle prodded gently.

"No," he responded after a moment. "Well, not entirely."

"Are you nervous about the wedding?"

"I am more nervous about her sister. Orabelle is nothing but trouble! All these rumors of her, of all the trouble she caused in Veruca, and now the latest rumor that she is with child? I worry what influence she has had on Maialen."

His mother laughed. "You are afraid that Maialen will turn out like her older sister? I should hardly think so. They are as different as night and day, those two. Though I happen to be rather fond of the Water Queen. She is quite entertaining, you know. There is hardly a dull moment when that one is around! Just like her mother when we were young."

Astraeus frowned and gave Irielle a reproachful look. "She is not the least bit entertaining, mother. The woman is nothing but trouble!"

"She is a good queen," Irielle countered.

"I don't see how causing a great rift in the Council is being a good queen. The Leharans are well, they prosper, trade is good, but there is more to it than that."

Irielle lifted her brows. "And of course I would not know anything about that? I have only been Queen of Samirra for more than twenty-five years."

Astraeus waved a hand at her. "You have been a queen, yes, but you have not been a Keeper. Father was the real ruler, not you."

"Oh, I see," she said, "and it was not me who made decisions when your father could not even remember where he was, or his own name?"

Astus, the former king of Samirra had been in decline for some years. Shortly after Irielle had married him, his mind had begun to deteriorate. It started with small incidents. He would walk into a room and forget why he had come, or he would stare at her, trying to grasp her elusive name from the fog of his memory. Gradually it had gotten worse. There were days now that he did not remember how to eat, who his son was, or that he had a wife.

"Father's illness comes and goes. I am sure that you helped him greatly, but you were not sole ruler. I am. My decisions will affect the entire kingdom. I cannot afford to make them lightly. Should I marry Maialen, I will then share the burden of responsibility for Orabelle. There are only so many things that I can watch over at once," Astraeus sighed, as if the responsibilities of the world had been placed on his shoulders alone.

"I see you are feeling very important today," Irielle murmured.

Astraeus smiled at her, missing the sarcasm, "Yes, mother, I am beginning to see that I have a great effect on the rest of Imbria."

"Have you thought of the effect that our low stores of grains will have on Samirra this winter?" she asked sweetly.

His smile faded. "Those damn Fomori are the problem! The farmers on the outskirts of the valleys were so terrified that most of them abandoned their crops. There have been three attacks now, mother. I have posted guards at lookout points but the farms are so large, they cover a vast area. We do not have enough warriors to watch over everyone. Thankfully, none of the raids have been as bad as the first, just a few small families being attacked, but still everyone is terrified! And now winter has come and the main villages are full of people who left their farms. They have no money and no food and no donations to the palace granary."

"Yes, my son, we are going to have to be very frugal this season. It will not be easy. Kymir, I am sure, would be glad to help us through this troubled time, especially since the Earth Queen will soon be your wife," Irielle said smoothly.

Astraeus frowned harder. "Perhaps I must go through with the marriage to Maialen. For Samirra's sake?"

"I thought you were fond of the girl. What has happened?"

"There is so much going on right now, mother, and so much hostility between the Council. The whole incident between Blaise, Orabelle and Tal would be enough to turn anyone off of marriage."

Irielle made a sound of understanding. "Yes, that was a very unfortunate incident. Poor Tal, he was such a good man."

"It is not good to fall in love with someone else's wife, or to father a child with a woman you are not wed to," Astraeus said pointedly. "Why do you insist on referring to them all as being so good? They are actually quite horrible if you think about it."

His mother laughed again. "Oh, my dear boy, when you are as old as I am you will hopefully understand. Do you think that Tal meant to fall in love with Orabelle? That he did it just to spite Blaise? Tal was already with Orabelle while the Fire King was still a grunt in the old man's army. They were companions for years. It was not something that happened overnight, not a weak moment of lust. The way he looked at her... But it is all rumor, my son. If she is pregnant I really would love to hear all about it! It must be such a romantic story!"

Astraeus groaned with disgust. "Mother, please. That is enough."

Irielle adjusted her skirts, her regal face still full of laughter. "I am merely cautioning you, my son, not to judge others too harshly, lest one day they stand in judgment of you."

# 22

"I do not wish to be here and I do not like being summoned by anyone other than my Queen."

Chronus swallowed the scathing remark that rose to his lips at the sight of the fastidious Leharan Captain approaching. He needed this man and he could not risk provoking him. "I sent Damek to request your presence, not to demand it. How was I to know that a ship with the royal flag of Kymir would be treated with hostility? My regent can be a bit sensitive to those sorts of things."

"Orabelle is not allowing ships in or out. You must have been aware of that and I could have been exposed," Colwyn told him, glancing around at the darkened woods. The leaves were browning with winter and they dusted the ground, rustling and crumbling under his boots as he shifted uncomfortably.

"Relax, my boy. She trusts you too much, you have nothing to worry about. I would not have sent the eagle for you if the nature of my query were not so disturbing. There have been rumors."

Colwyn frowned. "You brought me here because of rumors?"

"Don't pretend you don't know what I am speaking of! What is going on over there?" Chronus demanded, sick of having to deal with Orabelle and her wretched Leharans.

The Captain of the Guard hesitated, looking uncertain. "I am not sure what you are referring to."

"Listen here, boy, either you tell me what is going on or I will make sure that your Queen finds out about this meeting. I have nothing to lose, my daughter already despises me and I her, but you, you have much more to lose. Think what Orabelle would say if she learned that one of her trusted Guard were a traitor. Think what she would do. How the others would look at you."

"I am trying to help her! That is why I have done this, to keep her safe!" Colwyn protested, his face flushing.

Chronus laughed bitterly. "She will not see it that way. Neither will Damian. You think the two of them will let you live? You have seen your Queen's temper. Suppose I were to imply that you had already betrayed her long ago, that her beloved Tal's blood stained your hands as well. She would do worse to you than she did to Raynor. Don't be a fool, boy. You belong to me now, whether you like or not. So if you'd like to go on living you had better start being a little more forthcoming with the information that I ask for. "

"I did not betray Tal! No one would believe that and I am not your lackey-"

"Yes, you are!" Chronus practically spat at him. "If you so much as utter another word that isn't what I want to hear then I will see you buried. You will do what I say when I say it and you can be assured that if you are one day Guardian it will only be because I have allowed it, not because you have earned it. You will never be worthy of that title."

Colwyn's hand went to his sword and he was about to draw it from the scabbard when Chronus made a sign with his hand and arrow flew past, so close that Colwyn could feel the air move against his cheek.

"Now you will kill me?" Colwyn asked incredulously.

"This is not a game, you idiot! Did you think I would come out here, unprotected, and just do whatever you told me to? Your Leharan arrogance really is disgusting. You are surrounded by men who will not hesitate to put the next arrow through your heart if I give the right signal. Do not reach for your sword again, boy."

"What do you want?" Colwyn asked through clenched teeth, cursing himself for his stupidity. Of course Chronus would keep proof of their meetings, of messages sent. If Orabelle thought he betrayed her, or worse, that he betrayed Tal....

"What is happening to my daughter? Is she ill or is that just a farce?"

"She is not ill."

Chronus narrowed his eyes. "Do not make me ask unnecessary questions."

"She has given birth," Colwyn stated bluntly, hating himself for being trapped so easily by the old man.

Chronus nearly gagged. His eyes were huge as he grabbed the front of Colwyn's uniform. "What did you just say?"

"Orabelle has given birth to a child."

"It's not true," Chronus insisted, jerking Colwyn forward. The Leharan shoved his hands away.

"It is true. It is Tal's child."

"That damned, cursed witch! How could she? How did this happen?"

"I'm sure that you know well how it happened since you have two daughters yourself," Colwyn retorted.

Chronus's face was dark with rage. "This is not the time to be funny, boy."

"Believe me, I am not finding any of this amusing but there is one other thing you might find interesting."

"There is more?" Chronus cried, throwing up his hands and laughing bitterly. "What else could she possibly do? She is already a lying, deceitful, conniving whore who is well on her way to starting a war! I can't imagine what else she could come up with to ruin my life! Pray tell, what is the witch going to do now?"

"She is going to find the Fomori."

# 23

The planning for the journey to the Fomor Tribe was the cause of many arguments over the next weeks as I gradually became well again. Damian was still insisting that I not go, though my mind was made up. I was surprised that all of the Guard had volunteered to go with me. I had chosen half of them and would be leaving Colwyn there with the rest. Kaden was one of the men I was leaving behind. I still had no idea where Alita was but I did not want to take him away from her if they were able to see each other. It was sentimental and impractical, but I could not bear the thought of anyone else losing someone.

Damian was still arguing with me as we prepared to board the ship that would sail us to find the Fomor. We would be going to the southern wastelands, a desolate swath of land south of Veruca where nothing had grown or lived since ancient times. According to Damian, sandstone caves dotted the dead landscape there and led underground. The Tahitians would find these caves and use bait to draw out the Fomor one at a time, battling them for the right to claim themselves a warrior.

"It is winter, Damian. If we are going to the wastelands, now is the best time to go," I repeated for what felt like the hundredth time.

"We should at least wait for spring! You are weaker than you normally are. We should wait!" Damian was insisting.

"There is absolutely nothing that you can say or do that will change my mind, Damian. We cannot wait till spring. We are going now. The Council meets at the new year and it will be my only opportunity to stop Blaise without going to war. If he gets back to Veruca then he will not give in without a fight. In Kymir he will be away from his army, outnumbered and vulnerable. I must be able to prove to the others then that he has been trading lives to the blood-drinkers," I said patiently, speaking slowly and firmly.

Damian was glaring at me. "You do not need to speak to me like I am an idiot."

"Then stop acting like one! If you have a better idea I will gladly hear it but so far the only thing any of you say is to wait and I cannot do that! Now, please, can we get on board?" I asked, exasperated. He stomped up the wooden plank that led onto the ship and stood stubbornly on the deck with his back to me. Colwyn approached me anxiously, his eyes searching my face.

"We will miss you, my Queen," he said, squeezing my hands.

I forced a smile, feeling uncomfortable and trying to surreptitiously extract my hands from his though he seemed in no hurry to relinquish his hold on me. "I know that Lehar will be safe with you in charge," I told him.

His smile warmed and I groaned inwardly. Finally, I was forced to turn away so that he would have to release me or spin in a circle with me. Thankfully he let go. My eyes moved to Kaden who stood to his right. We looked at each other for a long while but I could not think of anything to say. The shadow that had been in his eyes since the night we left Veruca was still there and I wondered how many more shadows we would carry with us before this was through.

I gave a small nod and then started up the ramp to the huge ship. We were taking one of the biggest of our fleet, a massive three masted galleon that I hoped would intimidate the Fomor if they saw us coming. As I stepped onto the deck I stopped and looked back. Away from the crowd on the beach, near the line of the palms, I saw the frazzled grey head of Rashana, her bony fingers raised in salute. I raised my hand to wave back and my breath caught in my throat as I saw the dark head next to hers. Alita. In her arms was a tiny bundle of cloth.

I pressed my knuckles to my mouth and turned away from them, nearly colliding with Damian. "Stop sneaking up on me like that!" I ordered him.

"Start paying attention," he snapped back, wrapping his arm around my shoulders and guiding me below deck, away from the scene on the beach and the horrible gnawing in my gut.

The sail to the wastelands took days. I used my power when I could, guiding us through the roughest seas and pushing us along when it was too calm. As we drew closer the winds grew more and more fierce, buffeting our ship with hot, dusty air.

"The wind is worse than I expected!" I shouted to Damian over the roar of gusting air. We were standing on the deck watching the shimmering of land through the haze on the horizon

"Do you think it has something to do with Astraeus?" he asked me.

"I have never heard of the winds being so bad. We sailed near here from Veruca and felt none of this! His element seems to be running wild." It was taking a full crew to sail and I was trying my best to help soothe the sea but the wind ripped across the water, slashing at our sails from every direction. Around us, tunnels of air formed loose tornadoes of heated mist that rose and dissipated in seconds.

"You should rest, my Queen, we will be there soon."

I braced myself as a warm blast of wind slammed against me. "I am going below. Call for me if you need me!"

Damian nodded and stood resolutely, the wind seeming to bend around him. Being half his size I was not so lucky and nearly toppled over twice on my way to the stairs that led to my cabin.

The wind howled for hours and all throughout the night the ship was tossed across the waves. I was not sure what this meant for Astraeus, only that it was not normal. None of the crew who were experienced sailors had seen this kind of weather in this ocean. Had he lost some of his power somehow? I thought back to what Maialen had said when I had woken to find her in Lehar. *I felt something change. Through my element.*

I pushed the thoughts of my child aside as dawn rays broke over the horizon. The wind ceased its endless tormenting and was silent, the ship steady on gentle waves. I hurried up on deck to see how far we had come through the sleepless night. Damian was standing where I had left him, though he had donned the desert attire that his people had provided us. Long white robes over loose pants along with scarves to wrap over our heads and faces to protect from the sun. Winter did not seem to touch this place and the heat seemed worse than any I had felt on Lehar.

"Queen Orabelle," Brogan said with a bow, "the Captain wishes to know if you would like to anchor here?"

I made my way to the foredeck where the captain of the ship stood, surveying the sea ahead with squinted eyes. He glanced at me and grunted, which I had become accustomed to as his way of greeting me properly.

"Ever been to this part of the world?" he asked.

"No, I have not," I answered, wiping beaded sweat from my forehead. "We usually take the sea route around and avoid this coast."

"I have. Once, when I was a boy. Our ship was damaged we had been blown off course. It was damned difficult to get out of here with no wind."

"You have me for that," I stated the obvious.

He grinned. "Yes, yes, we do. Though I have to say, back then many of the men were terrified. Thought those Fomori were going to come up on us at any second and attack. They never did though. It's funny but I never imagined I would be sailing back here, actually wanting to run into them."

"Well, Captain, I can't say that I particularly *want* to..." I admitted ruefully.

He laughed. "We have half the Guard with us. And your big Tahitian. I am sure that we will put up a good fight if it comes to it. Shall I ready the skiff?"

"Yes, we will take a small group and go ashore for a few hours to look for signs of life. Damian!" I yelled back, then pointed at the harsh landscape that lay before us. He made a sign of acknowledgement and then began to issue orders and gather equipment. By the time we had dropped the anchor he was ready for us to go, along with two of the Guard, Brogan and Shemus. We piled into the small boat and rowed towards the shore. I reached over the side with my hand, guiding the water to help us along. It was not difficult, but not as easy as it should have been. I thought again of what Maialen had said. Was I merely still weak from the birth or had something changed? I had called my power and willed it to the child to help him live and now I wondered if it had that done something to him and to the rest of us.

Up close, the landscape was even more desolate than it had seemed before. The empty desert seemed to go on forever, nothing but sand, harsh sunlight, and cracked land.

Damian looked around us. "They cannot live out here. Nothing could survive. Their tunnels lead underground so we need to find their caves."

"How do we find anything out here?" Brogan muttered dismally. "And don't you know where they are?"

Damian shook his head. "The locations are not known. Part of the warriors trial is to wander this wasteland and search. I am trying to recall but it all looks the same. I had been hungry and thirsty, my mind played many tricks on me. I would not trust my memory for this. I know that we are looking for windworn rocks. There will be many formations but they can be hard to see because they blend in with the sand on the horizon."

I peered out from under the thin cotton layer of the scarf, studying the barren landscape. "We will keep going in the direction you think is best taking a steady course and see if we come across anything."

We continued on, the heat stifling and making each step heavier than the last. I tugged on the wrists of my sleeves, feeling the burn of the sun on my skin where it peeked through. My head began to ache from straining my eyes and my limbs grew weaker as we trudged on. We rested occasionally, taking long gulps of water, though our lips had already begun to crack even as we lowered the flask. The further we walked, the more disconsolate I felt. I had come all this way hoping to find proof against Blaise's treachery and all I had found was this nothingness that gnawed at my soul. Hopelessness settled deep in my breast, weighing me down even more.

A touch of wind played at the edges of the scarf that sheltered my face. I was grateful for it at first and tilted my face to feel the breeze, but the wind grew harsher. Bits of dust and sand were lifted off the ground and thrown into the air, stinging at my eyes.

"What is this?" I asked Damian as a low rumble echoed around us.

"I do not know but I think we should run," he warned, gesturing toward what appeared to be a massive cloud of dust rumbling towards us relentlessly.

We began to run and the hot air seared my lungs with each breath. I could feel my heart pounding in my chest. The air churned like it was on fire and the cloud of dust washed over us. I threw myself to the ground, yanking the scarf over my entire face and squeezing my eyes shut. I felt Damian's massive form covering me and we huddled there for what felt like an eternity while the sand storm rolled over us. Finally, the rumbling began to fade and the winds slackened, drifting further into the distance.

Damian stood, helping me to my feet. I tried to shake the sand from myself but it had invaded every fold and crevice of the loose garments.

"Orabelle." Damian stopped, pointing. "You don't see it?"

"I can't see anything anymore," Shemus spoke in frustration behind me, rubbing at his eyes.

"There, that dark shape," Damian insisted.

I shook my head and he grabbed my hand pulling me forward. After a few minutes I began to make out a rough outline that sat jaggedly against the white sky. I blinked hard, my eyes watering from the brightness, not trusting that what I was seeing was actually there or if it was my imagination that wanted so badly to find something.

"I think I see it too!" Brogan said excitedly, walking quickly ahead of us. We hurried to keep up with him as he strode at a brisk pace towards the shadow. I was not imagining it and as we drew closer a crag of windworn rock rose up before us.

"It could be just a rock!" Shemus called from the end of our short line.

"Well, it's the only thing we've found so it is at least worth a look," Brogan replied.

"Brogan, slow down," Damian commanded, pulling his great spear from the strap that held it across his back. "We should not proceed recklessly. Come here and stay beside the Queen. I will lead."

The other two men pulled their swords from their scabbards and flanked me protectively. My hand touched the hilt of the knife I had sheathed at my hip but I left it where it was. There was no need for it, at least not yet. I shuddered at the thought of the tunnels that might be awaiting us within the cauldron of rock. Since that day in the underground hollows of Veruca I had carried a weapon with me, something I had never done before. Damian had worked with me daily teaching me to fight so that I would never again feel the moment of helplessness that I had felt when I had been unable to call my element.

We proceeded towards the rock, the men moving cautiously. Damian broke off and jogged ahead, his massive frame barely visible through the haze of the blinding sun. Finally, he came back to where we waited.

"There is a cave there. I only went in a short way but it appears to lead further underground and most likely connects to a system of tunnels that runs underneath these lands." He looked up at the sky. "Daylight is waning. We may only have a few hours left. If we go too far we may have to stay there for the night."

"What about the smell?" I asked him. Fear laced through me and I shoved it away, trying not to think about the sharp-fanged beast that had pressed its jaws to my neck.

"There is a faint odor, but it is not strong. It is likely that they have used this place, or that it connects to the place where they are living but they are not nearby."

The entrance to the cave was a narrow gap where two enormous sandstone rock faces rested against each other. Damian squeezed through sideways and I followed him down a sloping path and into the cavern. The ceiling was low enough so that he had to stoop to walk but I was still able to stand upright. The room itself was maybe six feet wide and ten feet long, with a curve along the back wall that disappeared into darkness. I breathed deeply and the faint aroma of death tickled my nostrils.

"At least it is cooler in here and we are out of that wretched sun," Brogan said, sheathing his sword and rubbing his eyes vigorously. Shemus sat on the floor and began to massage his feet and Damian unwound the scarf from around his head, a tumult of sand spilling out from it. I passed around a flask of water and a chunk of bread and some dried pieces of fruit.

"So will we be exploring the caves tonight or shall we stay here and wait till morning?" Shemus asked, taking a huge bite of bread.

"I should not like to spend any more time here than is necessary. If you all feel up to it, I would prefer to see where this cave leads as soon as possible. Waiting here makes me feel too much like prey. Surely our scent is just as strong to them as theirs is to us. I do not want to wait here to be sniffed out by these dogs," I told them.

"I agree!" Brogan chimed in heartily. Shemus nodded his head, his mouth too full to speak.

"We shall rest here briefly then," Damian decided, settling himself against one wall, his spear laid ready on his knees. He pulled his long dreadlocks back and tied them behind his neck.

"How did the Fomori come to be here, anyway?" Brogan wanted to know. "I can't imagine that someone would actually want to live in this place."

"There is a story that the Samains of Tahitia tell," Damian said. I glared at him and he winked at me. "No, it is not that story, my Queen. Though the two are related, this one concerns just the past, not the future."

I made a rude noise but the two Guards were already looking expectantly at Damian, waiting to hear the tale. I waved a hand grudgingly for him to continue as I sat back against a rock, pulling at the edges of the scarf and continuing to glare at him from under the edge of cloth.

"Long ago, before there were the Element Keepers, the world was chaos," he began, his deep voice flowing around the cavern so that it seemed even richer than usual. "Men had been in great wars and had fought amongst themselves so much that they had destroyed much of the world. Food was scarce, people were sick and starving and the very air had become poisoned so that they could not walk around outside without covering their mouths. The gods had watched all of this sadly but without interference as they were showing men the consequences of their actions. The gods kept hoping that man would give them a sign, that they would begin to learn from their mistakes and they would turn from fighting and help each other. They felt that if they were allowed to wallow in their evil, that eventually they would see the need for goodness. There was one group of men who were particularly evil, who cared nothing for others and only for themselves. These men would roam the land, slaughtering, stealing and raping. They were feared everywhere. One of their practices was to eat the heart of a man they had killed, believing that they gained his strength from it. Eventually, as food grew even scarcer, these men began to eat more than the heart. The blood of others tainted them inside and they began to change, their bodies turning as twisted and evil as their minds. One day, there must have been someone or something who showed the gods that men could be redeemed. An act of kindness long forgotten that convinced the gods to give the world another chance. They came down to the world and forgave us, giving us the chance to rebuild, assigning Keepers to the Elements in order to protect the lands. However, as a lesson, they left the most awful of men to wallow in what they had become. The blood-drinkers were left as they were, forsaken by the gods and beyond help, to be banished beneath the land where they would live, isolated from everything and everyone with their eternal hunger. They are the reminder to us of what we can become. They are the consequences of our own actions."

Shemus let out a low whistle. "So they are the epitome of evil."

"And we are somehow supposed to convince the most vile men that have ever lived to stop being so mean and please help us?" Brogan asked, turning to me incredulously.

I scoffed. "Those are Damian's silly stories and they mean nothing. Besides, as I said before, if they are or were once people like us they must have some small part of them that is human."

"Not the part that eats people's hearts," Brogan pointed out.

I sent Damian another glare. "See what you have done?"

He shrugged. "They wanted to know. Now," he said, rising from the ground, spear in hand, "shall we get moving?"

The others stood and gathered their things. Brogan pulled a dry torch and a bottle of oil from his bag, dousing one end while Shemus used a flint to light it. We followed Damian around the curve at the back of the cave to an even smaller cavern that sloped down at a steep angle leading us further beneath the surface.

"Into the heart of darkness," one of the men muttered behind me. I could not agree with them more.

# 24

Chronus watched as Maialen tenderly adjusted the bandage on Gideon's shoulder, her gentle fingers working quickly to secure the knot.

"There, all done," she said with a smile, patting his arm. He flexed his shoulder and winced in pain. His arm still hung limply down by his side, useless. A worried look passed over Maialen's face but she covered it with a bright smile and turned to her father.

"He is getting better every day!" she announced.

Chronus met the big man's eyes and they shared a moment of understanding. Gideon had healed and would live but they both knew that he would never regain full use of his arm, no matter how much Maialen willed it. Which was going to be a problem as a one-armed Guardian was not what Chronus had in mind to protect his daughter. He turned away from Gideon and opened his arms to Maialen who hugged him happily.

"And how is your sister doing? I was told that was where you went when you ran off so suddenly," Chronus said with a soft reproach in his voice. "You know, daughter, that a Queen cannot afford to be so impetuous."

"She is fine now, father. She was ill and I was worried about her, that was why I left so quickly," Maialen explained, not meeting his eyes.

"Ill? What sort of illness?"

"A fever. Or something. Like that," Maialen said awkwardly, shrugging her shoulders and glancing over her father's shoulder and out the window.

Chronus frowned at her and seethed inwardly. She was covering for Orabelle. He was going to have to break the bond between them and the sooner that it happened the better off Maialen would be. He would not allow that witch to drag his youngest daughter down with her.

"Are you sure it was merely a fever, Maialen?" he asked with a look of concern.

"Well...I don't know exactly..."

"Maialen, it's alright. I know you want to protect your sister but I already know about the child. There is no need to lie to me," Chronus reproached her.

Her eyes flew open wide and stared at him, her cheeks flushing. Chronus recalled the meeting with Colwyn when he had told him of the birth. He could still feel the rage boiling inside him, nearly choking him with his desire to hurt Orabelle. She was going to ruin everything. He would see her dead, no matter what that idiot Blaise wanted. If he had his way he would go and find her himself and strangle her slowly, telling her that she was a whore just like her mother had been. But before she could die he had to destroy her. He could not make a martyr of her to Maialen or to anyone else.

"Are you very angry?" Maialen asked softly, interrupting his thoughts. He realized that he was breathing harder and forced himself to calm down.

"I am angry, yes, but the child is born and we cannot change that. All we can do now is protect it, and raise it as part of our family," Chronus lied, patting her hair lovingly.

She beamed up at him. "Oh father! You really mean that? Orabelle was so worried that everyone would be mad about it. I cannot wait to tell her that you will accept the baby!"

Chronus felt his stomach turn at the thought of accepting the bastard child into his family. It would never happen and as long as he was alive that child would never be an heir to any throne on Imbria. "Yes, of course I mean it, dear little Maialen. I want to see the baby as soon as possible."

Her face clouded over and she looked at the ground. He asked her what was wrong and she bit her lip, tears filling her eyes. "Orabelle has sent the baby away and she won't tell anyone where. Damian knows but he's.... well, you would have better luck getting her to tell than him. She wouldn't even let me see him."

"Ah, so it's a boy?" Chronus questioned with false enthusiasm. He cursed inwardly. Damn that girl, he should have killed her the day she was born. It had been a mistake to keep her alive, one that he was not going to repeat now. It was smart of her to have sent the child away but he would find it.

"Yes, I think that Damian said he. The old woman that delivered him said he has silver hair like Tal's."

"Maialen, please, do not mention that man. I can accept Orabelle's child because what is done is done but I forbid any mention of the man who violated my daughter in such a way."

"Yes, father," Maialen whispered in apology.

"There is something else that we must discuss," Chronus said, clearing his throat and preparing to plant the seeds of dissent between the two sisters. "Astraeus is having doubts about the marriage."

"What? Why? Have I done something wrong?" Maialen demanded.

"It was he who failed to protect her in Samirra!" Gideon spoke up from behind her, rising angrily from the chair.

"Actually, it was you who failed, as you are her Guardian and the one responsible for her safety," Chronus told the other man with a pointed look at the limp arm. Gideon's face reddened.

"No, father, Gideon saved me! He jumped in front of me-"

Chronus cut her off. "I am aware of what happened, Maialen. I am only pointing out that he should not blame others for what is his own responsibility. Now, if you would please send him from the room, I should like to talk with you uninterrupted."

Maialen turned to Gideon and squeezed his hand. "I'm sorry, I will talk with you later."

He did not return her grasp and she let his hand fall as he moved past her and strode out the doorway without looking back.

"Now, Maialen, about Astraeus, you are going to need to fix this between you two. It would be a great embarrassment if the Air King were to refuse to marry you."

"But I have not done anything that I know of!" she cried.

"No, it is not you that concerns him. It is your sister."

"Orabelle? What does she have to do with it?"

Chronus adjusted the gold cuffs on his wrists. "Your sister is out of control, Maialen, you must surely see that. She is acting very dangerously and very foolishly and there is only so much that the Council can be willing to tolerate. And now this thing with the child. I fear if Astraeus learns of it, it will be too much for him."

"I don't understand what that has to do with our marriage. I have done nothing," Maialen repeated again.

"Stop being naive! You know that your sister's actions reflect upon this family. Just because you are too caring to see her for who she really is does not mean that everyone else is fooled. She is selfish and willful and it does not matter in the least to her who she hurts. She thinks nothing of you, Maialen, or of your future."

"That is not true. Orabelle would never do anything to hurt me!"

"You really believe that? Did it not hurt you that she wouldn't even let you see her child? I saw the tears in your eyes, my poor darling. You, who have always been good to her. Did it not hurt you when she ran away after her Guardian's death without a word to you? When for months she ignored you and your messages and your pleas?" Chronus asked, allowing an edge of anger into his voice that Maialen would interpret as righteousness on her behalf.

She pulled at her thick braid of hair. "She was mourning, father, she didn't mean to. I can forgive her, she is my sister. And she is your daughter."

"Wake up, Maialen! Your sister is not the person that you believe she is! She is barely even your sister and she is no daughter of mine!" Chronus practically shouted.

"What do you mean?" Maialen was confused by the vehemence of her father's response.

Chronus covered his eyes with a hand. "Nothing. Nothing, Maialen, I should not have said anything."

"Father, please. I know she is not how you want her to be. That's what you mean, isn't it?" Maialen asked, taking his hand from his eyes and holding it in her own. Her stomach fluttered as she watched her father's tormented face.

"No, Maialen," he confessed, his voice anguished. "I mean that she is not my daughter."

Maialen released him and stepped back. "What are you saying?"

"Your mother, she was pregnant when I married her. I did not know of it. At first I thought Orabelle was mine, but then I learned the truth," Chronus let his voice trail off brokenly. He watched Maialen's face fill with sympathy. His daughter could not bear to see anyone in pain.

"No... how... I don't...." Maialen was stammering.

"Maialen, I am sorry to tell you this now but with everything that is happening with Orabelle I felt that you should know."

"Does she know?"

"Yes," he lied. "I fear that is one of the reasons that she cares so little for what happens to our family. She does not see us as her own."

"Who is her father?" Maialen wanted to know, her eyes once again filling with tears.

"I do not know," Chronus said sadly. "If Orabelle knows she is hiding him from us just as she has hidden her baby. After everything I have done for her she has ostracized us, treated us as outsiders. I always knew she hated me but I never thought she would turn on you this way."

"No, no, no! It can't... she wouldn't...." Maialen choked back a sob, tears falling down her face and she fled the room. Chronus let her go, knowing Gideon would be waiting outside to watch over her. She would go to her garden and cry and later he would speak to her again and comfort her. He would tell her that he would repair their relations with Astraeus for her, that he would fix everything as a good father should. He had already conferred with Irielle, the Air King's mother, and agreed on a winter tithe of food and supplies to Samirra as compensation to continue with the wedding plans. Maialen would see him as a hero and Orabelle would be left as the cause of all her problems, the thorn in their side. All that was left now was to find a way to discredit her to the Council and the rest of Imbria. Then he would see her, her bastard child and her accursed Tahitian dead before they could cause any more problems.

# 25

I stopped abruptly, the scent of decay rolling over me so that I gagged, swallowing bile. Damian shoved me behind him and the other two Guards flanked me from either side, forming a triangle. They held their swords ready and Damian grasped his spear tightly in his hands, shrugging his cloak back from his shoulders. There was a scratching noise ahead of us in the tunnel and I held the torch in white-knuckled hands, searching the edges of the orange glow for movement. We had been walking for hours, the smell growing subtly stronger till now, when it flooded our senses with the odor of death.

"Show yourself!" Damian called into the darkness. "I am Damian, Guardian of Queen Orabelle."

"What are you doing here, you fools? Have you a desire to be food for us? Ahh a Tahitian, come to earn your manhood with our slaughter," a sibilant voice echoed over the stone.

"We are not here to harm you. I have come to seek Carushka," I stated, my own voice steady despite the twisting of fear that curled through me.

"Carushka does not wish to be sought out," came the answer, slightly louder this time.

"Perhaps you should ask him."

The thing laughed, its hissing cackle sending chills down my spine. "What is it that you really want? If you have come to kill us you are sadly outnumbered. Surely you are not so foolish? We could have devoured you already but we get so few visitors here that our curiosity has gotten the better of us. Tell me, Queen, what would make you walk into your death?"

"I will speak only to Carushka. I am a Queen, I will not explain myself to you," I said haughtily. There was a long moment of silence.

"Very well. You may continue on. This route will lead you to a cavern. Carushka will be waiting."

We could hear it moving away. Damian glanced back at me, his eyes questioning. I nodded and we moved warily down the tunnel, eventually rounding a bend that opened up into a huge, cavernous space. I felt a wash of relief roll over me at the sight of a small pool in the center of the cave, the water dripping slowly from a great stalagmite that hung overhead. My relief at seeing a part of my element was quickly dampened as I noticed that the edges of the cavern were littered with debris that gleamed pale white in the torchlight.

"Are those bones?" Brogan whispered. I swallowed hard.

A new voice slid through the cavern. "Does it disturb you, to see the bones of your ancestors?"

The creature who spoke had the slight hiss that the other beasts had but this voice was deeper, more human. It held a hint of amusement, different from the malevolent laughter in the tunnel, and a faint accent that I had never heard before, as if the words were not native to its tongue. He stepped from the shadows, larger even than Damian, larger than any man I had ever seen. His heavily muscled body was covered in skin that was thick and grey. His hair was not a wild tangle like the creature that had attacked me below Veruca, but was long and combed, black and streaked with silver, tied back from his face so that the bright yellow eyes stood out dominantly. He had covered himself in a long robe similar to the clothing we had donned for the desert heat. He had full lips that held the barest hint of a smile and a straight nose with heavy dark brows that further accentuated the eerie icterine yellow of his irises. I met his eyes and their gaze held intelligence as well as something dark and forbidding.

"Carushka," I said.

"We meet at last, Queen." He smiled fully so that his sharp fanged teeth showed and he walked slowly toward us, his hands clasped behind his back. Behind him several other beast-men lined the wall of the cavern, watching silently. Damian tensed, his spear ready. Carushka looked him over. "There is no need to worry, Guardian. I will not kill her before hearing what she has to say. I cannot remember the last time we had such a lovely visitor."

His gaze traveled over me and I tried not to let my revulsion show in my face. "I would like to speak with you about your pact with the Fire King."

Carushka's eyes widened slightly. "So you know of that, do you? Let me guess, you have come here to plead peace with me, to convince me to not devour your precious people. Quite brave of you, really. Though not very practical, Queen. Would you ask the snake to not strike? Or a river to not flow? To destroy is our nature and the nature of things cannot be changed by pretty words from a pretty face."

"You were once human. That is your nature. What you have become now, it is not who you really are," I argued, taken aback by the intelligence the ancient being exuded.

"What do you know of who we are?" Carushka demanded. Sudden anger distorted his features. "You and the rest of them who forsook us! You who left us here to rot together while you made your world in the sun! Do you have any idea how long I have been down here? How many years I have spent in this darkness?"

I felt my own temper rising in challenge. "You are the ones who chose to be this way. You can choose to change."

He laughed, his eyes narrowing. "Do you think we chose this existence, Queen? We were branded, marked as evil by a world that turned its back on us when everyone else was forgiven! I assure you, we did not choose this life."

I held his gaze, refusing to look away. "You made the choices that led to this life."

He shrugged and began to pace, never taking his shrewd yellow eyes from mine. "There was much evil in the world then, Queen. Just as there is now. We did what was necessary to survive. Yet we were the ones blamed for all of it while the rest of you were allowed the luxury of forgiveness."

"I was not there to grant you forgiveness, Carushka. It was not my doing," I told him.

He stopped pacing and flung his words at me hatefully. "It was your kind that did it! You and the perfect people of Imbria betrayed us! You took your gifts, your elements, and you left us here to rot! Surely, Queen, you can smell us rotting. I can see it in your face and the way you breathe through your mouth. We are rotting slowly here but never dying! We are forced to live in the agony of darkness and hunger. And then one comes along and offers us food, he treats us as living beings, not just nightmares that haunt the outskirts of their villages, and you wish for me to give that up?"

"Blaise is using you to control fear. He is treating you like dogs, sending you out to attack as he wishes! You wish to be the dog of a vile man with a throne he doesn't deserve?"

"It is better to be a dog than a rat, ground underfoot and chased away like vermin," Carushka spat.

I stared at him incredulously. "Do you not realize what you are?"

"I know well what I am, Queen! It is you who has much to learn!"

"You stand here and lament that you are not accepted, that you were cast out and treated with abuse, but you can only blame yourself! You are a murderer! You slaughter people and you eat them! How can you expect to live among them?" I cried. "How could we say, yes, please come back and be part of our world when what you live for is death?"

"Death is a part of life! And so is pain!" Carushka growled. He threw an accusatory finger in Damian's direction. "His kind slaughters my people, they hunt us for sport, and yet you delight in his vile company!"

"You bring your suffering upon yourself!" I accused, stabbing a finger in his direction. "You blame others for the choices that you have made, for what you have turned yourself into!"

He moved as if to lunge at me and then stopped himself as the point of Damian's spear touched his throat. His eyes glowed with malevolence but he took a step back. Suddenly the anger seemed to pour out of him and his shoulders sagged. "What is it you want, Queen? I am tired of this conversation."

"I want to know about the pact with Blaise, as I said before. I want to know everything."

"And why should I tell you?"

"Can you truly not change? Could you not be contented with food other than humans? Have you tried? Or have you just accepted what you are as an excuse for evil?" I asked him.

He laughed again. "Let me guess. You wish for me to agree to a less... voracious diet. You will tell me that the people of Imbria will accept us if we do this, that we could once again walk among the living."

"Isn't that what you want most?"

Again, he stared at me, his yellow eyes searching mine. "I have done things more horrific than you can even imagine. I have killed more than you can fathom. I have drained them, eaten their flesh, torn their bodies apart limb by limb and you think that will all just go away? That by saying we are sorry, the past horrors no longer matter? The problem there, Queen, is that I am not sorry. As I said before this is our nature. I do not feel bad when I hear their pitiful screams. I do not feel regret when I see the light die in their eyes. I am not remorseful when after I have fed I look upon the remnants of what was once a young, strong body. Do you want to know what I feel?"

I shook my head, once more swallowing the bile that rose in my throat.

"I feel nothing. Nothing! For years I have felt nothing!" Carushka yelled at me, his face twisting into an ugly mask of torment as I tried not to flinch. "The only thing I can feel any longer is hate! Hate for your kind and hate for the ones that locked us in those tunnels in the first place! They were all given a second chance, all of them but us! They were allowed to feel happiness, joy, love. Yet we were only given misery!"

"It is not too late for you to change! Listen to yourself! You recall these emotions, even if you can't feel them any longer. By accepting that you are evil you have made yourself that way!"

"You humans are just as evil as we. We may be the ones that actually tear the flesh from the bone but you are the ones that provide it to us. Do you think that your Blaise is the first ruler that we have made a pact with? You lecture me on change, look at you! Will you go to war against the Verucan? You have already forgotten the lessons of the past, despite the fact that we have suffered for centuries as your reminder! You will fight amongst yourself, barter your flesh, just as you have before. You do not change, just as we do not change!"

"Well, if we are so awful, why are you so angry about being left apart from us?" I wanted to know.

"Because you are given a choice! You can choose where you go, how you live, what you do! You can choose to love or hate, to smile or to cry, you can raise your children, have your families. We have none of that! We have been left with nothing!" Carushka answered with a tortured groan as he turned from us, his head down.

I watched the proud figure bent in personal agony and before I could think about it I moved forward past Damian who still held his spear ready. He adjusted his stance slightly to let me pass, his eyes warning me to be cautious. I reached out a hand and though my stomach heaved and my fingers shook I laid it gingerly on Carushka's arm. His skin was hot and dry, and rough like hide under the soft layer of hair. He spun around, looking down at my fingers that now hovered in the air where his arm had been.

"What are you doing?" he hissed at me, for the first time sounding more like the beast that he was. His lips were parted and I could see his pink-stained fangs.

I dropped my hand to my side and stood my ground in front of him. A trickle of sweat ran down my back. "You must feel something to make you turn away like that. Something other than hate."

"Are you not afraid I will take a bite from you, Queen?"

I lifted my chin. "I am not afraid."

His bitter laugh resounded through the cavern. "Yes, you are. Don't worry, you smell a little too bitter for my tastes. Stubborn too, you would probably be very tough."

"If that is supposed to be humorous, it is not," I said with a baleful glare.

He laughed again. "Yes, my sense of humor is as foul as the rest of me, I suppose. Enough of this philosophizing, Queen. I am tired of arguing natures. I have been thinking this whole time. You plan on attacking Veruca, do you not?"

"Yes. Eventually."

"That is why you want my help. You can expose Blaise for the terrible man that he is without fighting if you can prove that he's been supplying us with....food. Your precious Council would have to take his kingdom away from him."

I waited without response, unnerved by the calculating glint that had entered his eyes.

He went on. "I am well acquainted with your Blaise and I can tell you that the Fire King will not give up willingly. There will be a fight. Now, as you are asking for my help you must be prepared to give us something in return, correct?"

"If it is something that I can agree to, then yes."

"I want Veruca."

I raised an eyebrow. "You want Veruca? You know that I cannot hand you over a nation of people."

"I do not want the Verucans. I want the city. I am tired of these tunnels, of this darkness. You can take the people of Veruca, spread them out over the rest of the land. We only want a place to walk outside, a place where we don't have to burrow underground like rats. If we would be willing to try a different sort of life, we could trade work in the mines for livestock that we can use as food."

"You would be willing to only eat animals?" I hesitated, wondering at the sudden turn in the conversation. "Moments ago you told me that you cannot change."

"Rash words spoken in anger. We cannot know unless we try. And if we fail then surely the armies of Imbria will be able to take care of us. You may kill us or chase us back to our tunnels," he shrugged. "I would, however, ask one more favor of you."

I frowned, sensing that it was going to be something I would not like. "What favor is that?"

"That you give us the spoils of all of your wars. The soldiers of Veruca, the dead and dying. It will be our last great feast," he said eagerly licking his lips, the icterine eyes shining.

Nausea crept over me once again. "And if we avoid war?"

"I said all of your wars. You will not avoid it forever, you cannot, that would be like asking the fish not to swim. You will fight each other, you will ravage the world as you always do, it is inevitable."

I hesitated. It would do no harm to agree with him now as I had no intention of honoring the agreement. I could deal with the Fomor later once Blaise had been stopped. I nodded. "Fine, the spoils of war go to you, Carushka, as will the lands of Veruca."

He smiled, a knowing look as if he understood my deception and had expected it. But even so he began to talk. "Good Queen. Let me tell you about Blaise. Where would you like me to begin?"

"The terms of your contract with him."

"He provides us with a certain amount of food every month, enough to sustain our people, though with his temper it is sometimes more than we need. In return, we stay quiet and underground if that is what he wishes, or we attack a ship or a village when he wants us to. I'm sure you have surmised all of this already, Queen."

"Yes," I said with a sigh, "I had, though I am still reluctant to believe it."

"You should be more concerned with how you will make the Council believe it. You, of course, expect me to go with you and divulge these delicious secrets, but that would be foolish of me, would it not?" Carushka asked. "Your humans will not be so anxious to allow one of our kind among them. There is also the chance that you would turn on me, kill me sometime during the voyage to Kymir, or that you will have a trap waiting for me there. It would bode well for you to be the one who defeated the leader of the famed Fomori."

"I will do everything that I can to guarantee your safety while you are with us. When we arrive in Kymir you may stay on the ship, under guard. I will bring the Council to you if that is what you desire," I offered.

He paced the floor with a thoughtful look. "I will agree to that."

"There is something else I wish to know about. Your bite is poison to us, is it not?"

Carushka nodded, touching his tongue to the tip of one of his sharp teeth. "Yes. As I told you, we are rotting. Those we bite will also begin to rot."

My eyes darkened with emotion. "Did one of you bite my mother, the Leharan Queen Ursula?"

He looked surprised. "Well, well, well. Clever girl, aren't you? However you ask the wrong questions. If you want to know about your parents there are things I could tell you. But, my dear, that was not part of what we agreed upon. I said that I would tell you about Blaise. I did not agree to anything else."

"Please, I must-"

"Begging will not help and it doesn't become you, Queen. I would not have expected you to be so sentimental. Your mother is dead, there is nothing you can do to change that. If you would like to know more, then you must offer me something else," he said, lowering his voice and leaning towards me. He breathed in deeply, closing his eyes. "There is something..."

"No!" Damian's spear was once again at Carushka's throat, the end of it digging into his flesh.

Carushka looked at him, his eyes full of amusement. "So you object, noble Guardian? I am afraid that you mistake my intentions. I have no desire for the young Queen," he paused, his gaze lingering on mine, "she merely reminds me of something that I have lost."

Damian twisted the spear in his hands so that a drop of black blood appeared at the other man's neck. "I will not drink your blood but I will spill it."

Carushka laughed, grabbing the spear and pulling it in further so that blood welled around the sharp point and ran down his throat. "You seek to frighten me, Tahitian?"

"Enough!" I commanded. "Please stop this."

Carushka released the spear and stepped away from me. "If you wish I have a safe place for you to rest for the night, Queen. The door can be barred from the inside."

"I do not trust them," Damian said to me, not bothering to lower his voice.

Carushka's eyes gleamed. "Of course you don't. But you really have no choice now, do you? Night has fallen and you will never make it to your ship in such darkness as exists out there. I offer you sanctuary."

"We have a compass," Shemus pointed out, eliciting a glare from the Fomor.

"A compass will not protect you. I can."

"Your offer does not comfort me," Damian retorted. Carushka ignored him and turned away, waving for us to follow.

The men hesitated, Brogan speaking up first. "If the door can be barred from the inside, as he says, then I agree. If he was going to try to kill us I think he would have tried already."

Shemus shrugged and Damian made a differential gesture towards me.

"We must stay somewhere," I answered.

We followed Carushka a short distance. He led us to a doored chamber and held the door open gallantly as Damian entered alone, surveying the surroundings. He quickly circled the room, testing the cavern walls and floor for traps and finding nothing save the two torches that lit the space. There was a long crevice in the stone ceiling overhead and a cool breath of fresh night air floated in from somewhere far above.

"Satisfied?" Carushka asked the Tahitian, a smile playing at his full lips.

Damian glowered at him. "Not in the least."

The Fomor gave a short burst of laughter. "I shall bring you blankets. Unfortunately, you must sleep on the floor. There is a draft here so you should be comfortable. Do not leave the room or unbar the door during the night. Wait till I have come for you in the morning. I can guarantee your safety if I am present but there are some among us whose appetites are harder to suppress."

We moved into the room and slid the heavy iron bar in place after Carushka had left. In silence we waited till he knocked again, his strange accent muffled through the thick doorway, "I have your blankets, please open the door."

He entered, passing a pile of tattered cloths to Brogan. "These are the best that we have. I'm sure you understand, Queen, that our resources are limited."

"Thank you," I said to him.

His yellow eyes glowed brightly in the torchlight. "There is no need for thanks, Orabelle."

I stiffened at the use of my name, the odd accent he spoke in making it sound foreign to my ears. He noticed my discomfort and gave me a small smile, then backed out of the room, pulling the heavy door shut behind him.

# 26

Irielle sat demurely, her legs tucked under her long skirts, carefully stitching a pattern of gold thread onto a piece of bright green cloth. She glanced up as her son entered the room and smiled as she continued her work.

"What is that?" he asked her, gesturing to the bundle of fabric in her lap.

"It is a wedding present for your bride."

"I see. So they agreed to the tithe?"

She nodded. "Of course they did. They will provide us a supply of food to get us through the winter. Hopefully, next season there will be more crops."

"There will be," he vowed confidently.

"Astraeus, there is something I wish to talk to you about." His mother folded the cloth gently and laid it aside on a table. "The merchant ships are complaining about the winds. They say they are blowing unpredictably, making it dangerous to sail."

He scoffed and threw his hands in the air. "Mother, I cannot be everywhere at once!"

"Yes, my son, I know that. However, the winds around Samirra should not require a great effort for you to control."

"What do you know of it? Besides, people are always finding something to complain about. If it wasn't that it would just be something else!"

"I am merely worried that if the merchants began to feel unsafe in our seas they will not want to risk bringing their cargo here. You could always speak to your father, he could help you with your control," Irielle suggested, smoothing her thick black hair away from her face.

"Father is a blubbering dolt! The last time I saw him he was ranting and raving about some boy he met and it turned out he was talking about something that happened thirty years ago! He is useless," Astraeus said disgustedly.

"Then go to the palace library. There are many records there from the past Air Keepers that may help you. And do not speak that way of your father." There was an edge of irritation creeping into her voice that she couldn't help.

"Mother, I have too many things to do to go digging through a mountain of dusty old books and scrolls. Have Favian or Zelia do it and then come to me if they find something." He kissed her quickly on the cheek and turned on his heel to leave the room. She started to call after him angrily but changed her mind, letting him go. It had been years since she had been in the library, though it had once been one of her favorite places to go. She loved the smell of the old parchments and the beautiful calligraphy of the writers. Samirra was the only kingdom that had such a collection and it saddened her that it was such a lost art. People were so concerned with their own lives, they no longer seemed to care what had happened to others before them.

As she made her way up the staircase that led to the great room, Irielle thought about the upcoming wedding between her son and the Earth Queen. While she enjoyed Maialen's company and her sweet disposition, she was worried that the two of them would not be able to stand their ground in the

Council. Chronus had already manipulated them into giving him the honorary title of High Regent. How he managed to make people listen to him was beyond her understanding. She had never cared for the man. In all honesty she rather detested him. Ursula had been a dear friend of hers and she could never forget how he had shut her away from everyone, claiming that she had some mysterious illness, though he was allowed to see her and he never fell sick. Irielle had watched as the two little girls had grown up without their mother, Chronus doting on the younger while the elder sister was raised with an iron fist.

"Ah, Orabelle," Irielle sighed aloud, coming into the library.

"Eh? The Water Queen is here?"

Irielle stopped short as the grey head of her husband peered over the back of the chair he sat in. The floor around him was littered with parchments and scrolls tossed carelessly about his feet. She made a disproving noise and started to gather them up.

"No, she is not here, Astus, I was merely thinking aloud," she explained as she rolled a scroll neatly and slid it into its case. "What are you doing with all of these?"

The former king looked away, his face reddening. "I...the things that I can't remember.... I thought reading these would help. "

Irielle frowned, setting the bundle in her hands aside so that she could put her arms around him. "In that case, make as grand of a mess as you'd like."

Astus chuckled. "You're a good wife, Irielle."

Her heart twisted that he had recalled her name. There were some days he could not remember her at all. Those days were becoming far too common. She worried that the same fate would befall their son, that perhaps wielding the element had somehow contributed to the former Keeper's madness.

"You are a good husband," she replied.

"Why were you thinking about the Leharan Queen? Has she gotten herself into more trouble?"

"No doubt she has! I am just waiting to hear of it. Now, tell me what you wanted to know that you couldn't remember."

"Our wedding day," he confessed, lowering his head dejectedly. "All of this talk about our son's wedding and I couldn't even recall my own, or when it was. I was just checking the records.... I am sorry, Irielle."

"There is nothing to be sorry for!" she exclaimed. "So, what did you find?"

"Not very much, actually. I did find something else interesting, though. Look at this!" he said, passing her a piece of old parchment.

She took it from him. "It's the record of gifts and services we sent for Chronus and Ursula's wedding. Why is this interesting?"

"Look at the date," he told her, his eyes shining. She smiled at him, glad that he was at least enjoying himself and in good spirits. There were times when his illness made him angry, his frustration with himself exploding in fits of rage.

"I still don't understand," she said with a shake of her head.

"Oh, come my dear, you love a bit of gossip! We were just discussing their eldest daughter, who was born in the summer," he hinted.

Irielle's mouth dropped open in surprise. "Orabelle should not have been born for months! Ursula said she came early, but to be that early the baby would not have survived."

"Yes, it appears that Chronus was not as chaste with his bride-to-be as he pretended!" Astus said with a laugh.

"Yes, it appears not," Irielle murmured. She thought of the way Chronus constantly deferred to Maialen, his contempt of Orabelle, the way he had always treated her as a chore. "Astus, where are the records of the visitors to the Royal Palace?"

He was already absorbed in some new bit of information and waved vaguely towards the rear of the library. She found them and began to pull out the ones from the year Ursula and Chronus married, running her finger down the lists as she searched. Something was nagging at her, a forgotten memory just beneath the surface. There was something about those months before their wedding. If she was recalling correctly, Ursula had spent a lot of time in Samirra.

"Aha!" Irielle said, slapping the page with her fingers. Ursula had been coming to Samirra every few weeks for nearly two seasons before she married Chronus. Could it really be that Orabelle was not Chronus's daughter? It would explain a great many things about their relationship. And if he wasn't her father, then who was? She and Ursula had been friends then but Irielle had been so wrapped up in her own life she had not noticed anything.

"Who would know something like that?" she wondered, rubbing her chin thoughtfully. "And if they did know and they have never told anyone all this time, would they tell me now?"

"Irielle, are you talking to yourself again?" Astus called. "And they call me the mad one!"

Irielle replaced the record and turned to her husband. Though she wanted to run out now and indulge herself in solving this mystery, she would stay there with Astus. There were too few times when he was like this and she missed her husband a great deal. She also wanted to talk with him about their son and his control of his element. With the weak crop they had that year they could not afford to lose any of the merchant trading as well.

It was nearly three days before Irielle found the time to go out from the palace and seek answers about Ursula. She still felt that there was something she wasn't recalling, something important, but it stayed just out of reach. The first place she went to was a nearby cottage. There was a woman there who had worked in the palace kitchens for years and was known for her vast knowledge of local gossip and secrets. She had been there when Irielle had first come as Queen of Samirra and a bond had developed between them as the girl could never be on time for the grand seated dinner that had been the tradition then. As a result of Irielle's constant tardiness she had been forced to eat at a small table in the corner of the kitchen with Raienna, the cook, as her companion. Irielle had been grateful when her husband had finally allowed her to do away with the horrible tradition, except on special occasions.

Raienna was sitting out front of her cottage, wrapped in a warm blanket, her spotted and rather unsavory looking cat perched in her lap. Her long hair was streaked with gray and pulled back tightly from her face, which was more lined than Irielle had remembered.

"Well!" Raienna cooed happily. "Quite a visitor I have today!"

"Hello," Irielle greeted her, smiling broadly.

The old lady shooed the cat from her lap and stood up, using a heavy stick to keep her balance. The cat hissed threateningly back at her and stalked off while Raienna cursed it soundly. Finally she seemed to remember that Irielle was standing there. "Oh yes! Come in for tea!"

Irielle followed her into the warm hut, glad to be out of the chill air. She sat beside the fire, taking the offered cup and exchanging pleasantries as the old woman settled herself beside her. The cottage was small and cramped, but cozy and kept immaculately clean.

"Now," Raienna said, blowing on her tea to cool it, "you must have come here for something besides the tea and the company. Have you been late for meals again and banished to the likes of the cottages?"

"No, it is not that," Irielle assured her with a laugh. "I wanted to ask you about something. Do you remember the year that Chronus married Ursula?"

The old woman narrowed her eyes and Irielle's heart leapt. She knew something!

"I remember their wedding. I traveled to Kymir for it to help prepare the wedding feast. I felt so sorry for that poor girl, if you don't mind me saying so."

"You can speak plainly with me, old friend. What about before the wedding? Ursula was spending a lot of time here. Do you recall what she was doing or who she spent that time with?"

Raienna shook her head, avoiding the other woman's eyes. "No. Nothing that would be of interest."

"Please," Irielle pleaded. "I am not merely searching for gossip to entertain myself with. If you know something please tell me. I'm sure you have heard that Chronus has weaseled his way back onto the Council. We should have known he would find a way to keep himself in power. If there is anything about them that could help Astraeus gain some sort of leverage I would be very grateful"

Raienna gave her an unfriendly look. "Ruining people's lives for the sake of your boy and his ambition is not something you should ask me to do, your Highness."

"I do not ask for his ambition but for his protection. And for those girls as well, for Maialen and Orabelle. I know you have no love for Chronus, you just said so yourself, that you were sorry for Ursula for marrying him."

The old woman gave her a long, searching look. "It is not a tale that will end well once it is told."

Irielle nodded. "I promise that I will not abuse the trust you bestow by telling me," she swore.

"Ursula was a Princess then, not yet a Queen. She was a beautiful girl, always laughing. And so kind. She may have been one of the happiest people I have ever seen. At least until she married that man. But you knew that already. I do not understand all this obsession with mingling the bloodlines and

Keepers marrying one another. Seems like too much power in too few hands if you ask me. You may want to think on that. But back to where we were.... one night she snuck out of the palace after everyone had gone to bed. I saw her because I had stayed late to clean up after a huge banquet given for the royals' visit. She begged me not to tell on her then asked me where I was going. I told her there was a celebration with singing and dancing going on in the village and that is where I was headed."

"She went with you, didn't she?" Irielle asked, sitting forward in her chair and listening eagerly.

"Yes, she went with me. I lent her clothing and we tried to make her look as common as possible, covering her light hair with a scarf so that from a distance you could not tell she was Leharan. I felt sorry for her like I said before. She was so young and sweet and already engaged to Chronus. I thought it couldn't hurt for her to go out and enjoy herself a little. Even then you could tell he was cruel. There was always something in his eyes."

"And no one ever knew?"

"No, we told the villagers that she was the princess's maid and the royals were always so busy with themselves they never noticed. Well, that night she met a young man. He was a quiet one, from one of the farms in the outer valley and I didn't really know anything about him other than he was very polite and very shy around people. Oh, and he had the strangest eyes. Every time you saw him they looked different."

"Did Ursula..."

"I do not know the details of what happened, it was none of my concern. I only know that the boy adored her. Many nights she would sneak out of the palace and change into my clothes so that she could go to meet him."

"What happened between them? Did they just stop seeing each other when she had to marry Chronus?"

Raienna frowned, her face folding into heavy lines. "I would have sworn that she was going to run away with him but she didn't. She married Chronus as she was told and the boy, well, no one really knows what happened to him after that."

"Really? Who was he, though?" Irielle wanted to know.

"Just a villager," Raienna shrugged, once again avoiding Irielle's gaze.

"You're lying!" Irielle accused her. "There is something else. What is it?"

"Since no one knows what happened to him, most of us assumed that he was dead after a time. I should not like to speak ill of the dead."

"Oh, now you must tell me. Please, Raienna. It is not speaking ill of the dead to simply tell me something about them."

She hesitated. "It would be if it were not true and I can't say for sure. But the young man, it was rumored that he didn't have a proper father."

Irielle tilted her head to one side. "I don't understand."

"He was without a father."

Irielle lifted her hands and gave the old lady a blank look. "Was his father dead?"

The old woman sighed. "No. The mother.... she was raped."

# 27

Carushka paced the deck of the ship nervously reminding me of a caged beast. He often paused, sniffing the air, his yellow eyes searching around him but it seemed to me that he was looking farther than the inky seas, seeing something in his past. The others kept their distance from him, the Guard constantly watching him in shifts, their swords always ready. Carushka would ignore them, staying by himself and not speaking to anyone, just pacing over and over. He seemed to grow more and more restless as we traveled further and I thought perhaps he did not trust me to uphold my end of our agreement. Which I could not blame him for since I had no intention of keeping most of my promises.

"I meant it when I said no harm would come to you," I said to him finally when his nervous prowling was beginning to wear on all of us. At least that much I had every intention of honoring.

He stopped and focused his inhuman gaze on me. "You will forgive me if I have my doubts."

I arched an eyebrow. "If you think that you have doubts try and imagine how I feel."

He laughed bitterly. "Yes, it must be difficult to attempt to trust our kind. After all, we are not to be trusted."

I looked out over the water with him. "You seem sad, like you are remembering something."

"When you have seen as much as I have, there are too many memories."

"I want to ask you something," I began.

"About your mother? I have already told you that I have no answers for you concerning that."

"Not about my mother. About the Solvrei."

Carushka's eyes widened slightly and a shadow passed over his face. He practically sneered at me contemptuously, "What do you know of that?"

"Not very much. Legends of the Tahitians and the ancient stories."

"There is a reason you ask. What is it?"

I shook my head. "I will not give you my reason."

"So, it is more than mere curiosity? Interesting but foolish. There is no Solvrei. Whatever you think you know is a lie and you would be wise to stray from those prophecies," the beast warned.

"Why is that? The Tahitians speak of a man who will unite the elements. One who will save Imbria."

Carushka seemed to bristle with anger and Brogan took a step closer to us. I lifted a palm for him to remain where he was while Carushka snarled at me, "Think about it, Water Queen. The Solvrei will save Imbria from what? From whom? From your silly Fire King? A worthy assassin could end that man's life in a matter of minutes. No, the legends of the Solvrei speak of a much greater enemy than that. They also speak of death. You hear the diluted tales from the Tahitians, repeated by old men as charming bedtime stories. What the legend really was involves things you should pray that you do not see in your lifetime. It would be the end of the Keepers, the end of the four realms, the end of the Fomor, the end of all of us."

"But the legend says that the Solvrei can save us," I argued.

"True. He can, but will he? That is what the Tahitians have forgotten, Water Queen. The prophecy of the Solvrei is the choice between good and evil. He is the one with the ability to choose what this world becomes. What if he does not make the choice you wish for?"

"They say he is the son of a god who wanted to help the mortals. If that were true, then why would he turn on them?"

Carushka made a sound that was like a growl deep in his throat. "I will tell you a secret, Water Queen, and then I am done with this discussion. The gods want to help only themselves and men are inherently selfish."

"But the-"

"I said that I was done! Now get away from me, I have not fed for some time and even the likes of you are beginning to seem edible." He stomped away from me and resumed his incessant pacing. I sighed and went to sit beside Damian near the helm.

"I gather that conversation did not go as you had planned," Damian remarked.

I folded my arms across my chest and glared at the ancient Fomor. "There are so many things that he knows and yet he won't tell me anything."

"You are his enemy, Orabelle. It would not be wise of him to tell you all that he knows for then you would have no more use for him," Damian pointed out.

I narrowed my eyes. "I would swear that you were born for this, Damian."

"I am not sure what you mean."

I waved a hand at Carushka. "This. All of it. Him, me, war, strategy. Your ability to think like your enemies, to reason. It's really quite annoying."

"I would have thought it would be helpful," he said with a smile, knowing that I was being petulant but at the same time telling him how much I needed him.

"It is. But it is also annoying."

"You are not always the most pleasant woman to deal with, either. So I suppose it is good that we must deal with each other for who else could?"

I couldn't help but smile back at him and as I looked up I saw Carushka watching me. I continued to smile and he turned away, his eyes again searching the nothing that surrounded us.

# 28

Blaise stared at the fire that burned brightly in the hearth. He watched as the flames swelled and shrank, devouring the wood that fed them. He was preparing to go to Kymir soon and could not help the anticipation that churned in his stomach. He wondered if Orabelle would finally consent to the marriage, or if she had found some other way to postpone it. He had waited for a message from Chronus as to the progression of their plan but none had come which increased his anxiety. He had learned nothing of the girl who had disappeared with the Leharans the night they had left or why they had taken her and his frustration grew daily. He had been a soldier before he was made king, a man of action and strategy and he disliked being forced to wait, put at the disposal of others.

On the floor across the room the boy, Akrin, sat playing with a horse carved from wood. He galloped it across the stones in front of him, back and forth, back and forth. The toy had reminded Blaise of one that his father had carved for him as a boy. He recalled doing the same thing as a child, rocking the toy back and forth on the dirty floor while his mother had watched him, a frown pulling down at her lips. He glanced up at her and grinned, displaying the horse proudly.

"Look! He can gallop and ride, just like father when he rides with the army!" Blaise had exclaimed, still basking in the delight of having received this recent gift. His father was a Verucan soldier and was often away but on every return he would bestow a new gift upon his sons that he had carved for them. Blaise kept the figurines arranged in a careful line along the edge of the window in the room he shared with his younger brother, Bastion.

"Your father should be doing better things with his time than carving silly figurines," his mother had snapped, snatching her skirts in one hand so that she could bend over and pluck the wooden horse from his grasp. "And you have better things to do as well. Go and fetch your books, you can practice your reading since you have so much time to waste. Someone must do something to better this family and your father is practically useless and we both know your brother will be no help to anyone."

"But-" he had begun to protest and she had snapped the horse in two like a twig. Blaise was crushed, his lip trembling as he stared at the broken pieces.

"If you do not obey me I will go to your room and inflict the same fate upon your other silly toys," she had practically shouted. Her eyes flashed angrily and her lips were pressed into a thin line that dared him to defy her. He was not afraid of her or her wrath and she knew it, and so her rage would not be directed at him, but at the innocent soul of his younger sibling. She knew that he could not stand to see his brother in pain and so that had become his punishment. He turned and hurried to where the stack of books sat upon the shabby second-hand table, picking one up and sniffing back his tears as he opened it and began to read.

"Out loud!" his mother insisted. Blaise threw a quick look at Bastion who sat in the corner watching. Bastion loved when Blaise read to him, but then Bastion loved everything that

Blaise did. Bastion had been born with what his mother called a defect. He was slower to learn than other children his age, and his muscles were soft and weak, his feet twisted in so that he shambled across the floor when he walked much to their mother's embarrassment. He would never run or be strong and he needed constant caring for. Because of this she had no use for him at all and therefore no love. She treated him as an unwanted burden she had been saddled with, like a cruel joke their father had played on her giving her such a son. She had been a bitter woman, angry at their place in life and angry at her husband for not doing better to elevate their status. She swore that generations before her family had been royalty in Veruca, and that her great grandmother had been a princess who had foolishly relinquished it all and abdicated her place in line to the throne by falling in love with a commoner. Whenever they would see the Verucan castle in the distance she would frown at it, deep lines furrowing between her brows, and exclaim how it should be she who was living there, surrounded by servants and adoration. Then she would become even harsher with the children, insisting that they be the best at everything, that they were more than common folk. Their father would try to coax her into softening, but she would have none of it. Poor little Bastion was merely a reminder to her of her failures. Blaise was the only one who held any hope for her and therefore he was the constant beacon for her cruel affections. Every day the burden of her misery and therefore the misery of the rest of the family fell on his shoulders. It was up to him to make things better, to become someone who would live up to her lofty ambition. Blaise remembered wiping away the last tears and giving his little brother an easy grin to let him know everything would be fine before clearing his throat and beginning to read. Bastion had beamed back at him, his heart too simple and loving to understand or care what else was going on. All he cared about was that his big brother was smiling at him.

Akrin broke through his reverie, asking if he could get a wooden man to ride the horse. Blaise nodded curtly and waited until the child began to play on his own again before settling back into his thoughts. He had never been comfortable around children after Bastion. Perhaps he just didn't want to relive the memories they conjured or be reminded of what had happened to his family. Even now as the faded moments began to crawl back he refused to see them and shoved them away into the dark corners of his heart. He would have preferred to pawn the boy off on someone else or have a servant watch over him, but until he could surmise the importance of Akrin's older sister he wanted to keep him close and gain his trust.

Blaise contemplated the idea of taking the boy with him to Kymir. Akrin would be able to identify his sister if she were there but on the other hand the child's presence could provoke Orabelle and show her that Blaise had an interest in the missing girl and the incident on the beach that night. That was not something he wanted brought up at the Council. Not just because it involved a dead child but also because he knew the smug look Chronus would give him. No, he would leave the boy in Veruca and tolerate him a while longer until he decided his usefulness.

One of his soldiers appeared in the doorway. "Sire, everything is prepared for the journey to Council."

"Very good. Does everyone understand their orders? I cannot afford any mistakes. The timing must be perfect," Blaise insisted in a firm voice.

"Yes, of course."

"You will be leading the second unit."

The man bowed deeply. "Yes, Sire. I will not fail you. We will be ready to attack at your signal."

Blaise nodded. "It is imperative that you not be seen by anyone. Your rendezvous point has been laid out carefully. There is no room for error."

The man bowed deeply and Blaise dismissed him. He was not going to be made a fool of again. If Chronus could not deliver Orabelle than he would take her from Kymir forcibly. His plan depended on his having her. She was the only true obstacle to his conquering of Imbria. The others were weaklings, they would fall easily before him, especially with his command of the Fomor Tribe. Astraeus's kingdom was already slipping into turmoil and the Samirrans' hopes depended on Maialen. With Chronus out of the way and Orabelle on his side, the Earth Queen posed no threat to him. And Chronus had dug his own grave long ago.

Blaise smiled to himself. He was toying with the idea of allowing Orabelle to kill her own father. It was somewhat poetic and knowing her temper he was convinced that she could be driven to do it easily. Perhaps it would bring them closer together. Though an assassin would be less complicated. He would have to decide soon on that course of action. As for the Water Queen, he had seen her weakness when he had found her cowering in the tunnels smeared with blood and terrified. He would show her how powerful he was, how he could bend the beasts from below to his will and control them. The blood-drinkers were becoming quite useful to him and he was pleased that he had agreed to the pact with them. Once he was ruler of all of Imbria, he would rule them as well. His own personal army of demons. Then there would be no more ridiculous Council, no more arguing or debating. He would be able to take action, to do as he wished unquestioned by the inept fools he was now forced to defer to. They would all bow to him.

"What are you laughing at?" Akrin asked, petting the wooden horse nervously.

"Nothing. Just a joke that I am playing," Blaise told him.

"I want to play too," Akrin insisted, his eyes brightening.

"We shall see about that," Blaise said, laughing again.

Akrin frowned sullenly. "Was that man your Guardian?"

"No. My Guardian is dead."

"Good. Then I can be your Guardian someday."

Blaise raised his eyebrows and stared down at the boy. "That is quite a responsibility. You will have to prove yourself very useful to me if you strive to hold that position."

# 29

The people of Kymir moved about their forests with an excited energy. The Council meeting and therefore the weddings were just a few days away and inhabitants of the other kingdoms had already begun arriving. Everyone bustled about making preparations, whispering to each other furtively and trying to guess what was going to happen. So much was going on. The rumors had spread that Astraeus had wanted to back out of the marriage to Maialen, though that was not nearly so talked about as the union between Orabelle and Blaise. There was also the lifting of the Tahitian's banishment to celebrate. People wondered if they would come and what they would do. Maialen wondered herself. To her, Damian seemed so violent and distant. Were they all like him?

Maialen twisted the emerald that hung from her neck, feeling the warm power of earth comfort her. The tightness in her shoulders eased slightly. All around her, people were gathering winter blossoms and tying the trees with ribbons. The air was cold and dry but no one seemed to notice as they bundled into their winter clothes and went on happily decorating. Her eyes moved to where Gideon stood, staring out into the forest. His arm still hung limply at his side and she felt a pang of sorrow for him. He had gotten the wound saving her life and although the Tahitian woman had healed him, he was no longer able to fight. What did a Guardian do that could no longer protect the one he guarded? Maialen didn't know but she refused to give him up. He would remain her Guardian for as long as they were both living.

A thin figure draped in black approached her. "Earth Queen! Are you here to admire the preparations?"

"Hello, Damek," Maialen answered without enthusiasm.

"Are you not looking forward to the upcoming festivities?" he asked, a sycophantic smile plastered on his face. His dark brown hair languished over his eyes but she could still feel them watching her.

She shrugged and looked around. "Should I be?"

"Considering that it will be your wedding, I should say yes. Your father has gone to a lot of trouble and expense for this day, your highness, it would be proper of you to show some gratitude," Damek lectured.

"You're always thinking of father, aren't you? I suppose you're right. I am being selfish. I just feel that there is a dark cloud hanging over everything these days. It is hard to feel happy when there are so many bad things happening."

"You are the Queen now, Maialen. Even if you are not happy, you should not walk around with that kind of morose look."

Maialen sighed and tried to smile. "Is that better?"

Damek gave her an exasperated look and started to bow away. Maialen stopped him, taking his spindly wrist in her hand.

"Damek, where were you coming from, just now?" she asked him, looking in the direction he had approached from. Behind the line of trees was the path that led to the tangle of growth where Tal had died. Maialen had forbidden anyone to go there.

"Me?" he asked in surprise. "I have been busy all morning with the festivities."

She gave him a stern look. "That is not an answer, Damek. You know I have forbidden anyone from entering those gardens. "

"I don't know what you are talking about, your highness," he insisted, his eyes darting around the clearing. "Ahh! There is your father! Chronus!"

Maialen glared at the man but he seemed not to notice as he bowed to her father, his eyes shining as the older man acknowledged him. "Damek, how are things proceeding?"

"Things are going marvelously. Everything will be ready as planned," Damek assured him. He glanced back at Maialen. "I have much more to do so I will take my leave of you now."

"Such a strange little man," Loagaire commented, twirling a strand of coppery hair around her finger.

"Loagaire," Maialen inclined her head slightly, noticing the fine shimmering golden cloth and modern cut of her gown which was no doubt a gift from their father. "I did not see you there, my apologies."

"She has come to attend the wedding," Chronus said.

"And to see what your wicked sister does, of course," Loagaire added, her full lips pulling into a smile. She was watching Maialen from underneath her gilded eyelashes. "I think that most of Imbria will come for that reason alone!"

Maialen looked at the ground and sighed heavily. "Yes, I suppose you are right."

"Dearest." Chronus put his arms around his daughter, hugging her sympathetically. "Do not worry. I will take care of you, no matter what Orabelle does."

Maialen nodded and felt tears sting her eyes. Everything was changing so quickly. Orabelle, who had once been her loving sister, was now a stranger full of secrets. Gideon had become a walking shadow. Her fiancé didn't really want her, he had to be bribed to take her. Her mother had a child with another man. So many awful things were happening and the only one who had remained constant was her father. She hugged him back, the solid strength of him comforting her.

"There now," he said, setting her back from him. "That is better, dear. You should be enjoying this time. Leave the worrying to me. "

Loagaire reached over and petted her hair. "I am here for you too now, Maialen."

"Thank you," Maialen whispered. "I think I will go back to my rooms now and lie down before everything begins."

She took her leave and threaded her way through the crowds, Gideon trailing behind her. They watched her leave, Loagaire running her fingers up and down Chronus's arm.

"It is a shame to see her so sad," she said to him.

Chronus stilled her hand. "Yes, but it is necessary. All of that sadness will be Orabelle's fault, then Maialen will be free from her."

"I still think it is a shame. It is always hard to watch the loss of innocence," Loagaire said, licking her lips.

"I doubt you ever had any innocence," Chronus replied, his words laced with condescension. Loagaire bristled inwardly but continued to stroke his arm, looking placid.

"Perhaps not," she agreed. "So are you going to tell me what you have planned? I know that look and you are up to something, aren't you?"

"Do not ever presume to know what I am thinking."

Loagaire laughed to hide her anger. "Of course not. I only meant that a man such as yourself is always prepared."

"You will see soon enough."

He walked away then, expecting in his arrogance that she would follow behind him. She watched him go, and once he was far enough away she let out the breath she had not realized she had been holding. She felt a pang of sympathy for Maialen for having such a man as a father. Why was it that parents were always inflicting their own miseries upon their children? They never seemed content to wallow in their own suffering, it always carried on to the next ones who would lift it like a banner hoisted into battle. Her thoughts skipped to her cousin and his ambition for power and rage, a gift from his mother, Maritka, that he could never relinquish. Blaise had been different before Maritka had sunk her teeth into him and distorted the man he could have been. Loagaire remembered that night, the last time she had seen the hateful woman, her cold body finally stilled and her red hair spread around her like blood from a wound. Blaise was staring down at her in horror. Loagaire had reached for him, taken his hand, and he had turned to her with a look of such abject terror that she had flinched and let go of him.

"What have you done?" she had whispered. He continued to stare at her with the raw torment of his soul exposed, his lips twitching as if he were going to say something but no words formed. He had looked so young then, still so innocent in his grief, the lines of his face unformed.

"Bastion..." he began, shaking his head. The shaking seemed to consume his whole body and he had fallen to the ground beside the corpse of his mother, pressing his palms to his eyes to try to stop the tears. He had never told her exactly what had happened that night but she suspected she knew. Bastion's absence hung heavy and silent in the air and Loagaire realized she had always feared that this day would come. She had waited until her cousin's tears has passed and then she had gotten a blanket and wrapped it around the cold body of her aunt.

"Blaise. Blaise look at me," Loagaire had coaxed. "We cannot leave her here like this. If your father finds her... they will know. We have to do something."

He looked over at the shrouded corpse and anger flashed through his amber eyes. "I know exactly what to do with her."

# 30

As we sailed into the harbor the tall masts of Leharan ships littered the skyline. Beyond that the treetops of Kymir rose into the air, their limbs nearly bare from the onslaught of coming winter. Carushka stood on the deck beside me, Damian on the other side of him. I was breathing through my mouth, a practice that had quickly become habit in the small quarters of the ship. The blood-drinker's smell had seemed to dissipate some during the journey and I wondered if it was because he had not fed from a human for some time. Or perhaps, I thought with a shudder, I was just accustomed to it.

"Are you sure that this is the course you wish to take?" Carushka asked, turning his yellow gaze to me. His strange voice was also becoming familiar to me. I noticed that his long hair was combed and plaited neatly and his grey skin scrubbed clean. It startled me to notice these little habits of grooming in such a beastly façade. He was a lesson in dichotomies, that much was certain.

"What other choice do I have? Blaise must be stopped," I answered him.

"Would you have gone to these lengths to stop him if you were not being forced to marry him?"

I looked up at him in surprise. He lifted one hand and waved it to include all of us, saying, "We are all selfish creatures, Queen. I am merely asking you to be honest with yourself."

"Yes, I would still stop him," I stated firmly.

Carushka watched me intently with unsettling intelligence. "I often wonder what it would be like to feel things like righteousness. Even before, that was not something I recall having felt in my lifetime."

"Is that what I feel? Sometimes it just feels like a great burden," I confessed.

"And yet you continue on with your path, even though it is burdensome to you."

"You also continue on even though you hate your existence. Perhaps that is just our nature, Carushka."

His yellow eyes widened slightly. "Those things are not the same, Queen."

I shook my head. "I know that. And yet, there are parts of myself that frighten me. I have a capacity for evil, for hate and sometimes I think that it would be easy to get lost there in the darker parts of myself."

"You hate the Fire King," Carushka began, "but you hate him because of love. He took someone from you that you cared for. If this had not happened perhaps you would not hate him. We, what I am, we do not hate for the sake of love. We hate simply because we are."

"Blaise is a vile person and he deserves my hate a thousand times over for the things he has done. I will do what is right, to protect others as well as to avenge myself," I vowed.

"But what is right is only right because you deem it so. Do not forget that no one begins the journey to being wrong with that intention. You are a very interesting woman, Orabelle. I am glad to have met you." Carushka spoke softly.

I lifted my eyebrow. "You are actually glad? Or just using the expression?"

"I am not sure. Perhaps it just an alleviation from the boredom of centuries. But now I think I will go below deck and wait so that I am not seen. Good luck to you, Queen." He bowed low, his plaited hair swinging over his shoulder and I inclined my head in return before he stalked away to go below deck. I watched the crew shrink away from him involuntarily. It must have been difficult for them to be in close quarters with such a monster and yet they had never complained. Even the grizzled captain who she thought would at some point raise concerns had accepted their passenger with as much grace as could be expected.

Damian leaned over the rail, pointing. "Look, there is a flag of Tahitia on that ship! So they have come."

"You can be very proud of what you have done for your people, Damian," I said to him, grateful that there was at least one thing to be happy for on this day.

"I am proud, yes, but now is not the time to be sentimental. We are about to walk into the snake's nest as you call it."

I took a deep breath to soothe my nerves. "Yes, we are. I will find Maialen and the others and denounce Blaise as soon as they are all there to hear it."

We pulled against the pier to disembark and were met by throngs of people who had anxiously awaited our arrival. The rest of the Guard was there waiting, led by Colwyn who gave me a brief update on life back on Lehar. He seemed nervous and the usual inappropriate warmth of his greeting was absent but I had no time to dwell on his sentiments that day. He led us through the crowd and into the city where we soon reached the clearing which was overflowing with revelers. Bright colored ribbons streamed from the trees and candles in tiny votives dripped from the leafless branches. It was a beautiful setting and I only hoped that Maialen would not hate me too much for ruining it. I glanced over the faces around me searching for her and could not find her in the crowd. A platform had been erected at one end of the clearing, just like at the last festival. It was draped with flowers and vines. Beside it stood Blaise and Astraeus who seemed to be ignoring each other, along with Favian and Gideon, whose heads were bent in conversation. I still could not see Maialen, though she must be close by. I began to squeeze through the crowd towards the stage. As I approached Chronus stepped onto the platform. I stopped short and waited to hear what he would say.

"People of Imbria!" his voice boomed across the clearing. A hush fell and people herded towards the stage to get a better look. I was pressed forward by the crush of bodies. "We thank you all for gathering with us today for this joyous celebration!"

A cheer went through the crowd and Chronus smiled benevolently, gesturing for them to quiet down. "However, there is another matter that has come to my attention that I fear cannot wait!"

I felt a knot forming in my stomach. What was he doing? What matter? People were whispering furtively to each other and Maialen was still nowhere to be seen. I met Blaise's eyes and his gaze burned through me. I held his stare, noticing the tightness in his jaw and the flash of annoyance in his amber eyes. So he had no idea what was happening either.

"Though it breaks my heart to say this to you, people of Imbria, I am afraid there is a traitor among us!" Chronus announced. "There is one among us who has made a pact with evil!"

The knot in my stomach churned and I gasped. My eyes flew from Blaise to Chronus and back to Blaise and I could see the fury rise in the younger man's face. I stood numbly, trying to piece together what was happening. Chronus was denouncing Blaise and helping me. My throat felt dry and I swallowed hard. Could I have been wrong about him this whole time? Had he been trying to set Blaise up for this? Or was he betraying him now for some other reason? My head swam with questions and I forced myself to focus on the scene that was playing out at the platform. Blaise had his hand on the hilt of the huge broadsword he carried, lip curled in disgust as he glared hatefully at Chronus, whose voice continued to echo across the clearing.

"This traitor has made an alliance with the blood-drinkers of the Fomor! They have used them to attack us, to inspire fear and hate! They have fed them their enemies as food! They are planning to use them to destroy any that will not bow to them!" Chronus paused, looking over the crowd who stared back in collective horror. He waited, letting their anxiety increase.

"Please," I murmured. "Please, father, just say his name."

"This traitor," he said, letting his voice drop and sorrow fill his face. "Is Orabelle, the Water Queen of Lehar."

"No!" My shriek of protest filled the air. The people around me shouted and tried to move away, fleeing my presence. I shoved my way forward in the confusion.

"There she is! The traitor!" Chronus yelled. "Take her!"

"Orabelle!" I heard Damian's voice and spun around but I could not see over the press of people that were grabbing and clawing at me, tearing my dress. From the edge of the forest a group of soldiers burst into the clearing. They had been hiding in the garden, Maialen's garden. Had she known? Why was she not here? The soldiers surrounded me, keeping the crowd at bay as they pushed me towards the platform. I was lifted onto it and shoved roughly so that I stumbled to my knees. Fury bit through me like a lance and my eyes flashed pale. The soldiers backed away quickly.

"What is the meaning of this?" Blaise snarled, leaping onto the dais and shoving the men back further as they recoiled from him in fear.

"Stay out of this, boy!" Chronus warned him. "I am cleaning up your mess! Make one move to save her and you will be sorry."

Chronus twisted a handful of my hair around his wrist, jerking my head back and snatching the Pearl from the clasp around my neck with his other hand. I uttered a sharp cry and clawed at him. "How dare you! You are a liar! How could you do this?"

"Quiet!" he snarled with a callous shake of my head. "Tie her hands!"

One of the men came and wrapped a rough length of twine around my wrists. The keen of the Sirens rose over the crowd and people began to wail in fright, running from them. Damian had a man by the throat and the other members of the Guard were struggling to move past the Kymirran soldiers. Amongst the cacophony I heard a boy I didn't recognize crying my name from the edge of the chaos that surrounded the stage.

"Enough!" Chronus shouted over the clearing. "Leharans you will lay down your arms now, or your Queen shall suffer for it!"

He pulled a short whip from his belt, the kind meant for unruly horses, and unwound it with a flick of his wrist, the tip of it dangling before my face. He moved quickly and the whip slashed across my back. I swallowed a cry and looked up at him, calling my power to me. He thought I needed the Pearl but I could feel it coursing through me even without my amulet. I would kill him this night, no matter what the consequence.

"Oh, no, no, my dear," Chronus whispered in my ear. "You will stop that right now. I have this whole clearing surrounded with men. If you so much as wave a droplet of water before your face I will kill every Leharan here and every disgusting Tahitian as well. You may be powerful but you could not save them all. How many would you be willing to sacrifice for your pride? Take your punishment and accept it, it is the best thing for your people."

"Why are you doing this?" I demanded to know.

"I should think that would be rather obvious to you. Power. You have too much of it, I'm afraid, and I cannot allow that imbalance to occur. Look what it has done to you."

"You are not a Keeper and you are not a god! You are a weak old man!" I said, spitting at his face. He struck me hard, the heavy gold cuff hitting my jaw and knocking me sideways.

Damian let out a cry of rage at my abuse and began pushing people out of his way.

"Stop there, Tahitian!" Chronus ordered with another flick of his wrist. This time the whip slashed across my right arm, biting through the skin. "Every step you take I will strike her again!"

"Chronus, stop this! What are you doing?" Irielle was now at the edge of the platform, her expression horrified. "You have no authority here to make such accusations or to carry out punishment!"

Astraeus caught her wrist trying to pull her away. "Mother, please, stay out of this! We need to leave-"

"I will not!" Irielle cried, shoving his hand off. She stomped onto the stage, her impeccably groomed hair beginning to come loose from the pins that held it. "Chronus you have no right!"

"Do not tell me what is right! She is my daughter and I will punish her as I see fit!" he yelled, bringing the whip down again. It tore open the skin across my back and I writhed in agony, biting my lip hard enough to taste blood to keep from crying out. I would never give him the satisfaction. He lifted his arm again and Blaise stepped forward, sparks dancing in the air and along the whip so that Chronus was forced to toss it away from his burning hand. He seethed at Blaise. "You will be sorry for that mistake, boy!"

"I'm right here, old man," Blaise taunted back, his easy grin playing on his mouth as he flexed his fingers, drawing his power.

"She is not your daughter, Chronus!" Irielle flung the words out. "And you know it! I order you to stop this at once!"

Another wave went through the crowd at Irielle's words. Chronus whirled on her. "What did you say?"

"You heard me, Chronus. She is not your daughter and you know it. You have always known."

I struggled to my knees, ignoring the pain. "What does she mean?"

Irielle looked past him to where I knelt. "Orabelle, I am sorry, he is not your father."

I felt the blood rush to my head and I closed my eyes to keep from fainting. He was not my father. Not my father. Not my father. The words repeated over and over in my mind. I finally opened my eyes. "You knew this?" I asked him.

"You are the bastard offspring of your whore mother! You are no daughter of mine! And now you have brought another seed of evil into this world!" Chronus turned to Blaise, his eyes wild and his finger pointing accusingly at me, "She has given birth to a child in secret! There is no end to her treachery! And you foolishly protect her? We should burn her while we have the chance!"

Blaise stared at me, his face going pale under his ruddy tan. "Is it true?"

"You dare to look at me like that?" I challenged him. "I never belonged to you! I was never yours!"

Chronus shouted to Blaise, spittle running down his chin, "Kill her while you can, boy. She has twisted your mind. She is the spawn of evil!"

"You are only too correct, Chronus," a strange voice rose from the darkness behind the platform. The smell of decay filled the air and I saw the yellow gleam of his eyes. Carushka.

Chronus spun around, "What are you doing here? Where are the soldiers that were protecting that area?"

"Dead, I am afraid. Along with another group that I had sniffed out along the way. Verucan, by the taste of them," Carushka said, moving silently through the darkness so that his voice carried from several places as he stayed in shadow. Blaise backed away and off of the platform, his amber eyes still fixed on me, burning with rage.

"Have you come to protect your witch?" Chronus demanded. "Proof that she is their ally! They have come to her rescue, killing more of our people!"

"You promised me that she would not be harmed," Carushka said, an edge of anger in his voice.

"Promised you..." Irielle repeated, incredulous. "Chronus, you couldn't have."

"He is lying! Trying to twist things around to save her!" Chronus insisted.

"You humans, so full of lies, and yet you accuse me? We are the most honest of all the beings on Imbria! We do not hide what we are. It is you, all of you, who hide from the truth!" Carushka said.

"You are the one hiding in the dark!" Chronus accused.

Carushka stepped from the shadows onto the platform. He towered above Chronus and Irielle, who nearly fell backwards, crying out at the sight of him. The people in the crowd began to flee, clamoring over one another in their panic. I saw Colwyn and Kaden using the panic to direct the Leharans back to the harbor. Carushka looked down at me, his eyes glowing. "She bleeds. You have broken your word and done her harm, as was expected of you, human."

"She deserves to bleed for what she has done! She is a traitor! She is a witch!"

"She is my granddaughter!" Carushka roared, silencing him.

Irielle gasped. "You! You raped the mother? It was true."

His icterine gaze swept over Irielle. "I had not known it was possible for me to have a child. Then my son was born."

"And your son was the one who fell in love with Ursula all those years ago."

Chronus's face nearly purpled with indignation as he brandished my amulet in his angry fist. "That whore laid with a beast! You have just admitted it! And her cursed offspring cannot be allowed to carry an Element! This woman is an abomination!"

"We had an understanding long ago. Then you, Chronus, in your jealousy, had my son killed." Carushka towered over him, his voice lowered menacingly. "And now you think that I will allow you to kill my granddaughter too? You think you can beat one of my own like she is your dog? That I will stand by and watch you shed her blood here before all these people? I have waited so long for this moment to come. Your insults are too many!"

He knocked the Pearl from Chronus's hand and fell on him with an evil growl, jaws snapping. Favian leapt at Carushka but the Fomor swatted him away like an insect, sending him flying. Irielle screamed and Astraeus grabbed his mother around the waist, dragging her off the stage just as Damian jumped onto it. Carushka ignored us, his attention entirely fixed on Chronus who was pinned beneath him.

"Now, finally, you are seen for what you are and you will die without redemption!" Carushka was snarling, his long fangs dripping with bloodlust. It sounded as if Chronus was arguing with him but I couldn't make out the words and I no longer cared. My father had betrayed me since the day I was born and the one who was my grandfather had manipulated me into bringing him here to kill him. Carushka would never have been able to reach Chronus in the safety of Kymir's Royal City if it hadn't been for me.

Damian cut the rope that bound my wrists and grabbed the Pearl from where it had fallen, then my Guardian hauled me to my feet and we were running to the back of the platform and leaping into the darkness of the trees. I could hear Chronus begin to scream and a spray of blood painted the tree limbs behind us and splattered my back in warm droplets

"Damian, we can't leave Carushka here, more people will die!" I struggled to pull my arm from his grasp. "They will attack him and he will fight back!"

I turned and hurried back towards the clearing, pushing through the trees just in time to see Maialen, her face white with fear and her green eyes huge. Her fingers shook as she released the string of her bow. The arrow imbedded in Carushka's thick skin and he growled in irritation, though he continued to tear at the carcass underneath him that was barely recognizable as Chronus. Maialen pulled another arrow and aimed again, letting it fly. This time it pierced his inhuman eye and he cried out in pain, turning to her.

"You. You are his spawn." He rose dripping with blood and yanked the arrow from his dark socket, tossing it to the ground as black blood oozed down his cheek. He started toward her as she stood setting her third arrow. She realized that she could not loose it in time and tossed the bow aside, holding the arrow like a dagger. I looked at the ineffectual object and the massive body of Carushka running at her. She may as well have been holding a twig.

"Maialen, run!" I shouted.

She stood where she was, calling her element. Roots shot up from the dirt snaking around Carushka's legs. He reached down and ripped them from the ground like weeds and raged towards her. I reacted instinctively, turning and grabbing Damian's short sword from its sheath at his hip. I leapt between them and swung the blade violently at Carushka as he lunged for her. His dark, foul blood gushed out of the wound I opened in his neck and he toppled forward, rolling onto his back so that he stared up at me with his one seeing eye. The sword hung from my hands, his dark blood dripping slowly from the tip of the blade.

"Orabelle," he rasped, his voice thick and choked with fluid. There were tears on my face as I watched him dying, the brightness fading from his yellow eye so that one feature of his was nearly human. His long fingers twitched and I knelt, dropping the sword, grasping his hand in mine. He was coughing, black fluid gathered at the corners of his mouth. When he spoke again his voice was thicker, heavier. "I told you before, you cannot change the nature of things. You have given me a great gift, my granddaughter."

"By killing you?" I asked, my own voice thick with conflicting emotions.

"Yes, for that. I have lived in my own hell long enough. But also for this moment. For your tears," he gasped out, his throat making wet gurgling noises. "Go now, and I shall die feeling almost as the man I once was."

I stood up from his body, settling his hand on his chest as his last breath passed across his lips. I turned and my eyes met Maialen's. She was still clutching the arrow in trembling fists, her face filled with horror. I would never forget the look that haunted her then.

"I'm sorry," I whispered to her. She backed away from me, shaking her head. I reached for her and she let out a cry of revulsion, twisting her body so that I wouldn't touch her.

"Orabelle," Damian said urgently. "We must leave."

"Maialen, please," I begged her.

"Don't come near me! You are a monster!" she screamed, her shaking hands holding the arrow in front of her to ward me off. The ground began to tremble beneath us as she called her element. Gideon was suddenly there, speaking to her softly and taking the arrow from her clutching grasp.

"Get out of here before anyone else dies," the big woodsman said to Damian.

"Orabelle, we must go now!" Damian grabbed my hand and dragged me into the forest. I followed him dumbly, not seeing where we were going, only seeing the look on Maialen's face as she had backed away. I was a monster to her now, the descendent of a Fomor. I was a monster to myself. I had been born with a legacy of rape, suffering, pain and death. I was part of all that was evil in the world.

"Over here!" Kaden's voice called and I shook myself from the darkness of my thoughts. We had nearly reached the ship, Damian still dragging me painfully along by my right arm, the one that bore the deep bite of the whip. Suddenly a group of men converged on the dock. Some of them wore the thick leather of the Kymirran archers and others were in the shining black armor of the Verucans. Kaden faced them alone, sword drawn and curving in wide arcs before him.

"Orabelle, stop them!" Damian ordered, dropping my arm and sprinting towards the men. I saw two more of my Guard leap from the ship, swords drawn. I breathed in the scent of the ocean and called my power to me as the men fell on each other. They were too close in combat, I would risk hurting my own men if I simply sent a wave down upon them as I had in Veruca. I needed to think of something quick.

I lifted my hands in the air and looked at the man who was slashing maniacally at Kaden. He stopped, dropping his weapon and gasping, his hands clutching at his throat. Kaden kicked him under the chin, sending him flying unconscious into the water. I moved on to the next two men who stood close enough together so that I could concentrate on them both. They both turned to look at me, their eyes bulging as I pulled the water from their bodies.

"What's happening?" someone cried out. "It's the Queen! She is doing it!"

The men fell back in fear as one by one the dried husks of their companions dropped to the ground. The voices of the Sirens filled the air with piercing wails and the last of the attackers' bravado was left on the docks as they scattered into the trees. We hurried to the ship and raced on board where I continued to concentrate on my power, the water swirling around us as I moved the vessel away from the dock. We had made a full turn when something banged against the side of the hull, the ship quaking and the smell of smoke and sulfur rising. I whirled around and there was Blaise on the shore, standing in front of his men, their flame-tipped arrows aimed at our ship. As they fired them, Blaise fed the flames so that they grew in midair to great fireballs that rained down on us. I flung my arm over my head and a rainbow of water arched over the ship, the fire sizzling and dying harmlessly against it. I heard Blaise shout with fury and another volley of arrows was fired. I held the cover of water but I could feel my strength ebbing.

"Get us out of here!" Damian was yelling. "The Queen is injured, she cannot hold them off forever!"

On the shore, Blaise was once again giving the signal for them to fire. He would know I was weakening. "Arrogant bastard," I whispered. I used the last of my strength to push the arch of water away from us and towards the dock so that it bore down on them. As I had hoped, the men fell back, dropping their unused arrows and hastily fleeing. The last thing I heard as we moved out of their reach was Blaise screaming my name, his voice burning with rage.

# 31

Maialen knelt beside the gored remains of her father, her eyes fixed on the jagged tear at his throat. She had heard him screaming as he died and she had been unable to reach him in time to save him. He was already gone when she had pushed her way through the fleeing crowds, ripped to pieces by the beast.

"Maialen," Gideon said gently, touching her shoulder with his left hand. His right arm still hung uselessly at his side and she looked up at him, at the long scar that was visible above the collar of his shirt. He knew what she was looking at and he turned away, his face reddening. As she watched him she felt hate rising inside of her. Those creatures had taken everything from her. They had ruined Gideon, murdered her father, and now they had claimed her sister as one of their own.

She stood up, moving quickly, and lifted Damian's sword that Orabelle had left lying on the ground beside the great monster. She gripped the hilt with both hands and plunged it down into the beast's body as hard as she could, then yanked it out and stabbed at it again, hacking at it mercilessly.

"Maialen, stop!" Gideon was trying to take the sword from her.

"No!" she cried. "I hate this thing! I hate it! I hate it!"

A boy standing near them made a gesture as if to stop her and Maialen screamed at him to get back. It barely crossed her mind how ridiculous it was that this boy stood there grasping a bunch of wilted flowers while black blood splattered his clothing.

"I will kill every Fomori in Imbria!" she shrieked wildly.

"Maialen, please," Irielle's soft voice spoke. The older woman reached for the sword, her face full of motherly concern. She took it from Maialen, passing it to Gideon so that she could wrap her arms around the Earth Queen.

"Why is this all happening?" Maialen sobbed as she let Irielle hold her.

"I do not know, my dear. I am so sorry," Irielle said.

Maialen pulled away so that she could look her in the eye. "How did you know? About Orabelle's father?"

"My husband was going through old records in the great library. There were things that didn't make sense so I talked to some of the elders and I pieced it together."

"How long have you known?"

"I just discovered it before we were to come here," Irielle explained. "There was no time to tell Orabelle or to find out what really happened back then."

Maialen looked at the bodies. "And now they're all dead and we shall never know."

Blaise suddenly came crashing furiously into the clearing, the soldiers he had taken following him at a distance, trying to keep out of the path of his rage. He strode up to Maialen, brushing Irielle aside rudely.

"You have some explaining to do, Earth Queen, and you had better start now!" he roared.

Gideon moved between the Fire King and the women.

"Blaise, please, she has been through enough for now," Irielle began, trying to calm him.

"This does not concern you, Irielle! Though I have questions for you too! I want to know what the hell is going on here!" Blaise seethed.

"I-I don't know any more than you," Maialen told him.

"You know something! Why weren't you here? Where were you? Did you know this would happen? Did you know that Orabelle was conspiring with those things?" he demanded, pointing at Carushka's body.

"No! I swear I knew nothing! I wasn't here because Loagaire said she needed to talk with me alone, somewhere we wouldn't be interrupted."

"Loagaire? And where is she?" Blaise asked, looking around. Of course his cousin was involved in this somehow.

"I don't know. I left her in my rooms when I heard the noise. She tried to stop me from coming but when I heard father screaming..." her voice trailed off and her eyes lost focus as she was haunted by the memory of Chronus's death.

"Blaise, please," Irielle begged. "That is enough."

"Look around you, Irielle! Now is not the time for hugs and tea parties! Chronus is dead! The leader of the Fomori is dead! We have no idea what is happening with Orabelle, and she is a Keeper. Does that not worry you at all?!" Blaise shouted at her.

Astraeus moved to stand beside his mother, taking her hand. "He is right, mother. Things cannot wait, there are matters that must be discussed now. Maialen, I am sorry for what has happened to you today but I suggest that we go to the Council chamber immediately and try to deal with this situation."

"Go then," Irielle said, nodding. "I will take care of this ... mess."

Maialen followed the men into the chamber and sat blindly in her chair, staring at the smooth marble of the table. Her head ached and she could not swallow the knot in her throat. She had no idea how she supposed to sit calmly and have a reasonable discussion when she had just seen her family destroyed in front of her. Astraeus sat beside her but made no move to touch or comfort her. She could not blame him. Favian and Gideon stood behind them and Blaise settled into the chair on the other side of the table, his amber eyes still burning hotly.

"Someone needs to start talking," he said, looking pointedly at Maialen.

"I told you before, I don't know anything," Maialen responded wearily. "None of you have been forthright with me. Everyone has kept me in the dark. All I know is that the last time I saw my sister she said that there was something about you, Blaise, that was terrible but she wouldn't tell me what. She kept saying for my sake she could not tell me yet. So perhaps you should be the one to start talking."

"It is no secret that Orabelle did not want to be my wife. I am sure that she was merely throwing out vague accusations to create sympathy," Blaise dismissed the idea with a wave of his hand. "The problem now is what she will do next. You do understand that we cannot allow her to continue to rule Lehar. She is the descendent of the blood-drinkers. She has made allies of them-"

"I do not believe that she would do that!" Maialen interrupted, her voice wavering.

Astraeus sighed. "I know you do not want to believe it but we all saw the evidence of it. She knew the beast. Even if she didn't know that it was her grandfather, she knew it."

Maialen shook her head. "It can't -"

Astraeus brought his fist down hard on the table. "Maialen, it was my kingdom that was attacked by those things! It is my kingdom that now suffers because of it! I will not allow that act to go unpunished just because of your sentimental loyalty to your sister! She had your father killed by that beast, Maialen! Open your eyes!"

"He is right," Blaise agreed. "And she cannot be allowed to continue. We need to take Lehar and her element from her."

"You will kill her," Maialen stated flatly.

"I do not wish her dead but we must protect Imbria."

Gideon spoke from behind them. "And who will control her element?"

"The Council as a whole can rule over her kingdom until that is decided," Blaise answered.

Favian shook his head, looking worriedly at his King. "That has never been done, Astraeus. You don't know if you can do it and if you cannot then there will be an element uncontrolled."

"I appreciate your concern, Guardian," Blaise sneered at the Samirran, "but you are not a member of this council."

"He has a valid point," Astraeus said. Though he would never say it aloud, he knew what Favian was concerned about. The Air King was having a hard time controlling his own element, how could he take on another? And Maialen had not even gone a full year as Earth Queen. Which left the balance of power tipped unevenly in Blaise's direction, something that Astraeus was not entirely averse to. It would leave the weight of responsibility on the Fire King and not on him, so that he could still focus on his own kingdom of Samirra.

There was a loud wail as the door of the chamber burst open and Damek rushed in, his dark eyes puffy and red and his face blotched. "What have you done?" he cried in anguish, moving towards the table. Gideon and Favian quickly intercepted him, though he tried vainly to push his way past them.

"Damek, please," Maialen began, rising from her seat, the knot returning to her throat as she watched the misery of the other man.

"What have you done!" he wailed again. "What have you let her do? Orabelle did this and none of you did anything to stop her!"

"That's enough," Gideon said firmly, taking him by the arm and steering him towards the door.

"Let go of me! I want to know why you let this happen!" he screeched at Maialen. "Your father loved you! He protected you! And you will let his murder go unpunished? You will let that whore do whatever she wishes? She will destroy you all, just as she destroyed him! She is poison! A vile, evil witch! She doesn't love you, Maialen, it was your father who loved you and she has killed him! She will kill you all! Let go of me!"

Damek shoved away from Gideon and ran at Maialen, grabbing at her clothes. His face was pale and sweaty as he shook her. Favian took his arms, dragging him from the room as he shouted back, "You have to stop her, Maialen! You must do it for Chronus!"

"He is right, you know," Blaise said after he was gone. "She has to be stopped."

Astraeus was hesitant. "But how can we attack Lehar? Our losses would be great, especially now that she has the Tahitians to fight for her as well."

"We do not have to attack Lehar," Blaise told him, his brows drawn together and his eyes smoldering.

Maialen shook her head, trying to clear her thoughts. Everything was happening too fast. She needed time to think and the only thing that her mind could see right then was her father's body. She needed to grieve, to mourn, to see him buried. Not to plan the death of her sister, her last living relative. She felt overwhelmed, lost. Her father had always been there to guide her and now she was alone and left to rule a kingdom alone, forced to be allies with a man she suspected was really a monster as well. So many changes, all at once. No one was who she had thought they were.

"Please explain," Astraeus offered to Blaise.

The Fire King steepled his fingers, his intense gaze encompassing all of them. "There is one thing left in this world that Orabelle hates more than anything. And that is me. We do not have to attack Lehar. She will come to Veruca, and we will be waiting for her."

# 32

I strode quickly through the hallway, my footsteps ringing across the coralstone floor of the Leharan fortress. Each step pulled at the fresh scabs that now covered the lashes on my back and arm. Over the past few days the bruising had set in around the wounds, making me stiff and my jaw was a mottled purple. I could hear the voices of the men and women inside the room talking anxiously and I paused outside the doorway, closing my eyes.

*Tal, if you are ever with me give me strength now.* I prayed silently, wishing with every fiber of my being that he was beside me this day. But he was not and I could not afford to think too much on him now. I pushed him to the back of my mind and took a deep breath, lifting my chin and swinging open the doorway. A hush fell over the assembly as I entered and moved to take my place at the head of the table. I looked at them, my eyes searching the faces of my Guard, the noble men and women, the regents of Lehar, the lined faces of the Tahitian elders. They all stared back at me, waiting.

"Thank you for coming," I began, my voice clear and steady. "I suppose by now all of you must know why you are here, but so that there are not any misunderstandings, let me explain.

I have called you today to petition that we go to war against Veruca."

"My Queen," spoke a man to my right. He was one of our best merchants. "You are the ruler of Lehar, what do we have to do with your decision?"

"It is your lives, or the lives of those you love that may be lost. That is why I am asking you today if I may have your full support," I answered him.

"And are we going to war just because you don't agree to this marriage with the Verucan King?" another man asked.

"Is she really a blood-drinker?" someone else whispered.

A murmur went through the room and Kaden stood up, kicking his chair back. "This has gone far beyond the Queen's marriage or what stories are spun about her lineage! Her mother was the Queen Ursula and her family has a long and prestigious history on Lehar. There is no foundation to their claims, no proof of who her father was and now they are all dead and their lies and secrets dead with them. What matters is who she is now. Think on it, Leharans! She has always ruled fairly, always looked after you. She has always protected her people! I do not question my Queen or her motives, for I have seen what the alternative is! I have been to Veruca, I have seen the way these people are treated. They live in fear and in poverty. Everything they have is given to the royal castle. You, merchant, if you were forced to give nearly all of your earnings to the Queen, if you were forced to do so using the threat of being fed to beasts in a dark tunnel, would you want others to just sit by and watch? If you were forced to sit quietly and say nothing while your child was fed to monsters or slaughtered on a beach, would you question us then? If you were one of the farmers in Samirra whose family had just been ripped apart, would you not want someone to avenge you? These things are happening!"

Brogan spoke next, banging his fist on the table and glaring angrily around the room. "My comrade is right. We are the Guard, we do not lie! We are men of honor! We have seen and heard for ourselves what is true. The Fire King is the enemy, not our Queen. I was there, in the desert with the Fomori, just as I was there in Veruca. If you do not take her word, then take mine. And if that is not good enough, then you should leave this island for good!"

Several people began to nod, whispering amongst themselves. Damian also rose from his seat, though without the righteous indignation that Kaden and Brogan had shown. When he spoke, his smooth heavy voice carried the words around the room. "The King of Veruca has committed atrocities that we cannot even fathom. He has ordered the attacks on Samirra that have been happening recently and he has been offering up his own people as sacrifices. If this were not enough, they tried to force the Queen to take the blame for what he has done. Look at her face. She was beaten, whipped like a dog. Your Queen! Beaten because she could not use her power for threat that you, her people, would be harmed. She did it to save you. She was treated without honor or respect, as was the Guardian before me. The Commander of your army, of Lehar, was murdered at the order of the Fire King. He has sought to kill the best of us, to break us, to turn the others against us. And he does so for power. We are the best army on Imbria! The Fire King longs for power that belongs to us, to the Water Kingdom! We are the strength, we are the opposition and we are also the judgment! If no one else will put an end to this man, then I say that we will!"

The entire Guard roared at once and people began to nod and cheer. I looked at Damian gratefully but he was still focused on the room, his face stern. He went on, "Leharans, what we ask you today is to do what is right. If you wish to live under the rule of a tyrant, then do not condone these actions.

If you wish to live in fear, then do not support us. But for those of you to whom freedom and honor are things of value, we ask you to stand with us now. The Guard, the most elite group of soldiers on Imbria, stands by its Queen. Tahitia, who has known the injustice of these men, will fight."

The merchant who had spoken first stood up. "My Queen, you have my full support and that of all the traders."

"The family of Havari supports its Queen."

"As does the village of Tascan."

I nodded at each of them as they stood, one by one pledging their allegiance and their support, till there was no one left seated save a lone figure in the corner of the room. The person was draped in a cloak, the hood pulled down low so the face was hidden in shadow. The gathered people all turned to watch as the mysterious person slowly stood up.

"I no longer speak for my kingdom, Orabelle, but you have my support." The hood of the cloak was pushed back and a cascade of dark hair fell over Irielle's shoulder. She smoothed it back carefully, watching my face.

I raised an eyebrow at her and bowed low. "I thank you."

Irielle smiled. "Besides, it is much more interesting here!"

"We will sail for Veruca in three days. Make ready. Damian, you and Colwyn will keep me updated on what is happening," I spoke rapidly to the men, then turned back to Irielle. "May I speak with you privately?"

"Of course," she said, inclining her head and following me as we moved out of the room. I led her down to the beach, kicking off my shoes and feeling the warm sand and the cool tide caress the soles of my feet. Irielle also slipped off the sandals she wore and fell into step beside me.

"How did you get here?" I wanted to know.

"I took a rowboat from the docks along with some of your tradesmen. It was quite an exhausting effort," she said, flashing me a brief smile.

"I'm sure it was," I murmured appreciatively. "And how is my sister?"

Irielle sighed. "She is not well, I am afraid. She is having nightmares and cannot sleep at night and during the day she walks around in a daze. Her Guardian watches over her but he is no better off than she. He grieves more for his arm than for anything else. I do not think the Kymirrans will have much involvement in what happens next. You cannot count on their support but I do not believe they would join the battle against you."

"What of your son? By your being here, can I assume that Astraeus has sided with Blaise?" I asked her.

"I'm afraid my son does not make the best decisions," she admitted. "He does not value my opinion on matters such as these."

"And what exactly is your opinion, Irielle? Why have you taken my side when it can bring you nothing but grief?"

She smiled sadly, her eyes following the waves of the sea. "I never had a daughter, Orabelle, but if I had it would pain me to see them suffer as much as you have."

I followed her gaze out over the water. "You pity me?"

She shook her head. "No. I merely want you to know that at least one person in the other three kingdoms knows the difference between what is right and what is wrong. I will stand by you because you are right. Not because I feel sorry for you. Even though Astraeus believes the lies of the Fire King, I do not. I will support those who will punish him for what he has done to Samirra, despite my son's foolishness."

"I can accept that," I responded.

"There is something else you need to know. Astraeus and Maialen were married. The day after you left. I thought it best for her protection. She was so lost and he gives her someone to hold onto. It was a very quiet ceremony, only a few of us in attendance."

I bowed my head. "I should have protected her from all of this, Irielle, but I did not. I only hope that your son does a better job of it than I could."

She hesitated. "What of the child, Orabelle? I had heard rumors and then your... then Chronus said you had given birth."

"I will not speak of that," I said firmly. I felt my eyes darken and my stomach fluttered. "My child is somewhere safe and even I do not know where."

"But-" she began.

I cut her off with a wave of my hand, "No, Irielle."

She ignored me and continued, "What of the other rumors? Of the stories about this baby and his father?"

"The father is Tal."

"You know what I mean, Orabelle," she said impatiently. "People are whispering of the Solvrei."

I shrugged. "They are silly stories, that is all. There is no truth to them, lest people make them come true."

"Even a self-fulfilling prophecy is still a prophecy. You must know the influence that carries over the common people," she pointed out. "Your son, if he is what they say he is, or if he becomes what they want him to become, what does that mean for the rest of us? The stories speak of chaos, of a time of despair. Is that what we are headed for?"

I stopped walking and faced her. A chill ran icy fingers up my spine despite the midday heat from the sun as I recalled Carushka's warning to forget about the Solvrei. "Are you questioning this attack against Veruca? You think I will plunge this world into a war from which it cannot recover?"

"I do not know what to expect or what to believe anymore but I do know that what you are doing must be done. If you don't they will eventually come here for you. My son is weak, your sister is broken and in no shape to lead. Even together,

Blaise will easily entrap them. We cannot let that happen. I only ask one favor of you, Orabelle."

"I am already indebted to you enough, I should like to return a favor," I said with a smile.

"Do not let my son be killed."

I gave her a long look. "It is possible that he will not even be in Veruca. That is what I am hoping."

"He will be there. They will be waiting for you."

"Yes, you are probably right. I will do everything that I can to see that Astraeus lives," I promised.

The next days passed in a flurry of activity. The war ships were made ready, the soldiers' armor checked and rechecked, their weapons sharpened. The Tahitians had come with their tall spears and were ready to sail with us. The healers had been busy making bandages and salves for the wounded. During the day I had walked through the fort looking at the faces of those around me wondering which of them would not be returning home. Night had fallen, and I stood on the deck of my ship unable to sleep. The cool ocean breeze moved through my hair and across my skin and I closed my eyes, breathing in the scent of the sea and asking myself again if I was doing the right thing.

Damian climbed the steps slowly to join me. I looked at his tall, dark form gleaming in the moonlight and remembered the other man who used to stand beside me in that spot, offering me reassurance when I doubted myself.

"I miss him, Damian."

"He is with you still."

I raised an eyebrow. "Do you really believe that?"

"There are worse things to believe in," he replied.

"I suppose there are. Though to be honest it does not give me much comfort. I cannot see him or touch him or talk to him. What is the good of his being there?" I asked.

"It is the sense of him that should give you comfort," Damian said.

I sighed. "I need more than a sense of someone right now."

"You are doing the right thing, Orabelle. It is the only thing you can do."

"But people will die, Damian. They will die because of me and because of Blaise and because of the Kings and Queens who came before us. They will die for reasons that have nothing to do with them."

He looked up at the moon. "They will die for a purpose. That is more than most people can wish for."

"Are you afraid of dying, Damian?" I wanted to know.

He did not answer for a long time. When he finally did, his voice was wistful. "No, I am not afraid. There are many here that I would not wish to leave but there are many others that I should like to see again."

"I wish that I had your faith," I confessed quietly.

"Then have it," he answered simply. "Now, my Queen, you should rest. We leave at dawn."

I agreed and grasped his hand tightly in mine. "Try not to die before I find my faith," I said with the ghost of a smile. "I would miss you terribly."

I released him and went below to my quarters. I looked at the bed but the thought of sleep seemed absurd. Instead I went over to the dressing table and lifted the lid of the heavy silver box that sat atop it. I began to pull out the objects in it one by one, laying them out carefully. There was the dried, crumbling remnants of a white orchid from my mother's funeral. I touched the disintegrating petals with the tip of one finger, asking myself what would have happened if she had lived, or if she had stayed with my real father instead of marrying Chronus. She would not have spent years in agony, wasting away in a forgotten loft, of that much I was certain.

My fingers moved away from the flower and over the brightly colored beads of a necklace Maialen had made for me when we were children. I could not stop the memory of her haunted face from returning and I prayed that one day she would look at me the way she used to, with love and adoration and trust. The truth was that she would probably never look at anyone that way again after all that we had put her through.

I set aside a scrap of lace that had been Alita's and the cloth Damian had given me the day I met him. Underneath it there was a faded silver ribbon, its edges frayed and yellowing. Tal had given it to me. Beside it was a lock of pale hair, something that Rashana had left for me after the baby was gone. These were the only remnants that I had of what should have been my family. The entire box was filled with sad little mementos of the way life should have been. I turned away from it and looked at my armor where it shone in one corner of the room. Tal had it made for me years ago and it was beautiful, the metal so bright that it was nearly white and carved with swirling designs that reminded me of the sea. I regretted that I would not be able to go my whole life without wearing it. I could only imagine how many more regrets I would have after tomorrow.

I took the silver ribbon and wrapped it around my hand, returning the other objects to the box. I closed the lid and pushed it away then climbed onto my bed and lay there, trying to relive the day Tal had given me the little gift.

It had been raining and I had been sitting inside this very room, watching the storm through the open doorway, enjoying the dampness in the air and the soothing fall of the water. Often I would sit outside in the rain, relishing the feel of it on my skin, but the day had been a cool one and I did not want to fall sick. My mother was still alive though she no longer opened her eyes and the sight of her would have made anyone hesitant to take risks with their health.

A shadow passed by the doorway and I waited but no one came in. I stood and went over, looking out through the rain. The deck of the shipwreck in which I lived offered few hiding places and I saw him immediately. He was standing halfway up the stairs but off to one side. His back was to me and he seemed to be hesitating.

"Tal," I had called to him. "What are you doing out there?"

He had turned to me, looking uncomfortable, a small box held in his hands. He did not speak, just looked at me as the rain soaked him, running through his pale hair and down his golden skin. I had stared back at him, thinking how perfect he looked standing there like that.

"Please, come in," I said to him, moving back into the room. He nodded and followed me, stopping just inside the doorway.

"Orabelle..." he began but once again he seemed hesitant. It was so unlike him that I wondered if something was seriously wrong.

"What is it?" I demanded. "Has something happened?"

"No! No, everything is fine," he had assured me.

I breathed a sigh of relief. "Then what is wrong with you today, Tal? You are acting very strange."

"My Queen, I know that tomorrow is your birthday, your twentieth, and a very important day for you. We will be at the Council and there will be so many people around us and I thought to give you a gift, but I did not see when we would have a moment alone," he said, his eyes on the floor.

"So you have brought me my gift today instead?" I prompted him.

"Yes."

"Is that it, that box in your hand?"

"Yes."

I raised an eyebrow. "Are you going to give it to me or must I beg you for it?"

He smiled and I felt my heart warm at the sight of it. He held the little box tightly in his hands. "I wanted to give you something, but now it seems so ... insignificant. You are Queen, after all, what could I possibly give to you that you do not have?"

"Tal," I chastised him, "it is not like you to behave this way. You are not the sort of man to doubt yourself and I do not care for it. Gifts are made special because of the way they are given, it matters not how lavish they are. I will cherish anything that you have thought to give to me."

He held out the box and I took it from him, smiling. I opened it and unrolled a long, silver ribbon that was nearly the exact color of his eyes. I spread it through my fingers, whispering, "It's beautiful."

"You are beautiful."

My head whipped up at his words and I frowned at him, thinking he was teasing me. When I saw his face I stopped, my breath catching in my throat. He stepped closer to me and I looked up at him with wide eyes while he reached to touch my face gently with fingertips that were still damp with rain. He was staring at me in a way that no one ever had and I felt myself tremble beneath his gaze. He cupped my face with both hands and leaned down so that his lips brushed mine. I fell against him and the ribbon had fallen to the floor, forgotten.

# 33

Gideon paced the floor, his agitation apparent in his halted steps. He wanted to grab Astraeus and shake him till he came to his senses then he wanted to bash that fool Blaise in the face. It was not like the big woodsman to be so angry, he was usually better at controlling his temper, but the sight of Maialen's pitiful face as they badgered her over and over again had pushed him beyond his tolerance.

That morning they had buried her father, or rather what was left him, in a quiet ceremony beyond the trees, in the square of land where her mother already lay. As soon as she had turned away from the grave she had to prepare for her wedding, a shallow ceremony that was devoid of happiness. When that had ended the two kings had begun their assault on her, insisting that she come to Veruca with them. They told her that they needed to present a united front against Orabelle, that by the other elements standing together they could convince her to give up her kingdom without bloodshed. Maialen had protested and they had dragged her down into a mired bog of hypothetical queries about what the dead would have wanted her to do. Gideon had watched her face as they had told her what her father would have done and they had cleverly placed the weight of his vengeance on her shoulders. They cared nothing for the fact that Orabelle was her sister, that she loved her, that she was all Maialen had left of her family. All those cowards cared about was themselves. They feared Orabelle and so they would destroy her.

There was a tentative knock on the door to his chamber. He strode across the floor and opened it, his eyes widening slightly in surprise.

"What are you doing here?" he asked bluntly.

Loagaire moved into the room, her wild mane of hair brushing his arm. He did not feel it and his irritation rose at the reminder of his injury. She looked down at her feet and avoided his eyes, smoothing the clinging fabric of her gown, her hands purposefully following the curves of her body in a gesture meant to look demur. "Gideon, I want to speak with you about Maialen."

"Please do not play coy or timid, we both know that it is an act."

She lifted her head and the corner of her mouth tilted up in a smile. "Very well. Most men prefer their women to be a little timid but I suppose you are not most men. You have become very bitter as of late, Guardian."

She ran a long fingernail over the scar at his neck and he pushed her hand away. "I do not care to participate in whatever game you are playing now, Loagaire."

She sighed, her lips forming a pout. "You judge me too harshly."

"What is it you want? If there is nothing then please go," he said rudely.

"Go, and leave you here to wallow in your self-pity?" she retorted. "Ha! Despite the fact that you will never be the fighter you once were, you can still make yourself useful to your Queen."

Gideon felt his temper rise another notch. "If you will not leave, then I shall," he said, pushing past her for the doorway.

"You cannot let Maialen go to Veruca," she called as he passed through the doorway. He stopped abruptly, turning to face her and she laughed. "Oh, now I have your attention?"

"You are trying a patience already worn thin," Gideon warned her, shoving a hand through his hair. "Please just tell me what it is you have come here for and stop with your torments."

"You have no idea how I could torment you, Guardian," she hinted, leaning close to him, her tongue touching her bottom lip.

"I am not interested. All I care about right now is the wellbeing of my Queen."

She shrugged. "Suit yourself. Now, about the sweet little Queen, she cannot be allowed to go to Veruca. We cannot let her go."

"Why do you care?" Gideon asked suspiciously. He did not trust this woman in the least.

"I care for Maialen as if she were my own sister! I merely want to look out for her."

It was Gideon's turn to laugh. "I am not so easily duped. Speak to me honestly or peddle your lies somewhere else."

Her eyes narrowed. "Have it your way. I am afraid that my cousin would not be averse to using an opportunity to see her dead. Putting her in a battle is like throwing meat to a wolf."

Gideon felt a wave of heat pass through him. "You're saying Blaise wants Maialen dead?" he demanded, grabbing her arm.

She pried his hand off. "No! He is happy enough for now about her marrying that idiot Samirran. I am merely saying that she should not be there. I do not think he plans her death, but he is an opportunist, and one who is hungry for power. Without her, there is a chance that he will not defeat the Leharans. You cannot let her go."

"You want him to lose?" Gideon asked incredulously.

"Do you think I am completely witless?" she hissed at him. "My cousin is a tyrant. He is cruel enough in Veruca where his obscenities can remain hidden in the mountains. Think what he would be like if he controlled all the kingdoms."

"You are not the selfless kind, Loagaire. There is something else you want. Tell me," Gideon insisted, watching her face carefully.

She smiled again. "You are a clever one, Guardian. Who knew that behind all that muscle there was a quick mind? What I want out of this little war, is Veruca."

Gideon was surprised at her candid response. He had assumed that was what she was maneuvering towards but he hadn't expected her to come right out and say it. "You want Veruca."

"Yes," she said vehemently. "I want the Fire Opal and I want the kingdom. I am Blaise's next living relative. If he does not name another then everything passes to me and he is too arrogant to think that way. He does not expect to lose so he will not think to name a successor."

"Had Chronus promised you the Fire Kingdom? Is that why you aligned yourself with him?"

"Chronus promised me a kingdom, though it was not Veruca."

Gideon nodded. "Lehar. You were going to take Orabelle's place."

"Now my cousin intends to keep the Pearl and Lehar for himself. Even though it was supposed to go to me," Loagaire said angrily.

"Lehar was never intended for you," Gideon replied. "You are much more suited for the element of fire."

"Then you will help me?" she wanted to know.

"I will help my Queen. You understand that the Fire Opal is not mine to give. I am merely a Guardian."

"You are the closest to Maialen. Let's not pretend, she barely knows her new husband. In her state she is vulnerable. She can be coerced into anything. I am presenting you with a better option. The rule of one kingdom as opposed to the oppression of all of them."

"You are counting on Blaise losing to Orabelle," Gideon pointed out. "There is no guarantee that will happen."

"Do not be a fool. Orabelle is more powerful than those two combined. As long as your Queen stays out of it she will not lose. And I have just the thing to make that happen," Loagaire announced triumphantly, pulling a little packet of folded paper from her bodice. She passed it to Gideon. "It is valerian root, anise, and other herbs. I will make her a tea from it and give it to her as soon as she awakens this morning. They plan on leaving soon and she will not be able to go. My little tea will put her right back to sleep and they will be unable to awaken her. Your Queen and the other Kymirrans will stay safely here."

"I am supposed to trust you? For all I know this could be poison and everything you are saying could be lies," Gideon claimed, trying to decide whether to believe her or not.

"If I wanted to poison her, would I have told you I was doing it? I would have just put something in her tea and left it at that. I want her as an ally and it seems to me that she is desperately in need of one. I would take some of the tea myself to prove it to you but there is no time. Make your decision, Guardian. It is me or the Kings. She can stay safely here, dreaming of pretty things and bunny rabbits, or you can send her to a battle where you know you will be unable to protect her."

Gideon looked down at the brown paper packet, running his thumb over the edges. He passed it back to her. "I will trust you."

She smiled. "Wise decision, Guardian. There is one other thing."

"We have a deal, Loagaire. There will be no more added terms," Gideon said firmly.

She waved the packet in front of his face. "Of course not, it has nothing to do with this. Just a little piece of information that someone, somewhere may be interested in. Haven't you wondered how Chronus knew the right time to denounce Orabelle?"

"What do you mean?" Gideon asked.

"I mean, don't you think it was odd that she was there with a blood-drinker on her ship the day that Chronus decided to reveal that she was a traitor?"

"Loagaire, I know you love to play at these things but please get to the point. I have no idea what you are talking about," Gideon sighed in exasperation. His head was beginning to ache and he was tired of her.

"Come now, Guardian. We both know the Water Queen was not allied with those beasts. It is not like her and it would have served her no purpose. There was another reason that creature was with her. A reason that she was never able to tell us because of Chronus's clever little ploy, though that did not turn out very well for him," she remarked, looking up at Gideon through her long eyelashes. "So ask yourself, how did Chronus know that Orabelle was up to something? How did he know that beast was with her? How did he know about her child?"

"Why don't you just tell me how," Gideon said.

"You are really no fun anymore, Guardian," she pouted. "He knew all of these things because there was someone in her Guard that was telling him. I do not know who, but that creepy little coward Damek does. "

"So there is a traitor among the Leharans."

She nodded. "Yes. One that should be exposed sooner rather than later, especially if they can decide the outcome of this battle. Do what you want with the information. Just remember our deal."

"It has been agreed upon. I will uphold my end of the bargain," Gideon assured her.

She leaned forward and pressed her lips to his, molding the curves of her body against him. "For luck," she said, tucking the packet of herbs back into her dress and laughing as she sauntered away down the hall.

He rubbed his mouth with the back of his good hand and thought over what she had said. He would send a messenger to Lehar warning Orabelle of the traitor in her Guard but he feared it would not reach her in time. Even if it did, the information could only distract her. He could not risk sending someone to Veruca for if they were discovered then he could be condemned for siding with her, depending on the outcome of the battle. There was nothing he could do but wait and see how things played out. At least Maialen would be safely away from the fighting, and that was all that mattered to him.

# 34

The day dawned bright and hot. The sun rose blood-red over the water, spreading its reflection like liquid flame over the sea. Blaise squinted against the morning light, peering out over the vast sea from where he stood in his black battle armor on the high wall of Veruca. His gaze moved to the cliffs that rose in a dark silhouette around the city. They would come from that direction. He wished that he had had more time to prepare. He could have arranged a nice rock fall as a greeting to the Leharans. But there had been no time. Reports had come that the islanders had sailed and he and Astraeus had raced back here, the Verucans on horseback and the Samirrans on their massive eagles. Maialen had conveniently fallen into a stupor which despite their efforts she refused to snap out of. She had mumbled at Astraeus incoherently and alternated between crying hysteria and fitful slumber. Finally, they had been forced to leave her. As Blaise had stormed angrily from her rooms, he had passed by Gideon, noting the look of satisfaction in the man's eyes. He had stopped in front of him, his eyes burning.

"Soon there will be no Guardians," Blaise had seethed at him through clenched teeth before stalking off, Astraeus hurrying to catch up with him. Now they waited with a third of the power he had planned on for Orabelle. He had still held on to the vague hope that she would surrender but without Maialen here he knew that was not likely. The Earth Queen had been his leverage against her older sister and now that she had been removed from the game the rules would have to be changed.

Blaise looked down the wall, past the archers whose flame-tipped arrows were ready and waiting, to where Astraeus sat atop his enormous eagle, its long talons gripping the wall as it waited anxiously for flight. He wore a gold helmet and breastplate, and his long broadsword was strapped to his side. Blaise grinned as he watched the other man's face and the look of intense concentration. Astraeus would try to be heroic in battle, he was that sort, but he would never be a leader anywhere else. His kingdom was doomed.

"There, sire!" a soldier cried out. The first sleek hull of the Leharan ships was coming into view around the cliffs.

"Took you longer than I thought, my dear," Blaise murmured aloud. "You must be saving your power."

He lifted his voice so that it carried down the wall to Astraeus. "Sound the drums! But do not fire till I give the order. We will wait until they are all in sight!"

They waited as the ship rounded its way to the shore and stopped. Several others followed it and Blaise waited impatiently for the rest of the fleet, but it did not appear.

"What is this?" Astraeus called to him. "She has only brought five ships?"

Blaise ignored him and peered down at the water, shading his eyes from the growing light of dawn so that he could see better. A lone figure was descending from the first ship that had reached the beach. They walked several feet towards the huge iron doors and stopped, looking up, their bright armor flashing white in the sun.

"Orabelle," Blaise said softly, never taking his eyes from me. There were two curved swords sheathed at my waist but

I raised empty hands, unarmed. He expected me to begin calling my power but he did not feel the rush of energy that the elements brought. Instead my voice rang out over the stones of Veruca.

"Listen to me! I have not come here to harm any of you people, I have come to try and save you! I know of the atrocities of your king! I know of the fear in which you live, of the threats he uses to keep you prostrate."

"What is she doing?" Astraeus asked stupidly.

"She is trying to undermine us!" Blaise told him. "Ready the arrows!"

I was still speaking from the beach. "Lay down your weapons and I promise you that you will not be harmed! How many of you are hungry? How many of you are afraid? How many of you have lost a loved one to the temper of your king?"

"Be silent, Orabelle! Or I shall have no qualms about killing you where you stand!" Blaise shouted down at me.

I glared up at him. "Astraeus! Take your eagles and your people and leave this fight. I ask this for your mother and for my sister, your wife. This does not concern you, Air King!"

Astraeus looked from Blaise to me and back again, his brow furrowed. Before he could answer Blaise said to me, "He cannot abide by the things you have done, Water Queen! None of us can. You will be the one to lay down your arms! If you do so now and you give the Council the Pearl we will have no need to fight!"

"Never!" I yelled, drawing one of my swords in signal as the Sirens rose screaming from the water. Men began to pour from the ships making a line of the beach and Blaise could feel me calling my power.

"Now!" he cried and the soldier next to him beat his drum. A volley of arrows burst into flame and showered down on the Leharans. As one, the islanders raised their shields over their heads and crouched under them as the arrows rained down upon them. I was standing in a huge whirlpool of water that spun around me like a typhoon. I raised an arm and flung it at the side of the mountain and Blaise felt the rock beneath him shudder. He cursed and yelled to Astraeus. "Go! Get down there and stop them before she causes the whole wall to collapse!"

Astraeus nodded and kicked at his eagle. It sailed into the air, the rest of his troop following. Blaise turned from them back to the little Queen who was still pummeling at the side of the cliff. "Damn you, Orabelle!"

I smiled at the sound of his fury and flung my arm again, putting all of my strength behind it. I had completely disregarded the iron doorway and was instead focusing on a bend in the wall where I had noticed, in my hours spent roaming the beach during my forced stay, a weakness in the rock face that rose all the way up the cliff from the ground. I heard a loud groan and felt the pebbled beach shifting. I slammed at the wall again and let out a cry of triumph as the great rocks began to shift and dislodge. I spread the water around us, keeping the rockslide from rolling over my soldiers and crushing them. Above, men were crying out and fleeing from the spot where the cliff was crumbling.

"Orabelle, look out!" Brogan yelled, running toward me and leaping into the air, his sword stabbing upward as one of Astraeus's eagle riders swung down. The bird ducked the weapon and the man atop it turned for another try.

"Get them on the ground!" I commanded, still holding the water as a barrier against the settling rock fall. Dust rose up everywhere around us, stinging our eyes and making us cough. Astraeus was calling his power and I felt the cool wash of air across my skin as the dust clouds swirled, growing thicker. The men were slashing at the birds, their forearms covering their mouths from the debris that blew on the air. The pressure on the water barrier eased and an entire section of the wall lay in a crumbled heap on the beach. I no longer had to hold it back and I turned the force of the water onto the Samirrans, shoving them from their birds who flew off in fear. As the men were knocked to the ground my soldiers fell upon them. The Sirens were with the Guard, one on either side of Kaden. I squinted through the dust at the right section of the wall and saw Blaise and the archers regrouping.

"Get over the wall and into the city now!" I ordered, clambering up over the rock as Verucan soldiers began to pour out to stop us.

"Orabelle!" I heard Astraeus's voice behind me though it was hard to see him through the dirty cloud that raged around me.

"My fight is not with you, Astraeus!" I told him. "I will not kill you but I will not let you stop me!"

"You will not win this! You have brought a handful of men! You have overestimated yourself," he sneered contemptuously.

"No, you have underestimated me, Astraeus. I ask you again to stop this," I repeated as we circled each other warily.

"You attacked my kingdom!" he accused and leapt at me, sword drawn. I spun out of the way, his blade clanging off the back of my armor. He swung again and I danced out of the path of his sword, countering his moves but being careful not to hurt him.

"Please, Astraeus!" I begged again. "Do not do this!"

He jumped at me and I had no choice but to stab him or to run under his sword and into him, taking the brunt of his fall. I could not stab him, I had made a promise. I rushed him and as he knocked me to the ground I punched his jaw with my fist and shoved sideways but he was too heavy. He fell on top of me, knocking the wind from my lungs. His sword lay near us on the ground and mine was still held in my hand though the blade was pinned underneath us. I let go of it and stretched my fingers toward his, hoping I could hit him with the hilt of it and get him off of me. He saw me reaching and snatched the sword before I could, pressing the blade against my throat.

"Give up the Pearl, traitor!" he shouted.

"I am not the traitor! You are being used," I told him frantically, feeling the skin begin to split.

"I ask you one last time then you die! Give up the Pearl and surrender!"

"No! I will die first!" I screamed at him. His shoulders flexed as he moved to draw the blade across my neck and then he was sprawling on the ground. He sat up, rubbing his chin as I scrambled to my feet, one of my soldiers standing over him.

"You dare to attack me, Leharan?" he raged at the man. "You would dare to kick me in the face? I am a King!"

The soldier backed up, their sword held protectively in front of them though they did not attack. I could not see who it was because of the helmet which covered most of their face. Astraeus turned his power on them, the wind lifting them from the ground and suspending them in the air. He laughed and the soldier began to claw at the neck of their armor frantically. Astraeus was pulling the air from their lungs.

I picked up my own sword but before I could lunge at him the soldier ripped off their helmet, desperate for breath. Dark hair streaked with grey spilled out and the regal features of Irielle were convulsed horribly as she struggled to breathe. She had disguised herself as a soldier and come to the battle without my knowing. She had come to protect Astraeus and in doing so she had saved me from him.

"Astraeus, stop!" I screamed at him. He looked at me with terrorized eyes, his hand trembling as he frantically grasped for his amulet that was trapped beneath his armor.

"I can't stop it!" he shouted over the melee around us. I watched Irielle, unable to reach her or help her.

"Astraeus for the love of Imbria, stop! It is your mother!" I was screaming at him. From the corner of my eye I saw the archers on the wall were setting their arrows. I was about to lift my arm and send a wave of water to quench the flames when a heartrending scream echoed over the rock cliffs and Irielle fell to the ground in a lifeless heap.

"No!" Astraeus bellowed in agony, throwing himself down beside the body of his mother, tears covering his face. Then he lifted his anguished eyes to mine.

"What have you done?" I cried.

"You!" he snarled. "You did this! I tried to stop! I tried to and I couldn't! This is all your fault!"

"I did not know it was Irielle! I would never have allowed her to do this!" I swore to him, my own grief welling up as I looked at the lifeless form that lay broken on the rocks.

"Liar!"

He ran at me, a hot wind tearing the air around him. I pushed at his power with my own, calling to the ocean. I backed away from him hastily, casting a quick look at the wall above us just as the Verucans' arrows rose into the sky. I turned my focus away from Astraeus and tried to deflect the attack but I wasn't fast enough and the blazing arrows hailed down on us. Astraeus was oblivious to the danger and dove at me, his sword skidding across the black rock as I dodged the blow. He slashed again and I felt the whisper of the blade as it passed close to my face.

"Damn you, Astraeus, stop this!" I cried.

"I will not stop till I see you dead!" he vowed. He came at me once more, unrelenting, and then Shemus was hurtling towards him. The Guard leapt on him from behind and I took advantage of the opportunity to call the Sirens. A wave surged underneath them, dragging Astraeus back towards the sea. He struggled against it, screaming curses at me. One of the Sirens moved, pulling him into the surf but keeping his head above the water, holding him down long enough for us to get into the city. The Samirrans converged on the Sirens to protect their king but their blows fell on the empty sea as my creatures left their shapes and reformed elsewhere around Astraeus, always holding the hysterical king at bay.

I turned away from the beach and gave Shemus a hasty salute before another volley of arrows rained down in a fiery curtain. Someone screamed and I saw one of the eagles burst into flame. Blaise did not seem to care who he harmed as long as he stopped me. I lifted my fingers and drops like inverted rain began to rise from the ocean, dampening the flames. My men were regrouping, the Samirrans still trapped by the Sirens in the shallow sea.

"Move!" I shouted. Kaden was beside me and we stumbled into the city, the others behind us. We stopped abruptly, faced by an unnerving wall of silent, black-armored Verucan soldiers.

"Damn," Kaden muttered under his breath. I agreed but remained silent, looking for the Fire King.

"Orabelle!" Blaise called from his place on the fractured wall. "You can see you are outnumbered. Give up now and do not make me kill you."

"Come down here and fight me yourself, coward!" I challenged.

He laughed. "You cannot win. You can see that."

"Can you be sure of that, Blaise?" I asked him. I motioned to Kaden and he let out a loud whistle. From the other side of the mountain came a rumbling sound that grew steadily louder.

"What is that?" Blaise demanded.

It was my turn to laugh at him. "That, Fire King, is the rest of my army!"

I grabbed my other sword from its sheath, curving them both in front of me. I glanced at Kaden. "Are you ready?"

He grinned at me and let out the battle cry that was taken up by the rest of the Guard as they rushed at the Verucans. Suddenly from behind the line of the soldiers another cry came as the Tahitians tore into the city from the overland path, Damian in the lead. The Verucans spun around, confused, their ranks broken apart as they were assaulted by the long spears of the Tahitians. Further beyond that Colwyn and a second rank of Leharans were advancing towards Blaise along the wall. The Fire King looked around, his face suffusing with blood. I could feel his amber gaze burning into me as I fell into the battle against the wall of black armored soldiers, slashing furiously at them. I was trying not to use my power as I had already exhausted most of its strength back at the beach. I saw Shemus's eyes go wide and he screamed as a man ripped an axe through him and he collapsed. Brogan was there, standing protectively over the body and shouting wildly, his sword slicing the air in skillful arcs. Kaden moved to stand beside him and they formed a deadly barrier over their fallen comrade.

I glanced up at the wall and Blaise was gone. Colwyn and his men had taken down the rest of the archers and they now stood on the highest point but they had not taken the Fire King. The signal that we had agreed upon was not given. Somehow Blaise had gotten away from them, though I could not imagine how as they seemed unharmed. He should have had to fight his way past them and Colwyn was not a novice swordsman.

"Orabelle!" Damian called.

"It is about time!" I snapped at him as he stood back to back with me. The Tahitians had begun to spread out among us which meant we had broken through the Verucan ranks. We were winning. "Where is Blaise? Colwyn did not give the signal so he must have gotten past him!"

"I don't know!" Damian kicked at a man and used his spear to deliver a solid blow to the Verucan's head. "But I would expect that he is coming for you!"

"Good," I said through my teeth. "I am ready for him."

# 35

Akrin huddled in a dark corner of Blaise's chamber in the castle, covering his ears as the sounds of the battle echoed though the walls. He was teary eyed and whimpering and at the same time hating himself for being afraid. His master was not afraid. Akrin had heard him shouting from the wall, brave and confident. He would be ashamed of the boy if he saw him now, hiding like this. Akrin forced himself to lower his hands from his ears and he crawled on all fours to the narrow window. He looked out over the city and the swarm of white armored soldiers that had converged on it. There were also huge, dark skinned warriors who wore no armor, just cloths wrapped around their bodies. He looked for Blaise but could not find him. He saw *her*. She was there with the men that had taken his sister and brother away. Her long pale hair had blood in it and she was fighting back a soldier twice her size, her body dancing around the swords gracefully. He had not thought that she would be such a beautiful fighter.

The boy ducked back away from the window in fright as he saw a man tumble from the wall, his head bashing on the rocks. Akrin was shaking again and hating himself for it. He needed to help his master, to defeat the witch in the white armor. But how? He was just a boy, what could he do?

He remembered Blaise sitting him down before the fire, his face full of concern. "I need to tell you something."

"What is it?" Akrin had asked worriedly. His master was not usually so concerned for others. Whatever it was, it must be terrible.

"It is about your brother and sister. I am sorry to have to tell you this, Akrin. Your brother did not die on the beach, as the rumors say," Blaise said, patting his head affectionately. "He was taken by the Leharan Queen and she has killed them both."

Akrin recalled the gnawing fear and the anger that had clawed at him at his master's words. He had tried to save his family that night on the beach but those people had stopped him. He had tried but what could he do against a witch and a Queen? He was just a boy. He crept to the window again to stare out at the hated woman. That was when he saw the bright red curls and shining black armor of his master moving through the confusion of men. He was heading straight for the witch.

"No! No, don't go near her!" Akrin pleaded aloud, wringing his hands. He looked around frantically, there had to be something he could do. Then an idea struck him and he ran out into the hallway and up to the heavy barred door that stood at the end of it. He pushed at the iron bars with all his might but they would not budge. He cried in frustration, banging angrily on the door with his tiny fists. If anyone could stop the witch, then the beastmen could. They did his masters bidding. They would save him. But he was too small to let them out.

There were noises from the other side of the doorway and Akrin covered his nose as a foul odor seeped through the edge of the door. He scooted away and a muffled voice called to him from the tunnels.

"Who is there?" it asked softly, its words sounding strange to the boy's ears.

"I-I want to save my master!" the boy said through his tears.

"Of course you do.... let us out we will help you," the voice promised.

"I can't! It's barred and it is too heavy for me."

The voice was silent, contemplating. Then it said, "There is another way, but you need a key. It's a large key with a yellow jewel on it. Have you seen it?"

Akrin sniffed, wiping his nose with the back of his hand. "Yes."

"Do you know where it is?"

"Yes."

"Good," the strange voice said happily. Go and get it and I will tell you where the door is that it opens."

Akrin scrambled to his feet and hurried to find the key.

# 36

I felt blood coating my skin and rivulets of it ran from shallow wounds on my body. I swallowed my nausea, my sweaty palms still gripping my swords tightly. The smell of burning flesh was close by and I saw Blaise throwing fire around him at any who got in his way. At first I thought he was advancing straight for me but then I realized his eyes were fixed on Damian. He burned his way towards us and a plume of steam from under the mountain ignited as one of his bursts of fire touched it. The ground rumbled under my feet.

"Blaise, stop! The mines!" I warned.

He ignored me, his focus still on Damian who had noticed his approach and was gripping his spear tightly, waiting.

"You think you can keep her from me?!" Blaise demanded.

"I can and I will," Damian told him. Blaise threw a whip of fire at him and Damian ducked it, rolling on the ground. I jumped back out of the way as another spout of vapor caught fire in the rock.

"Blaise, stop this, you will destroy the whole mountain! Your fight is with me, not with him or anyone else here. Let them go," I tried to reason with him.

He laughed at me and drew his sword, the blade of it igniting in glowing red flames. "My fight is with him, and with anyone else who has stood in my way," he swore darkly. He turned back to Damian.

As the two men circled each other warily, Damian never took his eyes from the Fire King. Blaise thrust at him and Damian knocked the burning blade aside, moving nimbly out of the way. Blaise grinned and struck out again. Damian deflected the blow easily, landing one of his own, the sharp point of his spear ripping through the black armor on the other side. Blaise glanced at the cracked armor of his side piece and grabbed it, tearing it off and tossing it on the ground. I could feel his temper rising. I ran at him and he flung his hand back at me, a burst of fire throwing me to the ground. I scrambled to my feet just as a great cry of panic arose from the soldiers nearest to the royal castle. The ground beneath me began to tremble and steam snaked up through the rock. I ignored the screaming men fleeing past me, my eyes intent on Blaise and then I smelled it. The foul odor of death rolled toward me and I fell back. The Fomori were tearing through the armies, clawing and biting indiscriminately. There were dozens of them descending upon us and I whirled at Blaise to see if this was his doing but his mouth was hanging open in surprise.

"What have you done?" I screamed at him. "Stop them!"

He shook his head. "It was not me! With Carushka dead they have no leader, there is no one to control them. I cannot stop them!"

"Then we have to kill them!" I shouted. I gripped my swords again and ran into the melee. Damian was close behind me. The first of the beasts that saw me advanced, jaws snapping, and I crossed my arms over each other so that my swords severed its head with a spurt of black blood. Damian had caught another with his spear and once again yelled his loud battle cry. It was taken up by the rest of the Guard and the men stopped retreating and gave up on fighting one another, the Verucans and Leharans both going at the blood-drinkers instead.

One of the beasts was running straight for me. I braced myself as it slammed into me and we went rolling across the ground. It climbed on top of me, clawing at my armor. It was too stupid to try and go around it and instead just kept tearing futilely at my heart. I dropped one of my swords and used both hands to raise the other behind my head, bringing it down with all my strength so that it cleaved the matted head wide open. I shoved the beast aside and kicked it off, rising to my feet just as another one grabbed my hair from behind, jerking me against it.

"You are the one that killed Carushka, you took him to his death!" the creature hissed, pulling my hair violently to one side and exposing my neck. I screamed and Damian lunged for me but another beast was in front of him, blocking his way. He was beating at it viciously, shouting in rage as he tried to get to me. The thing that held me laughed maniacally and bit down. I felt sharp fangs sink into my flesh and my whole body was racked with pain.

Damian roared in futile rage, still wrestling with the blood-drinker that had stopped him. Suddenly the jaws on my neck slackened and the beast fell backwards off of me. Blaise stood behind it, his sword covered in black blood. I stumbled, pressing a hand to my neck as the poison of the bite coursed painfully through my blood.

Blaise caught me and pulled me into his arms, holding me against him. "Orabelle!" he was crying frantically. He moved my hand and looked at the wound, relief washing over him. "It has missed the major bloodline."

"What...." I tried to ask but the words wouldn't form in my torn throat.

"Don't try to talk. I will take you to a healer," he promised, his eyes bright.

I wanted to ask him why he had saved me but my voice wouldn't come and I coughed convulsively, tasting blood. He lifted me in his arms and started to carry me back in the direction of the beach. Damian was screaming my name and I strained to see him over Blaise's shoulder but my vision was swimming in and out of focus.

I struggled in Blaise's arms, twitching violently as the waves of pain rolled through me. I tried to speak and my throat felt as if it was on fire. I swallowed hard and tried again, reaching up with my left hand to pull the Fire King's face down to mine. He leaned over me until our lips were mere inches apart. His eyes widened and flared with emotion as he moved to kiss me and I whispered to him, my voice a thick and rasping, "No."

I brought my right hand up, pulling the knife I carried from the sheath at my hip and plunging it into his side where he had thrown off the damaged piece of armor. I felt the knife glance off his ribs and I yanked it out with a cry of pain and shoved it in again. His face twisted into a mask of horror and he let go of me so that I tumbled to the ground, hitting the hard rock. He was looking down at his hands which were covered in his own blood.

"Orabelle..." he pleaded. "I was trying to help you."

"I hate you!" I spat out, blood running over my lips, the words tearing through my injured throat.

He stood clutching his wound and backed away. "I didn't kill him. It was never me, it was Chronus."

I was gasping for breath and I forced myself to stand. My vision blurred and I felt dizzy and I stumbled to my knees. I groped blindly for my swords along the ground, the noises of the battle echoing harshly in my ears. I rubbed at my eyes, trying to get them to focus. I heard my name and I looked up, defenseless. Blaise was moving towards me again, his sword back in his hand. I looked at it confusion. It was the wrong sword. The one that was flashing before me was not the dark steel of the Fire Kingdom. I blinked through the venomous haze that clouded my eyes and tried to understand what was happening. Then my vision cleared and I saw that it was Astraeus, his face contorted with grief, his sword moving through the air. I heard Damian screaming my name and I heard Blaise cry out in protest. I did not feel the blade as it bit into me, my body was already numb with shock from the poison. I looked down at the blood that dripped from under my armor and then back up at Astraeus. He was staring at me, his eyes wide and red and filled with loathing. He lifted his sword again, his lips pulled back from his teeth in a grimace as he swung at my neck. Kaden barreled into him from the side, sending him sprawling across the rock. He grabbed the Air King's sword and threw it away from him.

"Orabelle!" I heard my name called over and over but I could not speak through my torn throat. I fell forward and Damian's strong arms caught me, lowering me to the ground. I fought to keep my eyes open despite my body's desire to close them. Damian smoothed the hair back from my forehead as Kaden knelt beside him and unclasped my armor. They pulled it off and Damian looked away for a moment, then back at me.

"You are going to be fine, little Queen. It's nothing. I will take you to my mother and she will heal you. And then we will dance and sing and I will make you listen to stories that you hate and we will talk and laugh. And Alita will be there and your sister. You will hold your child and you will be happy."

I coughed and swallowed hard, trying to draw air to speak. I could not get a full breath but I managed to say to him, "You are a terrible liar."

Damian made a noise deep in his throat and stubbornly shook his head. I smiled at him wearily as a wave of exhaustion rolled over me.

"I am so tired," I told him, barely able to mouth the words, and Kaden began to cry.

I reached up and touched bloody fingertips to the young man's cheek and he grabbed my hand, kissing my palm.

"Your son will make you proud," he promised, his voice raw as he bent his head over my hand, hiding his grief.

Damian was looking up at the sky, tears dripping from his chin. His shoulders shook and I followed his gaze, a drop of rain falling softly on my cheek. Then another. Or perhaps they were his tears. I could not be sure. Darkness began to creep around the edges of my mind and I thought of my mother and her gentle smile, my father I had not known, the grandfather I had killed. I thought of my sister, of her laughter and the warm feel of her hug. Kaden and his ridiculous jokes. I thought of Irielle and Alita and the friendship they had given me, of Damian and his unbending faith, of my baby with the perfect grey eyes and all of the love I wanted to give, all of the times I wanted to hold my sweet child. I thought of Tal, the lines of his face and the feel of his skin, the way he had looked at me when he told me he loved me, the sound of his laughter and the taste of his lips. I thought of his smile that I longed to see more than anything else. The Sirens keened in the distance as I thought of all the things that I would miss the most, all of the tiny moments that had made up my happiness in this world, and then I closed my eyes.

Look for the **Keepers of Imbria** Book 2, **Maialen**, coming soon

Printed in Great Britain
by Amazon

18867174R00181